THE NOWHERE BONES

A NICK DRAKE NOVEL

DWIGHT HOLING

D1225552

The Nowhere Bones
A Nick Drake Novel

Print Edition
Copyright 2021 by Dwight Holing

Published by Jackdaw Press
All Rights Reserved

ISBN: 978-1-7347404-7-9

Cover Photo © by Bun Lee

For More Information, please visit dwightholing.com.

See how you can **Get a Free Book** at the end of this novel.

For Mary, Sam & Andrea Holing

1

THE STORM

Wildlife in Harney County signals the first day of spring with bright, bold displays. Male sage-grouse puff their tuxedoed chests and fan their spiky tails. Mule deer display antlers so new they're still wrapped in velvet sheaths. Goldfinches preen fresh feathers the color of sunshine after being cloaked in plumage as drab as winter.

The people of No Mountain don their own version of springtime finery to herald the vernal equinox with a special celebration. Blackpowder Smith stands on a rise with Steens Mountain at his back and faces a festive gathering. The store owner's billy-goat beard is neatly groomed and he wears a black frock coat and silk string tie for the occasion. November is by his side. Glass-beaded moccasins peek from beneath the hem of the old Paiute healer's handstitched ribbon skirt that is encircled from knee to ankle with bands of red, blue, and yellow.

I stand next to the pair and reach inside a brand-new suit jacket to scratch my shoulder as I tap my toes to loosen an even stiffer pair of boots. I try convincing myself my unease is due to the purchases being at least a size too small. Loq, my fellow

Vietnam veteran turned wildlife ranger, remains stoic as he nudges me with his elbow. The Klamath has used a store-bought equivalent of bear grease to make his long mohawk stand up and shine. The grizzly tooth that hangs from a thong around his neck gleams and a rakish slash of red paint adorns his high cheekbones.

"Breathe, brother, breathe," he grunts. "You look like you fell through ice."

"Clear a path, folks," Blackpowder shouts. "Here they come."

Loq trills, "*Wey heya, wey heya.*"

November shakes a gourd rattle and begins to sing.

The gathering parts down the middle as all eyes turn north. Wovoka, a buckskin stallion with black socks and tail, and Sarah, a sorrel mare with white daisies braided into her mane, pull a double buggy along the dirt road at a high-stepping trot. Pudge Warbler holds the reins. The lawman's short-brim Stetson is freshly brushed and the crown sharply creased. Pinned to his chest is the seven-point gold sheriff's star he reclaimed in the last election. It catches the afternoon sunlight and shines as brightly as his grin. His daughter Gemma sits next to him. Seeing her dressed in a white ruffled skirt and silk blouse with pearl snaps makes my jacket and boots pinch even tighter.

"Breathe, brother," Loq says between trills.

Pudge reins the spirited horses to a stop in front of us. Gemma steals a glance at me. Her eyes sparkle. "You ready, hotshot?" she mouths silently.

My throat is suddenly as parched as nearby Alvord Desert. The best I can do is nod.

"Who is giving this woman away?" Blackpowder asks officiously.

"I am, her father," the sheriff says. "But I got something to give first." Pudge hands the reins to Gemma, pulls a shotgun out of the buggy's scabbard, and holds it up for all to admire. It's a vintage Browning over-and-under, a 10 gauge from the look of the bores big enough to ram a broomstick down. The polished silver receiver with filigrees of intricate engraving shines.

He nods at his daughter whose curved belly straining against her silk blouse is plain for all to see. "If anyone here mistakes this fine piece of gunsmithing as meaning this is a shotgun wedding, it isn't. This is a prized family heirloom given to me by my father whose father gave it to him. Now, I'm proud to give it to my soon-to-be son-in-law and father of my soon-to-be grandchild." Everybody cheers.

The sheriff flips the over-and-under around and hands it to Loq. The Klamath grasps the butt and takes his time with the ritual inspection, complete with checking the twin cartridge chambers and sighting down the barrel. "It's a worthy gift," he says to me. I nod my assent. "The groom is honored to accept it," he says. Loq sets the Browning down and passes a framed pen-and-ink drawing I'd sketched to Pudge.

"Now, isn't this a pretty likeness of a bull elk, cow, and their calf," the sheriff says. "I'm grateful to have it to hang above my desk."

"That concludes the formal exchange of gifts," Blackpowder announces. "Let's get this pair hitched so we can start the hoedown and send them on their way proper like." That elicits more cheers.

Father and daughter step down from the buggy and the horses are led away. Pudge gives Gemma a kiss and me a firm handshake. Any dryness in my throat quickly disappears as I offer her my arm. Our shoulders and hips touch as we turn to face Blackpowder and November.

"You look more beautiful than ever," I whisper.

"You clean up pretty good yourself," Gemma whispers back.

Blackpowder perches a pair of half-frame reading glasses on the tip of his nose and opens a leather-bound Bible. "Dearly beloved, we are here to witness the joining of Gemma Warbler and Nick Drake in holy matrimony. Before they exchange their vows, I'd like to read a passage from the Good Book." He pauses to clear his throat.

"Most officiants would read chapter and verse about unfailing love and doing everything in the name of love and loving each other deeply because love covers a multitude of sins. All that's true, but I don't need to tell this couple how to love because it's been clear from the first time they set eyes on each other, it was love at first sight. It just took them a while to see what the rest of us saw from the git go." Murmurs and chuckles ripple through the crowd.

"I believe these words will serve them even more mightily in good times and bad." He lingers on the last word. "It's from the Old Testament. Book of Ecclesiastes. Chapter four. Verses nine through twelve."

Blackpowder waggles his index finger. "'Two are better than one, because they have a good return for their toil. For if they fall, one will lift up the other; but woe to him who is alone when he falls and has not another to lift him up. Again, if two lie together, they are warm; but how can one be warm alone? And though a man might prevail against one who is alone, two will withstand him. A threefold cord is not quickly broken.'"

"*Wey heya, wey heya,*" Loq trills.

Blackpowder goes on to read a poem by Elizabeth Barrett Browning about all the ways to count love before asking Gemma and me to promise to cherish each other until the end of time. When I slip the ring on her finger, she gasps. "My mother's! Where did you get it?"

I glance at Pudge. The flinty lawman appears to have a sudden urge to look down at his boots as if making sure the spit-shine still shines.

Blackpowder concludes the ceremony with, "Whereas and

wherefore the bride and groom have consented with all you fine folks as their witnesses, in the power vested in me as mayor of No Mountain, chief of the Volunteer Fire Department, and chairman of the Chamber of Commerce, I proclaim you husband and wife. You may now kiss the bride."

When Gemma's and my lips meet, November begins singing in *Numu*, her native tongue. Her lilting song rises skyward as the old healer dances a ritual circle around us, twirling and spinning to make the stripes on her ribbon dress mimic a rainbow. She throws pinches of yellow blossoms of brittlebush and silver-green leaves of sage she gathered at a sacred place somewhere out on the high lonesome. The mixture rains down on us as softly as a veil of lace.

I start to sway to the music and Gemma unclasps my hands from around her waist and places them on her stomach.

"Can you feel this?" she whispers against my lips. "The baby likes November's song."

Tiny feet kick beneath my palms and Gemma starts swaying too as the music envelops us. We're dancing now, Gemma, the baby, and me, three strands of a cord bound by the strongest power on Earth. I close my eyes and picture us dancing on top of the fluffy white clouds that make the big sky over Harney County seem even bigger. Slowly, softly, around and around, we move as one.

But suddenly the music stops and the clouds part and we fall out of the sky. Spiraling at first, then plummeting. Faster and faster. Too fast to scream. Then darkness. Sweet darkness that eclipses the horror and hushes the crescendo of screeching metal, splintering wood, and shattering bone.

My eyes blink open. As I try to shake the shooting stars out of my head, everything comes rushing back. The wedding ceremony and reception. The day after, when we leave No Mountain and fly over the southern Blue Mountains in Gemma's single-engine airplane to our new life together. An early spring storm with a dead-of-winter's punch coming out of nowhere. Towering black clouds colliding. Peals of thunder booming. Gemma fighting the yoke and working the foot pedals furiously to control the pitch and yaw of the little plane bucking up and down and from side to side in the violent sky.

A fiery blaze of lightning zigzagging close by. Too close. The starboard wingtip exploding. The plane folding like a shotgunned bird. Gemma desperately trying to level it out as we plunge. A thick forest sprouting up fast. Too fast. Spotting a glade covered in snow among the woods. Aiming for it. Hitting it. The wheels plowing through drifts. The landing gear buckling. The plane careening into the trees. The propeller shearing branches. Trunks clipping the wings. A thick limb lancing through the cockpit window. And finally blackness. Stillness.

It's quiet inside the twisted and broken cockpit. I taste iron and spit it out. Red gouts of blood splatter the bowed instrument panel. Breathe, Loq had taunted me only the day before. Breathe. I gasp. I sputter. My ribs burn. The seat belt strangles. I work the buckle free.

Gemma! She's on the other side of the limb that skewered the cockpit. I look over it and then under it. Her head is cocked back against her seat. Blood as red as slashes painted on high cheekbones streak her face. The impact drove the yoke against her chest. I can't see her curved belly beneath it. Can't see any tiny kicks.

"Gemma!" I shout. "Gemma, wake up!"

I reach beneath the limb and run my fingers across the instrument panel, feeling for the radio controls. I find them and grab for the handheld microphone. It's been knocked out of its cradle. I come up with the cord and reel it in. The black mike surfaces. I hold it to my mouth and click the side button. "Mayday! Mayday!" No chirp. No static. No nothing. I click again. I keep clicking while I twist knobs. "Mayday! Mayday!"

I drop the mike and suck in air. It tastes of gasoline. I hear the drips tick-tocking from the ruptured fuel tanks in what remains of the broken overhead wings. I have to get Gemma out, but the limb blocks me. I shoulder my crumpled door. Shoulder it hard. Again and again. Finally it pops open and I pop out and plop into the snow.

I roll to my knees and take a deep breath before standing. A hot blade stabs my chest. I take another breath. Another hot blade. I pause before trying to stand. The snow is soft. Soft like the clouds Gemma and I danced on. Soft like the last snowbank I knelt on. A snowbank at the Malheur refuge in the waning days of winter. It was only days ago. A lifetime ago...

2

The snow had blown in windrows that striped a field south of Malheur Lake. Though winter's final days were winnowing, the season was living up to a local's favorite twist of Mark Twain's adage: If you don't like the weather in Harney County, wait five minutes.

I was driving down the Central Patrol Road, a sometimes graveled, mostly dirt, and always potholed narrow track. The bed of my government-issued white four-by with the duck and fish emblem on the door was stacked with bales of hay. A nearby rancher had given them to me. To be precise, he'd given them to me to give to a herd of Rocky Mountain elk, the biggest and noisiest four-legged residents of Malheur National Wildlife Refuge.

The herd had hunkered down in a field to wait out a storm. The animals seemed unwilling to move on even after the snow had stopped falling and they'd stripped the field of its natural graze. Sworn to protect wildlife of every shape and size, I added the role of ersatz pizza delivery guy to my usual rangering duties.

Bucking heavy bales was mindless, finger-numbing work, but I welcomed the distraction. Ever since Gemma had told me she was carrying our child, I'd been doing way too much soul searching. Being a husband and father was something I'd never contemplated before. Not throughout basic training and the three years of combat duty I served in Vietnam leading long reconnaissance patrols, and definitely not during the six months I spent in a special ward at Walter Reed Hospital for soldiers suffering from combat fatigue.

Gemma and I had many discussions about the upcoming birth. Meaning, Gemma did the discussing and I did the wondering if I could handle being trusted to take care of something as fragile as a newborn after a recent history of not being able to take care of myself.

"Everybody's frightened about parenthood at first," Gemma said one night as we sipped lemongrass tea sweetened with sage honey beside the wood-burning stove that heated the old lineman's shack I'd called home since moving to No Mountain. "Do you think I don't lay awake at night and worry too?"

I gave her a squeeze. "You sure fooled me, especially the nights you sleep over." I mimicked snoring, but my attempt at a joke thudded. "What I meant to say was, I've seen you in action. Delivering a breech birth in the middle of a rancher's pasture? Taking care of a flock of lambs stricken with tetanus? You never lose your cool."

"There's a big difference between being a veterinarian and a new mother," she said archly. "I'll take a mare trying to kick me while I'm lifting her tail to insert a thermometer over walking an infant with a high fever any day of the week."

"You're going to be the best mother in the world. Besides, November will be there to help you."

"What about you?"

"Me too, of course, but there's still a couple of matters we need to iron out first."

"Such as?"

"Marriage, for starters. You haven't given me your answer. And then there's where we're going to live."

Gemma sprang up as if a red-hot ember had shot from the stove and landed on her lap. "I don't have time to think about such things. Last time I checked, I'm still the only large animal veterinarian in Harney County and there's still more livestock living here than people. Because of the storms, I've had to make rounds in my Jeep rather than my airplane. Do you know how long it takes to drive to Whitehorse Ranch in a blizzard? And then there's Pudge. Now that he's sheriff again and living in Burns most of the time, any free moment I do have is spent taking care of the ranch." She snorted. "As if I have time to plan a wedding."

"You're right, it can wait," I said. "But you know what can't?"

Gemma put her hands on her hips. It made her curved belly stick out even farther. "Let me guess. The call you got from your boss asking you to take on a district supervisor's job, which happens to be in Portland."

Regional Director F.D. Powers' request had come straight out of the blue. It was a mighty fast curveball thrown during a mighty complicated time. I chalked Gemma's chilly response up to hormones when I told her about it, but not making a decision was akin to having a loose shingle flapping all winter. I'd managed to stall Powers, but the politically minded bureaucrat who'd been appointed by President Nixon wouldn't stay ignored for long.

"I meant the baby," I said. "It's not going to wait. It's coming whether you or I or anyone else is ready or not."

Gemma's expression switched from annoyance to serenity in the blink of an eye. "The baby," she cooed, moving her hands from her hips to cradling her stomach. "I can't wait to meet it, and the sooner the better. The morning sickness was one thing and the mood swings another, but now these cravings." Her eyes fixed on the one-room shack's tiny kitchen. "Tell me you remembered to stop by Blackpowder's store and pick up the fixings for jalapeño poppers."

No less ravenous or demanding were the Rocky Mountain elk trotting toward my pickup. They showed little fear as I lowered the tailgate and started dragging out the hundred-pound bales with a pair of hooks. Two bulls that were always vying for dominance stood on opposite sides and started bugling impatiently. The largest, oldest, and crankiest of the pair pawed the ground and swung his massive head back and forth. Not to be outdone, the younger bull false-charged me.

"*Tenimayu,*" I said, using the Paiute word for "quiet down."

The cows weighed a couple of hundred pounds less than the seven-hundred-pound bulls, but they were even more pushy about getting their share of the hay. Most were surely eating for two. Rocky Mountain elk typically bred in the fall and gave birth in late May or June, but summer pregnancies and calving at the end of winter were not unheard of. One cow in particular appeared ready to calve. It wasn't only her swollen girth that made her recognizable. Her white rump patch was brighter and she bore scars on her left hindquarter that I was certain would match those of a cougar's claws. That she'd been able to buck off a big cat was testament to a strong will to survive.

As the herd grazed, I swapped the baling hooks for a pad of paper and began sketching. I'd taken up pen-and-ink drawing that winter as another way to distract myself. Though I was no Roger Tory Peterson, I was developing a knack for capturing wildlife, a result not from any latent artistic talent, but from being able to spend my days in the field.

After the elk finished eating and settled down to chew their cuds, I exited the refuge and turned onto the two-lane blacktop that led back to No Mountain. Within a mile I spotted a rusty sedan with a missing trunk lid stopped on the other side of the road. I U-turned and parked behind it. The open-air trunk was loaded with boxes. Tuhudda Will and his young teenage grandson were standing next to the car. A jack and spare tire lay at their feet.

"Hello my old friends," I said as I got out to lend a hand.

"I saw you in a dream last night, Nick Drake," the Paiute elder said in his slow, deliberate manner. "You were carrying an elk calf in the cradleboard Girl Born in Snow made for Gemma's baby. I do not know what the dream means, but if I have it again, I will ask the elk."

"As a matter of fact, I was just feeding a herd in the refuge, but there were no calves among them."

"Elk are wise. It must be a sign for them to have left their usual wintering grounds near Riverton."

"They came because they knew Mr. Nick would feed them, Grandfather," Nagah said.

"It's my job," I said.

The red bandana headband that kept Tuhudda's long white hair out of his eyes shook. "No, you do not do it for money. You do it because it is just. You will always seek justice because of what happened in the war in the green world. This is so."

"Grandfather and I got jobs and we are going to get paid too," Nagah said. "We are on our way there now."

I grabbed the tire iron and crouched beside the flat. The treads were nearly bald and the sidewall cracked. I started loosening lug nuts. "What's the job and where is it?"

"It is in Catlow Valley," he said.

"Where you take your sheep to graze in summer and fall, but that's still months away. I take it this job has nothing to do with shepherding."

"A man is going to pay Grandfather to identify old bones he found in a cave and pay me to help move rocks. He is a professor at the university."

"An archaeologist?"

"I think so. The professor heard about Grandfather. He drove to our camp yesterday on his way back from Burns where he was buying supplies. A woman was with him. She is his student. The professor said he would pay us, and so now we are going."

I fitted the jack to the frame behind the front wheel and started pumping the handle. The rusty sedan creaked and groaned as it tilted upward. Once it was raised, I removed the loosened lug nuts and tried to pull off the wheel. It wouldn't budge no matter how much I wrestled it.

"What is wrong?" Nagah asked.

"It's stuck. Sometimes rust gets between the wheel and hub and acts like glue."

I screwed the top lug back on, but only hand-tightened it. Then I hammered the bottom of the tire with the tire iron. That broke the corrosion seal. I removed the flat. The spare was nearly as bald, but it still held air. I put it on and lowered the car.

"You should reconsider going to Catlow Valley today," I said. "You don't have a spare now and I bet that cave with bones in it isn't anywhere near a paved road. The risk of getting another flat is pretty high."

"Then our own two feet will carry us the rest of the way," Tuhudda said.

Having to haul their gear in the cold with little chance of someone passing by to give them a lift didn't sit well. I knew better than to insult the old man by trying to talk him out of it. "I've always been curious about archaeology myself. How about if I follow you there? When I leave, I can take the flat tire with me to get it fixed and bring it back later."

"If it pleases you."

"It does. How long are you planning on staying there?"

A smile added another crease to Tuhudda's craggy face. "Until they run out of bones."

3

Professor Paxton Sizemore didn't look like he spent much time behind a lectern. If I didn't know better, I would've pegged him for a mountain climber. He had a chiseled jaw and cerulean eyes. Biceps pushed against the long sleeves of the flannel shirt he wore beneath a down vest. His Italian leather hiking boots sported red laces. The front pouches of the carpenter's belt strapped around his waist held trowels, spoons, picks, and brushes. A mattock with a foot-long handle hung from the hammer loop like a *High Noon* hogleg.

"Nick Drake," I said as we shook hands. His knuckles were calloused, his grip rock hard.

"Call me Pax. Everybody does."

We were standing at the dig team's camp as Tuhudda and Nagah unloaded gear from the lidless trunk of the rusty sedan that had made the fifteen-mile drive up a narrow rocky track without a blowout. It was parked next to a pickup with a cargo trailer hitched to it and a Toyota Land Cruiser. Both vehicles bore University of Oregon emblems. Beyond them rose a large basecamp-sized tent along with three smaller backpacking tents.

They were all arranged around a fire ring. A tool rack holding shovels, picks, and lever bars stood next to a stack of crates.

The professor took in my uniform and holstered sidearm. "You're a US Fish and Wildlife ranger here in Harney County?"

"Yes, I'm based up the road in No Mountain, but I patrol the refuges from the Idaho border to Northern California."

"That's a rich environment for Paleo-Indians, if you know what you're looking for." He paused. "Have you come across any pictographs and petroglyphs? Those are ancient rock paintings and rock carvings in layman's terms."

The condescension was hard to miss, but I let it go. "The closest to here are two miles to the west. A lizard, bighorn sheep, and a directional to a waterhole."

His blond eyebrows rose. "That's quite an array. I'd appreciate it if you drew me a map so I can take a look."

"I'll take you there, if you'd like. Are they your area of expertise?"

"It started off that way. When I was in high school, I talked my way into a summer job working on a project along the Columbia River east of Portland. The rising waters from the dam at The Dalles were flooding a canyon local Indians called *Tamani-Pesh-Wa*, or 'Written on the Rock.' Our job was to move the carvings to higher ground. All it took was one look at them and others nearby, including a woman's face painted in red called 'She Who Watches,' and I was hooked. The place is the prehistoric equivalent of the Sistine Chapel and Louvre all rolled into one. I needed to find out who painted them, when, and why."

"And did you?"

The professor shrugged. "I put my conclusions in a dissertation that earned me a doctorate and eventually tenure as a professor. Since then, I've devoted my career to unlocking the mysteries of early man in North America. Specifically, who was the first to get here, where they came from, and how they evolved once they did."

"I thought that'd already been decided—hunters who crossed the Bering Land Bridge chasing woolly mammoths during the Ice Age."

"Maybe the how, but certainly not the who and, more importantly, the when. Let me guess, you took an introduction to anthropology course your freshman year. What did you wind up majoring in, wildlife biology?"

"Staying alive. I was a sergeant with the First Cavalry in Vietnam."

Sizemore winced. "You were drafted?"

"I enlisted in '65. The draft didn't start until later."

He mulled that over. "People always talk about kids going to college in order to get deferments, but I've had students who were still drafted and ended up getting wounded or killed. That doesn't even count the kids who were on ROTC scholarships and became casualties. Here we are in 1970 and there's still no end in sight for that damn war. Even Neanderthals were smarter than that."

When I didn't comment, he said, "I don't mean to dishonor your service. It's that the whole political exercise confuses me. The war doesn't make sense from a societal or cultural standpoint. And it's certainly a big step backward in our evolution as the only species on the planet with big brains and opposable thumbs."

The throb of a gas generator sounded halfway between the campsite and a basalt cliff that rose hundreds of feet straight up. An electrical cord snaked from the generator back to the tents and a second toward the cliff. It disappeared into a hollow at the base. If not for the telltale cord, I might've missed spotting the opening.

I pointed at it. "Is that the entrance to the cave where you found the bones? It must be deeper than it looks to need power for lights."

"Technically, it's classed as a rockshelter," Professor Sizemore said. "Rockshelters range from an overhang to a shallow cave that has evidence of prior human occupation. This one's turning out to be atypical. Its considerable depth is one of the anomalies."

"Does that mean you're finding something other than a skeleton that's archaeologically significant?"

He pulled a tube of ChapStick from his vest pocket, unscrewed the cap, and ran the waxy bulb across his lips as he studied me. While the winter air in Harney County was as dry as summer's, I'd played enough chess to recognize a stalling tactic when I saw one.

"I need to correct you on a term," the professor finally said. "It's the teacher in me. We're conducting paleoanthropology here, not archaeology."

"What's the difference?"

"Archaeology is the study of human activity through the recovery and analysis of everything from pottery sherds to tombs. It's a subfield of anthropology, which is the study of human societies and their development. Paleontology is the study of fossils. Put the two together and you get what I do, which is basically working with fossils, petrified skeletons, bone fragments, and stone tools to understand hominization."

He paused and then smiled wryly. "My wife likes to remind me that I have a tendency to lecture. Hominization is just a two-bit word for how you and me and Tuhudda and his grandson over there evolved from the earliest members of our genus. Being a wildlife man, I'm sure you know where genus falls in taxonomy."

Kingdom, phylum, class, order, family, genus, species, I thought to myself. Another way I'd been distracting myself from dwelling on impending fatherhood was classifying all the creatures in the refuges and logging them in a notebook. I eventually planned to add sketches and create a working field guide. I thought of the pregnant Rocky Mountain elk with the cougar scars: *Animalia, Chordata, Mammalia, Artiodactyla, Cervidae, Cervus, Cervus canadensis nelsoni.*

He recapped the lip balm and slipped the tube back in his vest pocket. "How much do you know about early man besides being able to distinguish petroglyphs from cracks in a rock?"

"Not as much as I'd like," I said.

"And how about the native people of the Great Basin?"

"That's something else I'm trying to learn more about. What I know is limited to what I've observed since I moved here and what I've been taught by a healer who lives at the county sheriff's ranch."

"It's unusual for a native to share sacred cultural information with a white man."

"November is a very unusual person. She raised the sheriff's daughter after his wife died and taught her Paiute ways. The daughter and I are getting married. November wants to make sure I have my feet planted in both cultures to improve the odds I'll do a good job looking after her. I don't aim to disappoint either one."

"The healer's name is unusual too."

"It was assigned to her at a boarding school some sixty years ago. Her real name translates to Girl Born in Snow." I hooked my thumb at Tuhudda. "They're both revered tribal elders."

"Maybe I should've hired her too."

"It's better that you didn't. November wouldn't be keen on anyone poking around a gravesite, no matter if it is prehistoric. The spirit world is very real to her, very present."

"Well, the answer to your question is, yes and no. Yes, we did find human remains. By we, I mean, my two assistants and me.

They're working in the rockshelter now. Stick around and you can meet them. But as for the bones being a significant find, no, not really. They're not very old, at least not on any scientific timeline."

He gestured at the cliff. "The rock there is Steens Mountain basalt. It dates back to the Miocene and is approximately sixteen million years old, give or take a couple million. In geological time, that's the equivalent of a day since the oldest rocks on Earth are four billion years old. About ten years ago, a team working in Africa discovered the fossil of the oldest specimen ever found to be classified in our genus. It's called *Homo habilis*. It was dated to nearly two million years ago. In comparison to rocks, that doesn't even amount to a geological minute."

"And the bones you found?"

"Much, much younger than *Homo habilis*. I haven't done any testing, but I'd bet my tenure they're no more than two thousand years old. That's not even close to being Clovis culture."

When I gave him a questioning look, Professor Sizemore explained. "The Clovis are thought to be the earliest people to inhabit North America. Roughly fourteen thousand years ago. A site was discovered and studied near Clovis, New Mexico, in the 1920s, hence the name. Clovis are distinct because of the advanced stone projectile points they made."

"But you don't think the Clovis are the earliest to get here, do you?"

He stiffened. "What makes you say that?"

"If you did, then why are you out here freezing your butt off searching for something that's already been discovered?"

The professor chuckled. When I asked him what he really hoped to find in the rockshelter, he reached for the tube of ChapStick again. Before he could apply it, a woman's voice echoed from the far side of the generator.

"Hello the camp!"

"My assistants," he said. "They must've found something. Stephanie always has to be the first to let me know. She's working on her dissertation and is very focused, very competitive. Those qualities are as important as knowledge when it comes to conducting field study."

Two people hurried toward us. The woman appeared to be in her mid-twenties and wore a down parka and a soft Peruvian cap with silhouettes of alpacas on it. Long, braided tassels dangling from the earflaps batted at her shoulders as she made her way to camp. A man was losing ground behind her. He was heavy and had a scruffy black beard. His wool-lined barn jacket was unbuttoned and revealed a wide leather belt cinched beneath a sizable gut. Unlike the professor's tool belt, a holstered pistol hung from his.

"What did you find?" the professor asked the woman when she reached us.

It took her a moment to catch her breath. "Who's he?" she asked.

"Nick, meet Stephanie Buhl. Stephanie, meet Nick Drake. He's a ranger with Fish and Wildlife."

The young woman raised her hand like a stop sign. She wore wool gloves with the fingertips cut off. "But this isn't wildlife refuge land. I checked the jurisdiction, Pax. It's—"

"Nick's not here in an official capacity. He's a friend of our new helpers, Tuhudda and Nagah." The pair had lit bunches of dried sage and were blessing the campsite by blowing sweet smoke around it.

The second student assistant finally joined us. His breathing was labored. Despite the cold, he was sweating profusely. Flecks of spittle dotted his beard. "Jeez, you're killing me."

"Then don't try and keep up," Stephanie said.

The professor's frown was slight, but he quickly hid it. "Nick, this is Jelly Welch. He's a transfer student working to complete a master's degree."

"Jelly? As in, well, Welch's jams and—"

"That's right," the plump student said, jutting his beard at me. "And I don't mind the name one bit. In fact, I embrace it like a jujutsu move. You know, turn your enemy's force back against himself to throw him on the ground." He made karate chop motions with his hands.

"Professor Sizemore has been giving me a quick lesson in paleoanthropology," I said, "but he didn't mention that a Colt Python was a tool of the trade."

Jelly tugged the barn jacket to cover the holstered pistol. "We're working in a cave. You know what lives in caves? Rattlers. They ball up by the dozens during winter to keep from freezing. You don't want to wake them. You know what's also in there? Bats. They hang upside down by the thousands, dripping and drooling rabies." He shuddered. "I hate bats."

"Most likely they're brown bats," I said. "That's a species of vesper bats. Oregon has fifteen different kinds of bats." I winked at Pax Sizemore. "Sorry, it's the wildlife ranger in me." I turned back to Jelly. "Bats won't bother you if you leave them alone. Fire that cannon inside the rockshelter and if the ricochet doesn't hit you, the cave-in that the bang triggers will."

"Nick makes a good point," Sizemore said. "Remember the golden rule on any dig, safety first. Okay, people, tell me what you found."

Stephanie made a C with her thumb and index finger. "It's a rock yay long. The face is percussion-flaked. It also has flutes." She paused. "I think it's a Clovis projectile point."

"Think or know? Come on, Stephanie, you've studied hard. You've spent plenty of time in the field. Treat this as defending your dissertation. Which is it, yes or no?"

"I can't know for certain because I left the subject in situ without examining the posterior face to ascertain if it had identical percussion flaking." She'd adopted a formal tone and spoke as if reading notes. "I didn't dislodge it because the removal and examination must be supervised and witnessed by my field manager, namely you. However, my degree of certitude that it's a Clovis point is in the eighty to ninety percent range based on preliminary measurement, stone type, and the classic hallmarks of Clovis toolmaking, which includes grooves running from tip to base and pressure flaking on the edges."

Her delivery earned a smile from the professor. "Very good," he said.

"Wait a minute. I deserve some credit too," Jelly said. "It was in my quadrant."

Stephanie rolled her eyes. They were brown with gold flecks in them. "As if you'd know a Clovis point from an exclamation mark."

Sizemore cut off further bickering by saying, "Let's go see what you found." He turned to me. "Care to join us? This could be an enlightening introduction to early man for you."

"Lead the way," I said.

The entrance to the rockshelter resembled a gapped-tooth frown. Slabs of basalt had fallen from the top of the overhang and now stuck up from the ground. Professor Sizemore went in first, followed by Tuhudda. Everyone except for Nagah had to duck to keep from cracking their skulls. The steady thrum of the generator reminded me of a heartbeat.

A couple of yards past the opening, the paleoanthropologist stopped and reached into a cardboard box containing several flashlights. He picked one out and suggested the Wills and I do the same. "For emergencies," he said. Stephanie and Jelly were carrying their own.

"The ceiling's high enough to stand now," Sizemore said. "Turn around and look back at Catlow Valley. If this was your home ten, fifteen, twenty thousand years ago, you'd be looking out on a very different landscape. It was greener, lusher. The animal life was also very different. There were giant bison, sloths, and camel-like creatures roaming around."

He pointed his flashlight at the floor. "We've confirmed the discoloration you see here was caused by fire. The spot could've been used for cooking or keeping warm or leaving the prehistoric equivalent of a floodlight on at night to ward off wild animals. Saber-tooth cats—that's the proper name, not "tiger"—and dire wolves prowled southeastern Oregon back then. We've collected samples of residual charcoal that we'll carbon date later."

"Will that give you the age when the fire was first lit or the last time it went out?" I asked.

"More than likely we'll get a range of ages since there's every indication the rockshelter has been used over a period of millennia based on the human remains we found along with some newer artifacts. In other words, different people brought in different wood to burn at different times."

"That must make dating hard."

"It does, but that's the name of the game with paleoanthropology. Every site can be a box of pieces from different jigsaw puzzles all jumbled together. Carbon dating is one of the tools we use to sort them out, but it has its limitations."

I asked him how so.

"It can only be used to date items that contain organic materials such as plants, wood fibers, or bones, but it can't date anything older than sixty thousand years because of the decay rate of carbon. That's measured in half-lives of fifty-seven hundred years."

The handsome professor flashed a wry smile. "There I go again, lecturing. Think of it this way. You collect a bone fragment of an animal that died sixty thousand years ago. Every fifty-seven hundred years, half the carbon in the sample has decayed. Ten half-lives later, there's nothing left to sample. Make sense?"

"But what about the skeleton found in Africa? You said the scientists determined it was two million years old."

"His bones were fossilized, so they were able to use a different technique that dates the origin of rocks since fossils are rocks. It's called potassium-argon dating. It's accurate from four billion years ago to one hundred thousand years ago. At that point, the remaining potassium that hasn't decayed to argon is too small to measure. At least, by the means we have now. I've no doubt that will change. I also have no doubt that even older members of our genus will be found someday."

The professor flashed white teeth when he grinned. "Okay, class, the chemistry lecture is over. Let's keep walking."

He led and Jelly brought up the rear. I was second to last in line. Even though I was in front of the portly student, I could smell his body odor. He must not have believed in showering while camping. Daylight in the cavern continued to ebb until a string of caged work lights—like the kind home mechanics hang from the raised hoods of their cars when changing sparkplugs— took over, illuminating our way. The generator-powered lights flickered and cast our shadows on the rock wall in the herky-jerky fashion of an old-fashioned black and white film.

"You notice how Stephanie always makes sure she's right next to Sizemore?" Jelly whispered to me. "She gets any closer, she'll be wearing his shirt. She's always sucking up to him. She could hand in a shopping list for her dissertation and Sizemore would give her an A plus. Having a nice rack doesn't hurt, you know what I mean? There's a reason they call it teacher's pet."

I didn't bother to respond. I was concentrating on counting steps in case I ever had to make my way out of the cave in the dark. Old habits from walking night patrol were hard to shake.

Jelly said, "Did you hear what Sizemore called me? A *transfer* student. It was a total putdown. The department should've accepted all my transfer credits, but Sizemore blocked it. I could've had my masters by now, but no, it's all about him protecting the reputation of his precious program." He sniffed. "Protecting his grant money, more like it."

The professor halted again. We'd reached a fork in the

cavern. The left side wasn't lit. Professor Sizemore pointed at it. "That leads to the chamber where we found human remains. They're actually quite well-preserved because of the low humidity and constant cool temperature this far into the rock-shelter along with a lack of exposure to wind and sunlight. We minimize using light in there for conservation purposes."

He addressed Tuhudda. "I'm assuming they're Paiute because of the rockshelter's location and your people's long history in the region. As I said when we met, I believe it's only proper that a member of your tribe be present when we examine them. I've made that my policy even though it's rarely practiced at digs around the world."

Tuhudda's red bandana bobbed. "The ancient ones who walked the land we now walk should always be respected."

"Then, if it's all right with you, I'll show you the bones tomorrow. To put the remains into context, I first need your help identifying some relics that we found. They're back at camp. Let's go see what Stephanie found."

The professor turned toward the right-hand fork. "We'll need to proceed carefully from here. The floor has a thick vein of carbonate running down the middle with loose dirt and rock debris pockets on either side. Since the vein is too hard to dig without using jackhammers and explosives, we've let it be and use it as a path in and out. The floor on both sides have been gridded with strings as part of our mapping of the site. Please don't step on them."

We proceeded in the same order. A few yards in, Jelly started bellyaching again. "I don't get why you made such a big deal about my gun. You're packing too. That's a Smith and Wesson .357 mag, isn't it?"

He was right about my service weapon, but I didn't respond.

"For your information, I don't carry it only for snakes and bats," Jelly said. "I'm in charge of camp security. You ever heard of grave robbers? They're badasses who dig up artifacts and sell them. Get a good price too. The older the artifact, the more it's worth. I'm talking about a lot of money, the kind of money that might tempt somebody." He paused. "Know what I mean?"

Jelly waited for an answer, but when I didn't bite, he slapped his holster. "I catch one sniffing around the camp or in here, they'll find out who the real badass is. I'll add his bones to the old chief's back there." He snickered.

I blew out air. "Remember what I said about firing a gun in a cave?"

He huffed and then said, "You see all this white stuff on the ground? It's bat shit. Thousands of years' worth. I never look up when I'm in here because some bat might take a dump and it'd fall into my mouth."

"Another good reason you should keep it shut."

"Is that a putdown? It's a putdown, isn't it?"

"Only friendly advice."

"No, it was a putdown. A total putdown. You're like Stephanie and Sizemore. Trying to make yourself feel big."

The line came to a halt again. "Show us what you found, Stephanie," the professor said.

The grad student switched on her flashlight and directed the beam on a patch of ground inside a square of string tied at the corners to small stakes. The dirt resembled a layer cake with steps carved into it. She traced the outline of a dark stone imbedded in the dirt with the light.

"The subject is located in D one hundred and twenty-six," she began.

"Hold on, let me explain to the others," Sizemore said. "We gridded the site with an alphanumeric key. She's citing the exact location of the subject for use in the dig logbook and for cataloguing samples and artifacts. Go ahead."

"The subject is in a horizontal position," Stephanie

continued in the same formal tone she'd used earlier. "Surrounding debris has been screened and removed. The subject is likely obsidian, though it is possible it could be a dark-colored chert. It is spherical in shape and measures four and five-eighth inches long and one and one-half inches at its widest. It has a lance-shaped tip and a concave base. The exposed anterior face shows evidence of percussion flaking. Grooves run the length of the subject."

She leaned closer. The tassels that hung from the earflaps of her alpaca cap dangled just over the rock. She took a narrow camel-hair paintbrush from her utility belt.

"I am now going to clear around the subject to expose the edges." She brushed gently. Particles of dirt no bigger than grains of sand were swept into a neat pile. "The edges appear uniformly jagged and reveal pressure flaking."

The paleoanthropologist interrupted her again. He made a fist and mimed striking his left hand with it. "Percussion flaking is striking a rock with another rock to chip off flakes in order to shape it." He opened his fist and pushed his right index finger against the left. "Pressure flaking uses a sharp stick to do the fine-tuning by applying pressure at the edge of a flake to remove it. Advanced stone toolmakers could give a blade or projectile point a serrated edge much like today's bread knife."

Stephanie looked up expectantly. He put his hand on her shoulder as if needing balance and squatted beside her. They studied the rock intently.

"Let's turn it over to confirm the posterior," he said.

Sizemore pulled a tool that resembled a dentist's pick from a pouch on his belt and used the tip to circumscribe the dirt that framed the rock. With each turn, the tiny trench deepened.

"Clear debris," he said. Stephanie gave a few flicks with her paintbrush. "Trowel." She handed him a flat, triangular tool.

"Swab." He used the proffered square of cotton to dab at a streak.

"I'm now going to extricate the subject," Sizemore said. "Cloth."

Stephanie blanketed the rock with a small piece of white cloth. The professor held it in place with his finger and inserted the trowel's tip beneath the rock and gingerly worked it around. Slowly and carefully, he slid the trowel all the way under. Keeping his finger pressed on the cloth, he lifted, and then in a deft move worthy of flipping an omelet, turned the trowel over while still holding the cloth against the rock. He placed it on the ground and slipped his finger out. Stephanie brushed away a few particles of dirt that clung to the newly exposed face.

"It's your find," Sizemore said. "Tell us what you see."

"The posterior face of the subject shows the same level of percussion flaking as the previously examined anterior face." A noticeable quaver sounded in her voice. "There are the same fluted grooves running lengthwise."

"Don't leave us hanging, Stephanie. Tell us what it is."

"With visual inspection of both sides of the subject complete, I conclude that the flaking is bifacial and of an identical style. The subject is without question a man-made projectile point. Since it bears all the hallmarks associated with the toolmaking techniques of the Clovis culture, including percussion and pressure flaking plus grooves used to fasten the point to the wooden shaft of a spear or lance, I submit that it is indeed a Clovis point and its age is commensurate with the culture's known existence of between ten thousand and fourteen thousand years before the present."

"So witnessed by the field manager and supervisor," Sizemore said, adopting an officious tone. He clapped her on the shoulder. "Congratulations, Stephanie. It's a helluva find."

She leaned into him. "Oh, Pax. It's so exciting."

The paleoanthropologist who wore fancy Italian hiking boots and looked like a mountaineer threw back his head and yodeled long and loud.

As his cheer echoed through the cavern, Jelly muttered, "Teacher's pet."

5

A vented propane heater and cooktop provided both warmth and hot water for coffee inside the dig team's main tent. We sat on folding canvas chairs in a circle except for Stephanie, who pulled hers up to a work table, placed the Clovis point in a small cardboard box, and began writing in a logbook. Jelly slouched on the camp chair next to me. His BO grew even stronger inside the warm tent.

Tuhudda added two spoonfuls of sugar and a healthy dollop from a can of sweetened condensed milk to his coffee. He held the mug with both hands and slurped. A tin of shortbread was passed around. Nagah helped himself to one of the buttery Scottish biscuits.

"When do I get to move rocks?" he asked before taking a nibble.

"Tomorrow when I show your grandfather the bones," Professor Sizemore said.

"Are the rocks on top of them?"

"No. The skeleton is lying horizontally on a ledge in a cleft in a wall. The ledge may've been used as a bed or as an open-sided tomb. We don't know if he died in his sleep or was placed there."

Tuhudda shook his head. "*Numu* would not do that."

"Entomb the dead, why not?"

"Because caves are for giving life, not death. *Mu naa'a*, our creator, known as Wolf, made the world out of darkness. The first people he made were *Nuwuddu*, the animals. Then *Mu naa'a* created *Numu*, the second people." He pointed to Nagah and himself. "The people walked out of the darkness and into this world at the place white men call Malheur Cave."

"What can you tell me about how the Paiute of old treated their dead?" the professor asked.

"There were different ways for different deaths," the tribal elder began. "If a warrior died in battle, he was left where he fell to honor the battleground. If at home, he was seated in a hole in the ground with his knees against his chest and covered. If a woman died in childbirth, she was buried with her dead baby in her arms. An infant who died was buried in its cradleboard."

I thought of Gemma. She was strong and healthy and her pregnancy had been problem-free. The hospital in Burns was only a thirty-minute drive from the Warbler ranch. I could make it in twenty if need be. But Vietnam had taught me nothing in life was ever guaranteed.

"And the mourning rituals," Sizemore said, "what were those like?"

Tuhudda looked around the tent before he replied. He scanned the tables, the boxes of scientific equipment, and a makeshift pantry stacked with cases of canned food and bags of beans and rice. "There are as many different bands of *Numu* as goods you have here. We speak different words and have different ceremonies."

"But isn't it true the different bands held a mourning period that lasted for seven days? If a husband died, his wife would cut off her hair and lay it across his chest."

"Many *Numu* did that. Not only the wife, but the man's

sisters, daughters, and mother also. People would make drawings of him and those would be burned along with his wickiup.
Singers would sing. Dancers would dance."

"What about burying the body in a horizontal position?"

"Some *Numu* had to because they lived where the ground
was too rocky to dig. They covered the body with stones."
Tuhudda sipped more coffee. "When people were walking from
one place to the next and someone died, the body would be
burned and the ashes carried in a basket so the person could
complete the journey and not be left behind to become nowhere
bones."

Sizemore asked Tuhudda what kind of dances and songs
were performed.

The old man lowered his coffee cup. It was empty except for
congealed sugar at the bottom. He wiped it with his fingertip
and licked it. "Some *Numu* held a Cry Ceremony where they
sang the Bird Song and the Salt Song."

"Do you know how those songs go?"

"Yes."

"Can you sing them for us?"

"No."

"Why not?"

Tuhudda shrugged. "Because no one here is dead."

Jelly smirked and muttered so only I could hear, "He got
Sizemore there. A total putdown."

Nagah swallowed the last crumb of his shortbread. "Okay, I
am finished eating and ready to move rocks. Where are the ones
you want me to move? I will move them all."

"They're in the chamber where we found the bones. I have a
hunch the rocks might be blocking other clefts or even
entrances to other chambers," the professor said.

"And will there be more bones behind them?"

"Maybe. We'll have to find out."

"I am ready to find out now," Nagah said.

"It will be better if we start tomorrow when we're fresh."

"Will we move the bones too?"

Sizemore shook his head. "We can't rush that. If we do, we risk missing something that might help us identify them along with the cause of death."

"But I need to make money right away," Nagah said. "Our family does not have electricity at our camp. The winter has been long and we have run out of kerosene for our lanterns and oil for our heaters. There is not enough light for me to do my homework."

"Are you a good student?"

"I try to be."

"But school is still in session, yet you are here."

"Yes, because the teacher told me I could not stay in school if I did not do my homework."

"Couldn't you start on it earlier when it's still daylight?"

"My family's camp is in Harney Valley and the school is in Burns. It takes a very long time to walk there and back. I leave in the dark and get home in the dark this time of year."

"Can't someone give you a ride?" Sizemore asked.

"Sometimes Grandfather does, but now we do not have the money to buy gasoline to drive every day."

"There's no bus?"

Nagah hung his head. "It goes to the other neighborhoods, but not where we live on the reservation."

"How about this? I'll give you and your grandfather plenty of work so you'll be able to buy all the gas and kerosene you need. In return, you have to promise never to give up school. Deal?"

Nagah smiled. "You sound like Dr. Gemma. That is what she tells me also."

"Who's Dr. Gemma?"

"She is a veterinarian. Her father is Sheriff Warbler. She flies an airplane and said she will teach me one day. She and Mr. Nick are going to have a baby."

"I see." The professor turned to me. "Now I understand why November is in such a hurry to teach you Paiute ways." He turned back to Nagah. "You win. Are you ready to start making money right now? Not moving rocks—we're still going to start that tomorrow—but by helping your grandfather identify some items we've collected."

Nagah's eyes lit up. "Like the big arrowhead?"

"Actually, that's too big to be an arrowhead. It's a spearhead."

"Was it used in battle?"

"Most likely for hunting. The people who made it worked in teams to bring down big animals like mammoths and mastodons. They're the size of elephants. Mammoths had long, curved tusks. Mastodon tusks were shorter and straighter. They're extinct now, but if you come to my lab at the university, I'll show you some tusks and bones. I even have a mammoth skull."

"I would like that very much, but I will need to move many rocks to buy enough gasoline to get there."

The professor went to a stack of boxes and picked up the top one. He set it down and pulled a knife from it and held it out. The blade was made of black stone and attached to a white handle. He handed it to Tuhudda.

"Have you ever seen anything like this?"

The old man examined the blade and handle. He laid it across two fingers to find its balance point. "It is a very good knife. The blade is flint, the handle is the bone of a buffalo. *Bagootsoo*, in our tongue. It was made by *Numu*."

"How can you be sure?"

"My grandfather, *Padooa*, in your tongue, Bear, had one like this. Look here." He pointed to the butt of the handle. "That mark is the sign for *bagootsoo*. You see the hump? This knife was for cutting meat. My grandfather hunted *bagootsoo*. Many *bagootsoo* lived in the brown world during his time, but now they are gone."

Sizemore took the knife back and examined the handle's butt. "Well, I'll be darned. I mistook that for a scratch. It's a hump all right. I can see it clearly now."

I asked him how the blade was different than a Clovis point.

"It's not nearly as old, for one thing. While the same kind of percussion-flaking technique was used for shaping it, the fine-tuning of the tip and edges was done by grinding rather than pressure flaking."

The professor said to Tuhudda, "You say your grandfather had one? You're what, seventy, seventy-five years old? That means he was born a hundred, a hundred twenty-five years ago. Let's put his birth around 1840ish. Steel knives were widely traded among American Indian people even before then. Why did he have a stone knife? Was it ceremonial?"

"His father gave it to him and his before him. When my grandfather died, it would have passed to my father, *Tooonug-wetsedu*, known as Cougar. But it did not. Where did you find this knife?"

"It was in the rockshelter. We found it during one of our first explorations." Sizemore hesitated. "I apologize, I don't know all of the words in your language. You mentioned the translations for your father's and grandfather's names, but what do Tuhudda and Nagah mean in English?"

"Deer and Mountain Sheep."

"I see, your line honors animal totems."

"*Nuwuddu*." He pointed at the stone knife. "Whoever that belonged to would not have left it behind. He would not have forgotten such a valuable knife."

"Maybe he lost it in the dark and couldn't find it, Grandfather," Nagah said.

"He would have kept searching. To lose such a knife would bring much shame."

"I have something else to show you," Sizemore said.

He laid the knife down next to the box and pulled out two flat objects about eight to nine inches long and four inches wide. They were rounded at both ends and appeared to be made of plant material. When he held them up, I could see the ties at one end and a flap at the other.

"They're sandals," I said.

"Correct. They're made of—"

"Sagebrush bark," Tuhudda said before the professor could. "Bark was shredded and rolled into twine. Twining goes from heel to toe, heel to toe always when making sandals. I have never made such a sandal, but my grandmother, *Ohalune*, known as Yellow Moon, did. She wore them instead of moccasins because the sole was thicker. Sharp rocks would not poke her. Thorns also."

"Your grandmother made sandals like these?" When Tuhudda nodded, Sizemore called to Stephanie. "What was the age of the sandals Cressman found at Fort Rock?"

The grad student looked up from her logbook. Even though we were inside, she still wore the Peruvian cap with the alpacas. "They were radiocarbon dated to between nine thousand two hundred and ten thousand four hundred years ago."

"Fort Rock in Lake County, up by Christmas Valley?" I said.

Sizemore nodded. "It's not more than a hundred miles from here as the crow flies. The rockshelter there is an early dig site. My mentor excavated it. Luther Cressman. He's the father of Oregon archaeology. He founded and chaired the anthropology department—my department—until his retirement. He pioneered all the big digs around here. Dozens of sandals like this pair were discovered at Fort Rock."

I asked him if this pair was that old.

"I don't think so." He turned to Tuhudda. "If your grandmother made sandals like these, that links you and Nagah to the people who made the sandals at Fort Rock. The Paiute, along with all the other native tribes, are assumed to be descendants of the Clovis. And the Clovis had to descend from someone."

"The people you're trying to find," I said. "Do you have a name for them?"

Sizemore smiled wryly. "Not yet."

Tuhudda held the sandals aloft. "My grandmother wore hers always, even when she danced at Round Dance. She wore them the day she and my grandfather *Padooa* left our camp to walk to Fort McDermitt to visit family. I was a young boy then, but I remember them. Did you find these here also?"

"Yes. They were near where we found the knife with the buffalo-bone handle."

Tuhudda kept his eyes on the sandals. "What else did you find?"

Sizemore reached into the box and pulled out a roll of hide. It crackled as he unfurled it, revealing two rocks, a tuft of dried moss, a stick and a bowl-shaped piece of wood, and a drawstring pouch. The professor untied the strings of the pouch and used a long pair of tweezers from his carpenter's belt to extract two hanks of braided hair, each about three inches long. He laid them beside the pouch.

"What do we have here?" he asked.

Tuhudda stroked his whiskerless chin. "I have seen a bundle like this before. My grandfather had one. The rocks are used to start fire. One is quartz, the other jasper." He struck his balled fists against each other over the dried moss. "The moss traps sparks like clouds trap lightning." Then he pretended to take a pinch of dried moss and put it in the wooden bowl. He picked up the drinking straw-sized stick, placed one end in the wooden bowl, and the other between his palms and mimed rubbing them together quickly so the tip of the stick would drill into the bowl. "The stick and bowl are for starting fire."

Sizemore asked if the two braids of hair were also used as tinder.

Tuhudda placed the wooden fire stick down and leaned back in his chair. His shoulders slumped and his eyes closed. When he opened them again, they were moist.

"They are for a different type of fire. The one that burns in here." Tuhudda patted his heart. "The hair is from a husband and a wife. The man would carry them with him whenever he left camp to hunt or trade. No matter how far he walked or rode his pony, no matter how long he was gone, he and his wife would always be together. She would do the same."

The old man stared at the black flint blade with the white buffalo-bone handle, the pair of sagebrush-bark sandals, and the fire-starting bundle with the locks of braided hair. "I have seen all these things from my grandfather and grandmother's time. Who am I to say they are not theirs? When they set out to walk to Fort McDermitt, they were never seen again. My father and uncles searched for them, but found no signs."

He kept staring at the objects. "No one would ever forget they owned such things or leave them behind. Whoever they belonged to died where you found them."

"That's certainly possible," the professor said. "We found no human remains with the relics, but wild animals could've dragged them off."

Tuhudda crossed his arms. "I will go with you to look at the Ancient One in the morning. I will give him a blessing so he will no longer be nowhere bones like my grandparents."

"You've used that term twice now," Sizemore said. "What does it mean?"

"Nowhere bones are neither here nor there. Because no one was able to sing songs or dance to help send them on their journey to the spirit world, who is to say they ever completed it?"

"Ooh, ghosts." Jelly snickered and made hocus-pocus moves with his fingers.

Sizemore shot him a withering look.

Tuhudda sighed. "I wish I could find *Padooa* and *Ohalune* so my grandparents will be nowhere bones no more forever."

"Bear and Yellow Moon," Stephanie said, joining us. Her eyes were moist too. "It's a lost love story waiting to be found."

"This is so," Tuhudda said.

6

It was dark by the time I pulled up to the old lineman's shack and hustled inside to start a fire. I opened the wood-burning stove, made a log cabin of kindling, and touched a match. As I watched the flames lick and readied to feed in quarter rounds of split ponderosa pine, I replayed the unsettling conversation I'd had with Pax Sizemore after I bid everyone good night. The professor got out of his camp chair and offered to walk me to my pickup. When we reached it, I said, "What do you want to tell me that you didn't want the others to hear?"

Sizemore handed me a scrap of paper. "That's the radio channel we use. Protocol is for me to check in with my department daily, but transmission and reception can be hit or miss with the Cascades running between here and the campus in Eugene. Since you're on the east side of the mountains and relatively close, I could radio you and you could telephone in our status. That is, if you don't mind."

"It's not a matter of minding, it's a matter of being available. When I'm at the refuges, the reception is usually pretty spotty too. I also spend a fair amount of nights away. My beat is the size of a lot of states. When I'm patrolling Deer Flat along the Snake

River or the Sheldon refuge down on the Nevada line, it's typically a two-night stay, if not longer."

"Even in winter?"

"Year-round."

"I was hoping I could count on you."

I could tell he was concerned about something other than abiding by protocol. "Go ahead and try radioing me. If I don't pick up, then call this channel." I scribbled it down. "It's the sheriff's office in Burns. Orville Nelson will likely answer. He's the department's newest deputy and Sheriff Warbler's right-hand man. I'll let him know about our arrangement when I'm in Burns getting Tuhudda's tire fixed. If a day goes by and we don't hear from you, we'll radio you. Be sure to pick up, because if you don't, then expect a visit from the sheriff's office."

"That's more than I hoped for. Thanks."

"Now is the time you tell me why you don't want to miss a daily check-in. Does it have to do with grave robbers? Jelly told me about them. He also said he's in charge of security."

The professor groaned. "That would be a self-appointment. I appreciate you trying to teach him a safety lesson. Jelly gives new meaning to a loose cannon."

"If he's a risk, why did you bring him along?"

"I didn't have a choice. He'd filed a formal complaint with the anthropology department earlier in the year and the powers-that-be came up with the bright idea of offering him a field job if he agreed to drop it."

"Was it about his transfer credits?"

"Jelly told you about that too?" Sizemore shook his head. "The department couldn't accept them because they were for classes he took through an unaccredited correspondence school. He said he earned them when an illness forced him to stay home a year. I'm starting to think the illness was mental rather than physical. That thing he said about balls of rattlesnakes? Ophidiophobia isn't his only anxiety."

"The fear of snakes," I said. "His fear of bats is chiroptophobia."

The professor's eyebrows rose. "You do know your taxonomy."

"Is his phobia about grave robbers imagined too?"

"They're real enough, but it'd be highly unusual for someone to strongarm an active site. Your typical looting takes place long before a dig even starts. Someone gets wind of a rock-shelter and goes in with heavy equipment and wreaks havoc while the dig plan is still on the chalkboard. They usually destroy more than they steal."

"If it's not grave robbers, what is it that made you leave a warm tent to make sure you didn't go a day without being heard from?"

"I've received some threats of a personal nature. They're probably nothing, but it'd be irresponsible to ignore them. I have the safety of my team to consider."

"Who's threatening you?"

"Two people, I'm embarrassed to say. The first has to do with Stephanie Buhl. Well, not Stephanie, specifically, but her boyfriend. Ex-boyfriend, actually. His name's Philip Carson, but he goes by Flip. He's a throwback to a different age."

"You've met him?"

"Unfortunately, and more than once. Flip and Stephanie grew up in Springfield. It's a mill town that shares a border with Eugene but the two are worlds apart. Flip and Stephanie dated in high school, or at least the two years Flip attended before dropping out to work on a logging crew. Stephanie, on the other hand, was class valedictorian and won a full-ride to the university. She earned her baccalaureate in three years and went straight to grad school."

"Paleoanthropology is a pretty obscure field. I doubt she got much exposure to it growing up in a small town."

"The magic of higher learning. It opens doors. Stephanie took an intro to anthro course her freshman year to fulfill an undergraduate requirement and realized Springfield was a microcosm of hominization. One course led to another and eventually to a seminar I was teaching. I'd like to think I was an influence, but that would be taking credit away from her. Stephanie has a real gift and is well on her way to a stunning career as a paleoanthropologist."

"And that leaves little room for Flip the logger," I said.

"Stephanie outgrew him the first year at the university. Dating the proverbial bad boy may have been exciting while in high school, but once she embraced her intellect, there was no going back."

"But Carson hasn't embraced her evolution, has he? If he's threatened you, he must think you're more than her professor."

"Believe me, that's all I am. Our relationship is strictly professional. I'm happily married. Flip operates under the assumption that every man lusts after what he does, or, more to the point, what he wants and can't have. I'm not the only professor who's had to deal with this sort of thing. There's always some boyfriend or girlfriend of a dig team member back at home who starts imagining what goes on in a tent way out in the desert. It's a situation as old as robbing the pyramids."

"But Carson does more than turn green, right?"

"Do you know which species of the *Homo* genus is the most violent? It's us. *Sapiens*. There's a reason we're the only one left. We killed off the others. We haven't even evolved from killing our own kind."

"How violent is Carson?"

"Very. The first time I met him, Stephanie and I happened to be leaving a lecture hall at the same time. Flip was stalking her and got the wrong idea. He all but bared his teeth and drummed his chest at me. Recently—and, mind you, it's been years since she broke up with him—Flip stormed into my office while I was working late one evening and grabbed a three-thousand-year-old stone axe from an examination table. He screamed he was going to split my skull in two unless I admitted I was sleeping with her. It was quite a dilemma, you see, since I'm not. I had no doubt he'd do more than bash my head in if I lied and told him I was."

"How did you get him to back down?"

"Luckily, a custodian came in to clean my office. Flip dropped the axe and stormed out. Thank goodness the blade didn't break when it hit the floor. It's quite valuable."

"Did you tell campus security?"

"Of course, but they were already aware of him from previous run-ins."

"What kind?"

"It always had something to do with Stephanie. Stalking her, harassing her, making a living hell of her life and that of anyone around her that he suspected had designs on her."

"What about the Eugene police department?"

"Yes, I filed a report with them, but now I've learned they arrested Flip on a drunk and disorderly charge since we've been in the field. He was banging on the front door of a house. The police locked him in the drunk tank and he made bail the next day. Later that day, they realized it was my front door he'd been trying to get into while my wife was home alone."

"Did the police go after him when they found that out?"

"They tried, but he's disappeared."

"Does Stephanie know?"

"She knows he barged into my office that night, but I haven't told her about this latest incident. It could be very disruptive to the limited time we have here."

"Does Carson know where the dig site is?"

"The only one who knows the exact coordinates is the head of my department, but it's no secret this part of Oregon is a hotbed for Paleo-Indian digs, what with Fort Rock and Paisley Caves nearby."

I asked him to tell me about the second threat.

"It has to do with my work at Paisley Caves. That's a complex of five rockshelters in Lake County. My mentor, Professor Cressman, did most of the exploratory work there in the late thirties. I was awarded a grant to conduct a follow-up study a couple of years ago. I presented what turned out to be groundbreaking findings that extended the original estimation of human habitation there. An associate professor in the department challenged me. He offered laboratory results that contradicted my findings and accused me of falsifying data. My grant was rescinded and my reputation put on the line."

"You fought back."

"Darn right I did. I arranged for another laboratory to independently redo all of my tests and they came up with the same results as me. At the same time, I did a different type of digging. I uncovered evidence that proved my accuser had rigged his data to bolster his false claim against me."

"Why did he have it in for you?"

"Competition for grant money, secure tenure which I have and he didn't, professional jealousy, resentment, rivalry, take your pick. I brought the independent lab's findings to the American Society of Paleoanthropologists along with proof that my accuser had falsified his tests. The board ruled in my favor and my reputation was preserved."

I asked him what happened to the other professor.

"He was discredited, of course. He lost his standing with the society and his assistant professorship at the university."

"What sort of threats is he making?"

"It started as a whisper and letter campaign. He said I was a fraud, that I bought off the society, and I cheated him. Later, he escalated it to in-person confrontations. He barged into a society meeting ranting about me. He staged a one-man protest of his firing at a university board of trustees meeting. A few days ago, a student of mine overheard him at a tavern in Eugene. He was saying he had a surefire plan for my current dig that would, quote unquote, blow it and my reputation to kingdom come."

"Do you keep dynamite at the camp?"

"Pardon me, but I need to correct you on a term. When explosives are used at a dig, it's TNT, the same explosive miners use. But, no, I don't use explosives at all. You can never be sure you won't destroy what it is you're looking for. Why do you ask?"

"Maybe he was being literal. Have you spoken to campus security?"

"Yes, they're aware of it along with the other things he's done, but in their estimation, it doesn't rise to anything more than an academia squabble."

"What's this professor's name?"

"That's *former* associate professor. Cecil Edwards Oliver."

"I'm going to pass this information onto Sheriff Warbler. Pudge doesn't like surprises."

"If you think that's best."

"If Carson or Oliver show up here, radio the sheriff's office right away. Day or night. Ask Tuhudda and Nagah for help too."

"What can an old man and a boy do?"

"You'd be surprised. The Paiute have managed to survive in a harsh land for thousands of years because they're smart, resourceful, and very brave."

I put the conversation with Sizemore out of my mind and added a couple of pieces of pine to the fire and closed the load door. The biscuits and coffee I'd had at the dig camp weren't enough for supper. I set a pot of leftover stew on the burner to reheat. While it warmed, I turned on the radio. The DJ was spinning a new album by Van Morrison. The Irish singer-songwriter had incorporated soul, jazz, and rhythm and blues to his compositions about love, spiritual renewal, and redemption. The title track had become Gemma's and my favorite, and on the nights she stayed over, the song usually sparked us to slow dance around the wood-burning stove before bedtime.

The phone rang. I answered by saying, "Perfect timing. They're playing our song." I held the receiver toward the radio and then brought it back and started singing along. "*Well, it's a marvelous night for a moondance, With the stars up above in your eyes.*"

"Maybe yours, not mine," Loq grunted and then began talk-singing, "*From the Halls of Montezuma, To the shores of Tripoli.*"

"Once a Marine, always a Marine." I turned the radio down. "I thought it was Gemma."

"Where is she?"

"At a ranch up by Pine Creek. A herd came down with *Pasteurella haemolytica.* She said it could take a couple of days before she brings it under control."

"They give a disease a name like that, it's got to be bad."

"So Gemma tells me."

"When she's doing all that telling, she happen to tell you if and when she's going to marry you?"

I lowered the flame beneath the pot of stew. "She's been pretty busy."

"You might want to hurry her decision along if you still want me to be your best man. When the spring migration starts, I'll have my hands full at the refuges."

"I don't recall having asked you."

"You two are so busy trying not to make decisions, I went ahead and asked me for you. By the way, I said yes."

"I'm honored. Is that why you called?"

"That and to say we got a problem at the Klamath Marsh refuge. The water that's supposed to stay in it isn't."

"There must be a break in one of the levees. Beavers have always been hard on them. Badgers too. Did you check for burrows?"

"I found a break made by animals, all right, the two-legged kind. How soon can you get here?"

"I have a couple of things to do in Burns first thing in the morning, but I could be there by noon."

"See you then, Moondance."

I turned the volume on the radio back up. I watched the stew bubble as the DJ cued another track from the new LP, this one called "Into the Mystic." As Van Morrison put his heart and soul into crooning about a couple born before the wind and younger than the sun, I thought of Gemma—her laugh, the sparkle in her eyes, and the way she tried to help me make sense of why I was a magnet for violence.

"That's an easy one," she'd say. "You went to Vietnam because you couldn't turn a blind eye to people in danger. You came back thinking it was all a big mistake and so you tried to forget why you went in the first place. But you can't forget who you are. You have a need to help people. It's a big reason I fell in love with you."

I looked up from the stew pot. Steam had fogged the kitchen window. Van Morrison was singing passionately about wanting to rock her gypsy soul. As he hit the chorus, "*And together we'll float, Into the mystic,*" I reached over and began wiping the pane to clear it, wishing that Gemma was on other side smiling back at me.

7

THE WICKIUP

I press my face to the plane's window and shout, "Gemma!" I try the pilot door's handle, but the crash has compressed the fuselage and clamped the door tight. I need something to jimmy it. Splintered branches and limbs litter the wreckage, but they're either too thick or too supple.

Something glints in the snow. It's half of the propeller that snapped off when we plowed into the pines. I grab it and jam the tip into the gap between the door and fuselage. I pull on it. Nothing. I push against it. Still nothing. I dig in my boots and put my shoulder to it. My ribs burn. The door frame groans. The gap widens. I shove the prop blade in deeper and continue pushing. The screech of metal grinding on metal makes the fillings in my teeth ache. I don't let up. The metal buckles, the locking mechanism springs, and I wrench the door open.

Neither the ungodly screech of metal nor the cold mountain air wakes Gemma. I can see how close the limb that lanced through the windshield came to striking her. The blood that streaks her cheeks and chin is dark. Her half-open eyes are unseeing.

I reach for her wrist. Her fingers are still locked around the yoke, the small plane's equivalent of a steering wheel. The gold band on her ring finger gleams like her father's badge. I feel for a pulse. Her skin is cold—cold as the snow on the ground. I place my ear to her lips and listen. "No!" I shout. "Not now. Not here. Not this way."

I slide my thumb up and down and around on the inside of her wrist. Snapshots begin blinking as if I'm fanning the pages of a photo album. There's Gemma standing with her hands on her hips and glaring at me suspiciously the first time we meet, the night Pudge finds me in the middle of the high lonesome and brings me to his ranch house with my Triumph motorcycle strapped down in the bed of his pickup. Then it's Gemma laughing as she teaches me how to ride Wovoka. And Gemma pensive and understanding as I tell her about the ambush that killed everyone in my squad but me and how I tried to silence my guilt with heroin. Then Gemma all business as she works to save a wild filly foal I found among a poisoned herd of mustangs. And finally Gemma beaming as she says I do.

I keep rubbing the inside of her wrist. Something moves. Faint. Slow. But there. A pulse. I'm sure of it. Then something brushes my ear, something softer than a thread of cobweb drifting in a summer breeze, softer than the clouds we danced on. Faint, slow, but there. It's her breath. I know its touch. I'd know it anywhere.

"Stay with me," I urge. "Come on, you can do it. You and the baby. Come back to me."

But all I get is the faint pulse and shallow breathing. I tell myself it's something. I can work with something.

I quickly check for wounds. There are no signs of deep punctures, no compound fractures with jagged bones sticking out, no pools of blood gathering in the pilot's seat or on the floorboards. The crash knocked both of us out, but I came to. Why didn't she? Maybe the limb gave her a glancing blow. Maybe she struck her head against it when whiplashing. I slide my palm between her curved belly and the cockeyed instrument panel. I hold my breath and count. Ten, twenty, thirty seconds. Nothing kicks back. I tell myself it doesn't mean anything. Hours can pass without the drumbeat of tiny hands and feet. Days, even.

I try to recall what the book said about kicking in the third trimester. The book. Gemma gave it to me one evening at the lineman's shack after we'd gone several days without seeing each other. "Catch," she said, and tossed me a thick paperback. I snagged it before it hit the floor. When I saw the cover, it grew heavy.

"Does this mean what I think it means?" I held up the copy of *Baby and Child Care* by Dr. Benjamin Spock. Gemma said, "For a wildlife ranger, you're not very observant." I replied, "But how was I supposed to know?" The horse doctor's teasing expression turned into a sly grin. "Why don't you come here and kiss me, and we can review how the birds and bees work."

I only read the first two chapters. I should've read more.

I exhale and suck in air. Fuel. I can taste it again, hear the drips. I back out of the cockpit and go around to the passenger side and try sliding my seat forward, but the track jams. I push on the hinge lever to make it fold forward. It's jammed too. I shove my arm behind the seat and pat around the floor. I recognize the feel of my duffle bag and give it a hard yank.

It's not the one I'm searching for and I toss it aside. I shove my arm behind the seat again and fish around. I come up with another duffle bag, this one smaller. It's Gemma's. I toss it aside and reach in again. The horse doctor never travels anywhere without her medical bag, never takes off without making sure the plane's emergency kit is aboard. The two have to be back there somewhere, but the rear of the plane is jumbled. I need more time, but the tick-tock of leaking fuel shouts I don't have any.

I scurry back to the pilot's side while recalling the short course of battlefield first aid I took in basic training and later practiced in country. Memories of applying compresses and carrying wounded men in firefights flicker like the shadows of people projected on a cave wall by a string of hanging work lights.

Moving Gemma could be the biggest mistake of my life. A broken rib could puncture a lung. A fractured femur could sever an artery. If her back is injured, I risk damaging her spinal cord. I flash on Deputy Orville Nelson hurtling through the sheriff's office in his wheelchair.

I feel around Gemma's feet to make sure they're free of the pedals. Her right ankle is twisted and the foot points in an unnatural angle. I unlock her fingers curled around the yoke. Then I reach down and work the lever to slide her seat back in the tracks. Unlike the passenger seat, it moves a couple of inches before jamming. It isn't much, but it's enough to put distance between the buckled metal and the baby in her belly.

I slide a hand under her and the other behind her shoulders and gently pull her close, backing up slowly, careful not to catch her skin on any metal edges or bang her head. I carry her down the path carved by the plane to the clearing where we first hit. Still holding her, I kick together a pile of sheared pine boughs and place her on top of them to keep her off the snow. I run back to collect the two duffle bags and yank out coats and sweaters to blanket her.

Only a couple of hours of daylight remain. It's going to get a lot colder once it turns dark. The snow stopped, but odds are it will start again. I can sit next to Gemma and wait for the air cavalry to come swooping in and medevac us like they did in Vietnam, but I know doing is better than hoping when lives are on the line.

I begin gathering downed limbs about the size of the one

that sticks through the cockpit windshield. I hack off branches using the broken propeller blade as a machete. As I work, I envision the wickiup next to Tuhudda Will's single-wide trailer. I once spent a few days inside it. Tuhudda's slow, deliberate way of speaking echoes in my ears as he described how he built it the same way *Numu* had been building wickiups ever since *Mu naa'a* created the first and second people.

I select the three thickest and longest limbs and lash their tops together with one of the duffle bag's shoulder straps, leaving a foot of their tips extended. I stand them up in a tripod and pack snow around their bottom ends as foundation blocks. Then, I stand the other limbs on end and lean their tips in between the crotches at the top of the tripod. I leave small gaps between every third and fourth limb and form an opening at the bottom to use as a doorway. I thread saplings in and out of the gaps to belt the entire structure together. I finish by chinking the shelter with handfuls of moss and pine needles.

Night falls by the time I cover the floor of the wickiup with a thick bed of fresh pine boughs and carry in Gemma. I lay her down and blanket her with clothes again before tying the shoulder strap of the smaller duffle bag across the top of the opening and drape the now-empty bags over it to fashion a door.

It's pitch dark. As Blackpowder recited at our wedding, if two lie together, they are warm, and so I scooch gently next to Gemma. The surge of adrenaline sparked by the crash begins to ebb. The stabbing hot blade in my rib cage returns. Along with the discomfort comes the crushing weight of our situation: no one knows where we are.

Gemma filed a flight plan for Portland before we took off from the dirt airstrip at the Warbler ranch, but when we don't arrive, someone, somewhere, will sound the alarm. A search will be launched, daylight and weather permitting, if not tomorrow, then the next day, or the next.

While it sounds good, I take little comfort in it. The ferocity of the storm surely blew us off course. If Gemma were conscious, I doubt she'd be able to tell where we crash-landed. Her eyes were glued to the altimeter spinning backward and the gyro horizon turning somersaults as she fought to pull us out of the death spiral. Keeping track of the heading indicator, airspeed, and turn coordinator was the least of her concerns. The black clouds and suddenness of the dizzying plunge prevented me from seeing any recognizable landmarks too.

The truth grows as frigid as the night air. We could be anywhere, from the Blue Mountains to the Ochoco Mountains to the Cascades. For all I know, we could've been blown all the way east to the Wallowas. We could be on the side of a peak or in a steep mountain ravine. We could be anyplace except where we're supposed to be.

I stare into the black and assess the situation the same way I used to peer into the dark pool of a jungle night. I clear all thoughts of fear and focus only on the steps needed to survive. It means stripping everything down to the basics. Water. Food. Shelter. Fire. It's no different than the Clovis people did in a rockshelter in Catlow Valley.

I vow to keep vigil throughout the night and make sure Gemma stays warm. Then I'll return to the plane in the morning and retrieve the emergency kit and medical bag, that is if the plane doesn't blow up. I'll gather dry wood and make a fire. If the emergency kit doesn't contain matches, then I'll use moss to capture a spark created by striking rock on rock or rubbing two sticks together. With a fire, I can boil snow for water and get Gemma to drink some so she won't dehydrate. I'll find my sidearm that I put in the back of the plane on takeoff. If it fell out during the crash, then I'll make a weapon and go hunting. I'll clean and cook what I kill.

I'll keep on doing it until help arrives. And if help doesn't, then there's only one answer. Do whatever it takes to keep us from becoming nowhere bones.

The wind turns from a whistle to a howl. Trees groan under the weight of falling snow. There will be no sleep for me. Not tonight. Maybe not for a long while. I pull Gemma close to share our body heat and wait for morning to see what first light and the rest of my life will bring...

8

The lineman's shack still held heat from the wood-burning stove when I woke at dawn. Van Morrison's "Brand New Day" played in my head as I slathered a sourdough biscuit with blackberry jam spooned from a Mason jar. I ate standing up while waiting for the coffee to brew. With a full thermos in hand, I grabbed my holster, and headed out.

The two-lane leading from No Mountain was empty. Sagebrush sparkled with frost as the sun began to crown behind the Stinkingwater Mountains. I sipped coffee and wondered if the herd of elk would still be in the field next time I patrolled Malheur. While I'd miss being able to sketch them if they weren't, I couldn't go on feeding them forever. It was a fine line between helping animals and conditioning them to take hand-outs. A bale of hay strewn as bait by a poacher would make them easy pickings.

The stoplight on the outskirts of Burns was still flashing yellow, but traffic was starting to increase on the main street through town, Highway 20. The transcontinental highway started in Newport, Oregon, and terminated at Kenmore Square in Boston. The feed and grain store was open. So was a coffee shop and a gas station. I pulled in to fill up and see about getting the flat from the rusty sedan with no trunk lid fixed.

"Even if I could patch that hole, it'd spring another," the mechanic drawled when I rolled the wheel into his bay. "A pencil eraser has more rubber."

"What's a new one cost?"

"About a nickel," he deadpanned before slapping his knee. "Gets 'em every time. As for a tire, a new four-ply run you thirteen dollars. You want it in whitewall, it'll cost you two bucks more."

"Black's fine," I said. "I'll swing by in an hour to pick it up."

"We'll get 'er done."

With a full tank, I turned up North Court Avenue. The pink stucco sheriff's office was on the corner of West A Street. It was no surprise to find Sheriff Pudge Warbler already at his desk. He looked up from a stack of papers.

"You know, son, after taking a bullet that led to me losing my star to Bust'em, I told myself becoming a part-time deputy was okay because the top job was more politics and paperwork than policing anyway. Now that the good voters of Harney County saw fit to return me as their sheriff, I've been reminding myself being half-retired wasn't half-bad."

"Speaking of Burton, what's he doing now? I haven't seen him around."

"That's because the little pissant's career of kissing everyone's behind paid off big time. The attorney general went and paid some fancy law enforcement expert to come up with the not-so-bright idea of reorganizing the state's sheriffing system into regions."

"And Burton got himself appointed to oversee one?"

"Not any old one. He's got the Klamath, Lake, Harney, and

Malheur County sheriff's departments all under him and a new title to go along with it. Southeast Region Commander Sheriff Buster Burton. I beat him in the election fair and square and Bust'em still wins."

I started to say how my own dealings with having a regional director had grown even more testy with his job offer, but Pudge didn't seem to be in a mood for commiserating.

"I stopped by to share some information on a situation down in Catlow Valley. There's an outside chance it could turn dicey. I'd thought you want to know."

Pudge sat up. "Now that sounds a lot more interesting than pushing paper. What's it all about?"

"It involves a university professor who's conducting a dig in a rockshelter. That's a cave to you and me."

"Archaeologist, huh? They've been doing that kind of work over in Lake County for decades."

"The professor—his name is Paxton Sizemore, goes by Pax—has made a couple of enemies during his career. One is a rival professor. The other is a jealous ex-boyfriend."

"Whose boyfriend?"

"One of the two student assistants who's at the site with him. Her name is Stephanie Buhl. The professor swears there's nothing going on between them, but the girl's ex isn't buying it." I gave him a recap.

"Who's the second student assistant?"

"His name is Jelly Welch. He's the kind who's always looking for the easy way. He packs a Colt Python he says is for rattlers, bats, and grave robbers—"

The sheriff cut me off. "But you think it might also be for getting something the easy way. Like what?"

"Jelly mentioned relics bring a good price on the black market. He may have been testing me to see if I was interested."

"I've said it once, I've said it a hundred times. You got what it takes that makes you my kind of lawman. Namely, built-in suspicion. Sure wish that wild mustang daughter of mine would hurry up and pick a date so you two can get married and settle down to raise my grandchild. Having another mouth to feed is reason enough for you to accept my offer to sign on as a deputy. It pays better than what you're earning." He patted the seven-point star on his chest. "Play it right and when I retire for good, this could be yours."

When I didn't respond, Pudge sighed. "Okay, have it your way. Who's the second enemy the professor made?"

"An assistant professor by name of Cecil Edwards Oliver." I gave him the rundown and the threats Oliver made at the tavern. "He blames Sizemore for costing him his job and reputation."

"A three-namer, huh? Probably a case of a little rooster flapping his wings at the big rooster over a seat in the hen house. This Flip Carson character is the one who gets my attention. Rage goes with jealousy like robbery goes with greed. I don't want some caveman thumping a girl on the head and dragging her off by her hair anywhere near my jurisdiction. I'll give a call to the Eugene PD and see what's what."

"Sizemore said he also reported the incident to campus security. They should be able to tell you about Professor Oliver too."

"See, you're already telling me how to do my job. A born deputy."

"One other thing. Tuhudda and Nagah Will are at the dig site too. Sizemore hired them to help identify artifacts and human bones."

"Human? How fresh?"

"Not very. The professor estimates them to be a couple of thousand years old."

Pudge whistled. "Well, isn't that something. But how that man died or who put him there is way beyond my jurisdiction."

I told him about the daily radio check-in arrangement.

"Go ahead and tell Orville. I swear, ever since I made the college boy a deputy, he's working harder than ever. He never slept much when he was an intern, and now he's sleeping even less. Orville spends so much time here, the cute gal whose mom owns the boarding house where he bunks is bringing him homecooked meals."

"Lucy Lorriaga," I said.

"That's the one. She says it's the only time she gets to see him." Pudge patted his paunch. "Truth be told, I'd hate to see that romance break up. Lucy brings me a plate while she's at it. I do love Basque cooking."

"I'll drop by his office on my way out. I'm headed to Klamath Marsh. Loq called about somebody busting a levee. After that, I'll head down to Catlow Valley to take Tuhudda a new tire. If you find out anything from Eugene, I can relay the message for you."

"Fair enough, but don't stray too far in case my grandchild decides to make an early appearance."

"You'd know that before me. I'm last on the list to hear anything."

"If it's any consolation, I'm second to last. November knows everything first. That old medicine woman knows things before they even happen. She knew Gemma was with child before Gemma did."

Orville Nelson was in his new office, a considerably larger space than the file room he'd been relegated to as an intern. It accommodated a huge desk comprising three tables pushed together to form a U. Electronics covered all three surfaces. The first time I'd seen it, he told me he'd modeled it after the command center on the *USS Enterprise*, the starship in his favorite TV show, *Star Trek*. He told me he called his desk "The Bridge" too.

"Pudge told me you never leave work," I said by way of greeting.

"Ranger Drake, a pleasure to see you. Yes, since being deputized and taking on the responsibility of bringing the department up-to-date with current criminal science technology along with all of my other duties, I find there is not enough time in the day."

I still wasn't used to seeing him dressed in khakis with a deputy's star on his chest. The entire time I'd known him, he'd worn a skinny black tie and buttoned-down white shirt to work. It was the uniform of an FBI agent, a job he'd hoped to get someday until a bullet to the back rendered him a paraplegic.

"Your desk looks more crowded than usual," I said. "Have you talked more inventors into letting you try out their gadgets?"

"Indeed, I have. I am putting one through its paces now. It is the latest generation of the scientific calculator the Cattleman's Association gave me for helping bust the rustling ring. The improvements include a light emitting diode screen, expandable memory cards, and connection to a thermal printer. The engineer who designed it says one day machines like it will design even smarter machines. He calls it artificial intelligence."

I pointed to the multiline telephone and police band radio. "Today's intelligence is enough to suit my purposes." I filled him in on my arrangement for daily radio check-ins with Professor Sizemore.

Orville typed on his new machine while I spoke. He asked for the spelling of Stephanie Buhl's last name. I gave it my best guess. Jelly Welch's was easy.

"I will do a background search on all the parties," he said. "You never know when
that sort of information might come in handy."

As I drove back to the gas station to pick up Tuhudda's tire, I mulled over what Pudge had said about the right traits for being a good cop. Orville Nelson had them in spades. He was honest, diligent, fiercely loyal, and dedicated. He'd finally received a vehicle with hand controls and learned to fire a service weapon that he kept in a shoulder holster, but it was his curiosity and fearlessness about applying new technologies to investigate crime that made him so well-suited for the job—perhaps even sheriff one day.

9

The three-hour drive to Klamath Marsh National Wildlife Refuge took me through Christmas Valley. When I approached the turnoff to Fort Rock, I was tempted to take it and swing by the rockshelter Professor Sizemore had described as the equivalent of a time capsule left by people who wore sagebrush sandals and flung rock-tipped spears at woolly mammoths. But visiting yesteryear would have to wait. The problems of today beckoned.

The wet meadows and high spots in the open-water wetlands of the forty-thousand-acre marsh came into view as I drove down a gravel road after leaving the blacktop at Silver Lake and crossing into Klamath County. The marsh was the most northerly in a chain of five national wildlife refuges that had been established in Klamath Basin. A drainage twice the size of New Jersey, it ran southerly between the Cascade Mountains to the west and the Basin and Range Province to the east. Migratory birds and waterfowl followed it like the watery equivalent of a highway map as they traveled between Latin America and Alaska. The five refuges acted as rest stops where the birds could recharge and refuel before continuing their epic journeys.

The two Oregon refuges in the chain—Klamath Marsh and Upper Klamath Lake—had been the westernmost part of my beat during the first year or so on the job. After Loq was hired, regional director F.D. Powers assigned us the three refuges in Northern California too. Adding Lower Klamath Lake, Tule Lake, and Clear Lake expanded our beat by two hundred square miles.

Loq was waiting for me beside a bubbling spring. The water had traveled underground from nearby Crater Lake that was formed in the caldera of a volcano that Paleo-Indians witnessed erupting more than seven thousand years prior. The spring was the headwaters of the Williamson River, a hundred-mile-long artery that ran through marsh, forest, and ranchland before emptying into Upper Klamath Lake. It carried a lifeblood of rich nutrients that supported aquatic creatures, from tiny tadpoles to large redband rainbow trout. Beavers, mink, and muskrats found it a welcoming home. So did egrets and herons that stalked its shallows.

Both the river and marsh were sacred to the Klamath, or *Maklak* as the people called themselves. I knew Loq would've arrived early. He'd been born in nearby Chiloquin and lived there before and after his service in the Marine Corps. We'd been in country at the same time, but never met on a battlefield. It was a different story when we got back home and buddied up patrolling the wildlife refuges.

"Did you offer tobacco?" I said after parking my rig and joining him.

"Of course. I blew smoke in the four directions and asked the river for its blessing." He paused to eye me. "I also asked the river to help my partner quit asking me questions he already knows the answers to."

"They're called icebreakers," I said.

"It's still winter. We got all the ice we need."

He said it without grinning, but I flashed one in return. "Okay, show me what you found. I'm in a hurry to get back to Catlow Valley." I gave him the lowdown on the dig team and Professor Sizemore's concerns about Flip Carson and Professor Oliver.

"They're digging up ancient ones?" Loq's long mohawk rippled as he shook his head. "That's bad medicine any way you look at it. We need laws against people disturbing our burial grounds."

I agreed with him. "Where's the break in the levee?"

"Follow me."

We rolled out on foot, Loq fast-stepping and me matching his pace. In the sixteen years since the refuge had been dedicated, a network of levees and channels had been built to protect multiple springs to ensure the marsh a year-round water supply. The sound of gurgling water reached my ears before I saw the break. It was a couple of feet across.

"When did you first notice it?" I said.

"When I nearly drove into it." Some of the levees doubled as single-track roads. "I thought a culvert had rusted out until I took a closer look. I found pick and shovel marks that someone tried to conceal. I waded in and found a hump of mud—a shovelful toss from shore. The snow on the other side of the break has been brushed with a sapling. They quit too soon. There's boot prints fifteen yards out and the sapling chucked over the side. Another hundred yards out I found tire tracks."

The embankment on the northside of the impoundment had a dark line two feet above the water's surface like a bathtub ring.

I gauged the water level on the southside. "You'd think it'd be higher with new water pouring in, but it isn't."

Loq pointed across the marsh. Sunlight dappled the water

and cattails waved. "There must be another break over there that's keeping it level."

"Let's go see if you're right."

We returned to our pickups and drove convoy style. The *Maklak* led and didn't need a map to find an alternate route on the maze of levees. The rattling of our vehicles sent a trio of American coots paddling away furiously. The squawking mud hens were averse to flying and lived in the marsh year-round. We flushed a couple of mallards, their glossy green heads signaling their gender.

Loq's brake lights flashed. I stopped and got out. The levee was cut in the same manner as the last breach. Loq plucked a pair of green hip waders from the bed of his rig, pulled them on, and snapped the straps to the belt loops of his jeans.

When he'd waded into the marsh several yards, he stopped and cupped the water. He sniffed it and then sipped it. "Still has the purity of *Gii-was*," he said, using the *Maklak* name for Crater Lake.

Loq reached into his shirt pocket, pulled out a bird feather, straightened its quills, and placed it on the surface. We watched as it was borne away by the current. The feather served as a compass point. I scanned its heading with my binoculars. Another dirt embankment hemmed in the marsh on the far side. It bordered a field with a forested ridge rising on the left.

"Looks like the water is being diverted to that field," I said. "Maybe it's being used to irrigate crops or support livestock."

"If it is, then it's being done illegally," Loq said as duck-walked back. "No one on that side of the marsh holds a water use permit."

"I don't see a road leading there from here."

"There isn't one. We'll have to go the way you drove into the refuge and then find a logging road that follows the ridge down.

The forest in there is crisscrossed with them. Most aren't signed."

We drove convoy style again. Snow dusted the higher elevations. The first gravel road we tried dead-ended in less than a hundred feet. The second was a loop with no forks. The third led into a maze of narrow tracks. After taking a few false turns, we split up and kept in contact by radio. I finally found a long stretch of road that paralleled the west face of the ridgeline. The farther I drove, the more the forest of lodgepole pines and white fir became checkerboarded with clearcuts. In one cut, old logged trees littered the ground like giant pickup sticks. In another, blackened stumps on a clefted snowy hillside reminded me of the time a drunk jutted his stubbly chin in my face and dared me to take a swing.

I stopped and radioed Loq to say I'd found the main road and would wait for him to catch up. I got out to stretch my legs. Both sides of the road had been cleared. No hawks perched. No woodpeckers pecked. Loq arrived and joined me.

"I was only a boy," he said, "but I still remember my people wailing the day Washington passed the law that terminated our tribe so the big timber companies could steal our land."

"But now logging is restricted in the forests closest to the marsh," I said.

"Maybe on paper. This butchery has the look of gyppo loggers. They treat rules the same as poachers. They kill everything, take only the choicest cuts, and leave the rest behind to rot."

"I'll call a Forest Service ranger I know and see what he has to say. He's been working with some organizations that are promoting alternatives to clearcutting. Selective logging, I believe he called it. There's nothing we can do about it now, but maybe we can do something about the stolen water."

We got back in our rigs and drove. The road had a couple of

more forks. I chose the right ones by following the ridge's natural fall line. We ended up at the embankment that separated the marsh from a large field. We got out and started walking on the borderline between wet and dry.

Twenty, thirty yards in, Loq halted. "Sounds like my mother's kitchen sink when she pulls the stopper."

The burbling led us to a sluice gate that been installed in the levee. It was raised and lowered by a handwheel that operated a grease screw. The head gate was partially open and water was running into a wooden sluice that poured into a ditch alongside the edge of the field. Hand-lettered "Keep Out" and "No Trespassing" signs with crudely drawn skulls and crossbones were nailed to posts stuck along the near side.

"Not very neighborly," Loq said.

The field had a thinning cover of snow with patches of rabbitbrush and clumps of bunchgrass sticking up. "The water's not for irrigating this field. It hasn't been plowed or grazed for years," I said. "Let's follow the ditch and see where it leads."

I pulled the 12-gauge pump shotgun from the rack in my pickup. Loq looked down his high cheekbones at me.

"One of the students at the dig in Catlow Valley told me about rattlesnakes that ball up in wintertime," I said. "You never know what could come rolling out of the ditch."

He stayed put for a few moments before taking the government-issued lever action Winchester .30-30 from his rig's rack. "In case we spot it rolling toward us from a distance."

The field was shaped like a kidney bean with the ridge pinching it in the middle. We followed the ditch as it curved around the ridge. Sunlight striking the surface of a pond glistened at the far end of the field. A shack stood at water's edge. The diverted water from the marsh was being funneled onto a set of paddles mounted around an upright wooden waterwheel.

The wood creaked and water splashed as the wheel rotated, while a high-pitched whine pierced the air.

"The wheel is spinning a generator inside that shack," I said. "Somebody's making their own electricity."

"Somebody who has eyes on us," Loq said. "You feel them?"

Before I could answer, two rifle shots rang out. Loq fell to the ground as I dove for cover.

10

"Speak to me, brother," I said as I searched the shack for movement and gun flashes. I was on my stomach behind a clump of bunchgrass. It wasn't much cover. "You hit?"

Loq finally answered. "Been calculating the angle of fire. It's not coming from the shack. The shooter's got the high ground. Shots came from eleven o'clock thirty yards upslope."

"Roger that. Somebody's moving there now."

"Got him." Loq was also prone, propped on his elbows with nothing in front of him. The Winchester was tight against his shoulder as he sighted. "No clean shot. He ducked behind a tree."

"Maybe he was trying to warn us off."

"Marines don't do maybe."

"Best way to find out is ask him. Lay down some distraction fire so I can get into the woods."

"You think if he couldn't hit you standing still, he won't hit you running?"

"Only one way to find out."

"Have it your way. Go!"

Loq pulled the trigger. I jumped at the bang like it was a starter's gun, hurdled the ditch, and stayed low as I sprinted for the woods. Loq levered in another round and fired again. No one shot back.

I ducked into the pines, stood behind a tree with my shotgun at port arms to catch my breath, and then began climbing quickly at an angle to get fifty yards above the pond so that I'd be higher than the shooter when I reached eleven o'clock from Loq's position.

When I got there, I stood against a trunk to guard my back and picked another in front in case I needed forward cover. I waited and watched. Loq fired again, this time below the shooter to drive him uphill. A stand of vine maple rustled as somebody scrambled toward me. When the shooter was ten feet away, I stepped out and pointed the shotgun.

"Drop your weapon! Do it now."

The shooter looked up in surprise. He was only a boy, thirteen, fourteen years old tops. "Don't shoot," he cried.

"Drop your weapon," I barked again. "Now!"

He was clutching a deer rifle. "I drop it, it could fire."

"Then lay it down slowly."

He did as he was told. His hair looked as if it'd been shorn with sheep shears. He was wearing a dirty gray sweatshirt under a denim jacket with frayed cuffs. His jeans had patches on the knees. "I wasn't trying to hit you, only scare you off. You can't be here."

"But I am. My name's Nick Drake. What's yours?"

"I can't tell you."

"Why not?"

"I'm not supposed to talk to nobody."

"But here we are talking and I'm the one holding the gun. Tell me your name."

He hung his head. "Silas."

"What's your last name, Silas?" The boy hesitated. "Go on, tell me."

"It's Grazier."

"Where are your parents?"

"Can't say."

"Can't say or won't say?"

"Both, I reckon."

"I know you don't live alone. I saw the sluice gate and the waterwheel."

Silas stared at his feet. "I don't know nothing about nothing. And I'm not supposed to say nothing neither."

"Says who?"

"Daddy. His orders are never talk to nobody. Don't trust them neither 'cause everybody's out to get us." He cowered. "Are you here to get me? Are you gonna hit me?"

"Of course not. I need to speak with your father. Where can I find him?"

"I can't tell you that 'cause that's how they'll get him. Daddy says so. You should leave right now. He'd've heard the shots and come running."

"Good. It'll save me the trouble of having to find him. Sit down cross-legged. Away from that rifle. Put your hands behind your head and lock your fingers."

"Do I have to?"

"Yes. I'm a federal officer and ordering you to."

He sniffled. "Daddy's gonna be mad. Real mad." He started shaking.

"Don't be scared. Everything's going to be okay. Leave your father to me."

"You don't know him. My big brother neither."

"What's his name?"

"Ebal."

"Who else do you live with, Silas? Your mother? Maybe a

sister?" His expression turned from fright to sorrow. "What's your sister's name?"

"Rebekah," he said in almost a whisper, "but she's dead."

"I'm sorry to hear that. Was she older or younger?"

"Older."

"You two were close, weren't you?"

"We was."

"Did she die here or in a hospital?"

His shorn head went back and forth. "Can't go to no hospital. Can't go nowhere where people are. That's where they're at. Daddy said so."

"Who's they?"

"The ones out to get us."

"Is she buried here?"

"Yep, but it's hidden so they can't come get her."

"They," I said.

"Yep. They."

"And what about your brother Ebal, are you close to him too?"

"Nobody's friends with Ebal."

"How come?"

"Because he won't let you be his friend."

"And your mother? Where's she at?"

"Home."

"Which is where?"

"I won't tell you and you can't make me."

"Can you at least tell me what you're generating power for? I saw the waterwheel, heard the generator."

"Stuff."

"Electricity for the house? Maybe a sawmill?"

Silas raised his chin. "We ain't loggers. It's for the garden, but I can't tell you that. Daddy says so."

An owl hooted.

I tightened my grip on the shotgun. "Are you supposed to hoot back?"

"Whatcha talking about?"

"That's a great gray owl's call, but it's broad daylight. Either your father or Ebal made it. They're calling to each other or you."

The hoot came again twenty yards across from me. I repositioned to put a tree trunk between the hooter and me.

"Mr. Grazier," I called out. "Nick Drake, US Fish and Wildlife. I'm here with Silas. I only want to talk."

Something directly uphill from me moved. It was another person staying in the shadows. The hooter moved again too, no doubt trying to keep me in a crossfire.

"Don't make a mistake here," I said. "Right now all we're doing is talking."

"Who are you?" a grown man's voice said from the uphill position.

"I told you. Nick Drake. I'm with Fish and Wildlife."

"Anybody can say that. You're with them, aren't you?"

"If you mean Fish and Wildlife, yes, that's who I work for. I'm a wildlife refuge ranger."

"Prove it."

"Come down here and I'll show you my badge."

He scoffed. "Badges can be bought at a candy store. Shots were fired at my son."

"They were only warning shots like the ones Silas fired toward me. No one's hurt and no one needs to get hurt. Come on out so we can talk."

"I'll do no such thing. This is my land and you're trespassing. I'm within my rights to defend it. That's the law."

"And the law also says shooting at a federal officer carries a mandatory sentence, but I'll overlook it seeing as Silas meant no harm."

"Anybody can put on a uniform and pretend to be someone they're not."

"I'm who I say I am. I'm not here to take anything. I'm not here to hurt anyone. All I want to do is talk about how we can resolve the water from the marsh coming onto your land. Maybe you didn't know, but that's prohibited. I have a simple solution. We shut the sluice gate, repair the levees, agree that it doesn't happen again, and everybody goes on about their business. Sound fair?"

"That water's mine as much as anybody's. It'd be flowing here like it used to if they hadn't penned it up. Now it's no good to anyone."

"If you want to lodge a complaint, there's a time and a place for that, but it's not here and it's not now. Tell your son Ebal to lower his rifle. Yes, I saw him duck behind the tree across from me."

"How do you know his name?" Grazier asked suspiciously.

I started to say Silas told me, but held my tongue. "It doesn't matter. Tell him to put his rifle down."

"I got a bead on him, Daddy," Ebal said without showing himself.

"Either he puts it down now or my partner will put him down. He was a sharpshooter in the Marines and has your son in his sights."

"He's lying," Ebal said. "Nobody's near me."

"Your call, Mr. Grazier. If Ebal shoots me before my partner shoots him, I'm apt to pull the trigger by reflex and shoot Silas. Your sons will both be dead. Over what, water?"

"I can take him, Daddy," Ebal said. "I can."

Moments passed but Grazier remained silent.

"Now," I said, but I wasn't talking to him.

It sounded like a watermelon being thumped, followed by "Ow!" I kept my shotgun trained on Grazier's position as a teenager who looked a few years older than Silas stumbled from behind a tree rubbing the back of his head. His homemade haircut and patched clothes were similar to his brother's. Loq gave him a shove with the Winchester. He was holding a second rifle too.

"About time you showed up," I said.

"I was checking out the waterwheel. Reminds me of the ones in 'Nam."

"Stay away from my property!" Grazier shouted.

Loq ignored him as he pushed Ebal down into a sitting position next to Silas.

"Now you know I wasn't lying about my partner and I'm not lying about only wanting to talk," I said. "If you don't come out right now, I'm going to come get you. We'll arrest the three of you for threatening the lives of federal officers and I'll also arrest your wife for aiding and abetting."

"How do you know about my wife? You better not touch her, I'm warning you."

I noticed Silas flinch as his father spoke. I also noticed he had bruises around his wrists and a cauliflower right ear.

"I'll go get her," Loq said, though he made no move to do so.

It did the trick. Grazier stepped out from behind a tree. He was buggy-whip thin and wore a floppy felt hat and had shoulder-length hair and a full beard but no moustache. His jacket and pants were patched like his sons' clothes. A pistol with a walnut grip was stuck in his belt at the front of his waist.

"Keep your hands where I can see them," I said.

Grazier halted, but his eyes didn't stop shifting.

"You stashed your long gun behind the tree," Loq said to him.

"How do you know that?" Grazier said.

"You just told me."

"That rifle's my property, the same as this land."

"But the water in the marsh isn't," I said.

"Then go ahead and shut it off. I'll find another way to get what I need."

"Not if it means destroying levees and stealing water from the marsh."

Grazier's eyes shifted back to Loq. "How do you like working for the *man*, Uncle Tomahawk?"

The Klamath's skin tightened over his high cheekbones. I braced for him to strike Grazier, but he didn't. He yanked the walnut-gripped pistol from the bearded man's belt.

"Sell out," Grazier hissed. "You're like an apple. Red on the outside, white on the inside."

Loq looked back at me and tilted his head. Someone else was uphill. He brushed past Grazier and disappeared into the woods without rustling a branch or stepping on a twig.

"Where's he going?" Grazier said.

"To collect your rifle. He'll be right back," I said. "Why don't you tell me why you're taking the water. Are you trying to live off the land, grow your own food?"

Grazier yelled at Silas. "What did I tell you about trusting people and talking to them? Especially the ones who look like him. I warned you about the *man*."

He lunged at the boy and made to slap his right ear, but I knocked Grazier's wrist away with the barrel of my shotgun. The man cried out. "That's my son. He disobeyed me. It's my right to punish him."

"Not with your fist. Now, tell me about the waterwheel and generator," I said.

"The only thing I need to tell you is get the hell off my property. You had your say about the water. Go ahead and turn the spigot off on your way out. But don't come back. You do, it won't be warning shots you hear."

"You tell him, Daddy," Ebal said.

I turned to Ebal. "Have you ever shot anyone? You're what, seventeen, eighteen? That's around the same age as a lot of brave soldiers I served with in Vietnam. The ones in my squad all shot men. They didn't like it, not one bit. They never crowed about it, never got used to it. They did their job and couldn't wait to go home."

"I should've known it," Grazier spit. "You're not only the *man*, you're a baby killer too. Get off my land. Now!"

"I'll go after you answer a few questions. Civilly. How long have you lived here?"

Grazier kept his hands at his side and was clenching and unclenching his fists over and over. They kept time with his twitching eyes. "I don't have to tell you anything. You can't make me."

"Were you living here before the marsh was made a refuge?"

Grazier's hesitation was guarded. "Why do you want to know?"

"Depending on the time, it might give you prescriptive rights to the water. Do you know what that word means?"

"Of course I do. I went to college. I was an engineer before, well, before. Why should I believe you?"

"Because I'm trying to help you."

"You're up to something, I know it."

"Do you want my help or not?"

He stared at me, tightening his fists until his knuckles whitened. "We came in the fall of '62, but my wife's uncle owned this property free and clear for forty years. That's long before the marsh was established. I'd say that means our rights to the water are grandfathered in."

"1962? I remember October of that year. Kennedy and Khrushchev were staring each other down over missiles in Cuba. Your kids were probably doing duck-and-cover drills at school."

"That's right, but it wouldn't've saved them, would it? Whole world could've been blown to smithereens. Still could. No desk or bomb shelter in the basement is going to help against nuclear-armed missiles. I know. I worked in defense."

"As an engineer," I said.

Grazier's twitchy eyes glowered. "Armageddon is coming. You better believe it is."

"Is that why you moved here, you think it's safe from the missiles you helped build?"

He started breathing heavily. "You see any cops cracking skulls with billy clubs for protesting the war, any National Guard troops shooting college kids to death like they did in Ohio last May? Smartest thing I ever did was quit working for the *man* and move my family here. Escape all the madness."

"And your wife's uncle, does he still live here? Maybe he has a copy of the deed. It might say something about water rights on it."

"He passed a couple years back, but he left the land to my wife and me. The title's in our name, if that's what you're wondering. We own it free and clear."

Checking for a property deed would be child's play for Orville Nelson, I thought. "What line of work are you in now?"

"The none-of-your-business business."

The whole time Grazier and I were talking, Silas and Ebal stayed rigidly still, but never took their eyes off their father as if watching a house on fire and waiting to see if the gas main would explode. The fact was, I'd grown tired of talking to him. I was anxious to get back to Harney County to see Gemma and take Tuhudda his new tire. I was also looking forward to talking with Pax Sizemore some more and explore the rockshelter again.

Loq appeared as quietly as he'd left. "Time to move out." He glanced at Grazier. "I'll leave your pistol and long gun down by the waterwheel." Grazier started to say something, but Loq cut him off. "Don't!" He marched off without another word.

"Consider yourself officially warned about violating the laws that protect the marsh, Mr. Grazier," I said. "If you believe you have water rights, you'll still need to file for a use permit and abide by the specified amount allowed." I collected the boys' rifles. "I'll leave these for you down at the waterwheel. Don't be in a hurry to come collect them."

Grazier spit. "There's your permit."

I ignored him. I was in too much of a hurry to catch up with Loq and find out what he'd seen that made him rush off.

11

Loq was waiting for me beside the waterwheel. I added the boys' rifles to their father's guns.

"What did you see back there?" I said.

"Grazier's wife. She was watching from behind the trees. I left so I wouldn't take it out on him in front of his sons."

"Why, what did she say?"

"Nothing. She didn't have to. The bruises on her face said it for her."

I grimaced. "I stopped him from backhanding his youngest son."

"I saw his ear, but thought he'd gotten it from wrestling with his big brother, the way brothers do. When I saw his mother, I knew differently."

"How come she didn't scream when she saw you?"

"The same reason the enemy sometimes freezes when you have the jump on them. They're either too scared to fight or too used to losing."

"Did you see where they live?"

"I followed her when she took off through the trees. Pigpens are cleaner. There's an old cabin and a converted school bus with bunks in it, but it hasn't been on a road for years. The tires are nearly rotted off. They're not using the generator here for power up there. Not an electrical wire or lightbulb in sight. No indoor plumbing either. The outhouse reeks."

"Grazier told me he was once an engineer. You'd think he'd keep his place more shipshape than that."

"You mean, they're city people who dropped out?"

I nodded and told Loq about Grazier wanting to escape the weapons he'd helped build and his suspicion that everyone was out to get him. "He reminds me of some of the GIs who were at Walter Reed with me. It was all they could do to keep their shit together. The slightest thing would set them off. This one grunt was convinced the orderlies were Viet Cong. He refused to take his meds, said they were trying to poison him. A nurse told me he'd been diagnosed as a paranoid schizophrenic, that he'd always need to be institutionalized for his own safety."

"Nobody sees the world the same after they've been in war," Loq said with a grunt.

"I know, but Grazier seems as shell-shocked as if he'd been in the blast zone caused by his missiles. Somewhere along the line he stopped believing the arms race was intended to save lives, not take them."

"So, he did an about face. What's that protest sign say? Make Love, Not War."

"Did you notice his eyes? They never stopped moving. And the thing he was doing with his hands, clenching and unclenching? It was all he could do to hold on."

"He's lucky his eyes aren't black after I saw what he'd done to his wife and the way he's forcing his family to live," Loq said.

"I got a bad feeling about this. Silas told me he had a sister named Rebekah, but she died and is buried somewhere up there. Mrs. Grazier's uncle owned the land, but he's dead too."

Loq looked uphill. "That explains why I felt the spirit of death around the cabin. I didn't see any graves."

"Let's check out the shack here and see if we can figure out what he's generating power for."

The door was unlocked. Inside, the grinding of gears and the whine from a spinning shaft made the fillings in my teeth hurt. The generator was hooked to a dozen car batteries by a spiderweb of cables.

"This is a page right out of the *Whole Earth Catalog*," I said. "Have you ever seen a copy? It was started a couple of years ago as part of the back-to-the-land movement. Has everything in it from instructions on how to build a shelter to shopping lists for tools to tips for raising your own food."

"That looks like a water pump," Loq said, pointing to a small motor connected to one of the batteries. "There's a pipe coming in from the pond and then going out the back of the shack. Electrical wires too."

We went outside and followed the pipe and wires up an incline and into the forest. The trees had been cleared a couple of rows in to create an opening no bigger than a half-acre. Straw and mulch covered the ground, but nothing was growing.

"I wonder why Grazier planted a garden up here when he has that big flat field down below," I said. "He wouldn't need to pump any water, just open the sluice gate and irrigate it by gravity feed."

"Over there, in the trees," Loq said. "A light."

We beelined toward it. Another shack was hidden in the forest. A bright white line outlined a door that fit loosely in its frame. Loq pulled the handle. Fluorescent lights in ballasts hung from the ceiling. They shined on tables and shelves built from wooden planks. The surfaces were covered with tin cans. A small green plant sprouted from each.

"Those aren't tomato starters," I said. "It's marijuana."

"And a plenty big crop too, more than one pothead can smoke, no matter how much he likes getting high," Loq said. "Grazier starts them in here to get a jump on spring and then transfers the seedlings to the field. A little clearing in the forest like his would be hard to spot by a drug enforcement plane. He's cultivating for selling."

"No wonder why he's paranoid. He gets caught with this much dope, he's looking at serious prison time. I'd heard about illegal pot farms on national forestland in Northern California, but always thought it'd be too cold up here. This greenhouse solves that problem."

"Yeah, but it creates a different sort of problem. He's making his wife and kids accessories to a felony."

"Let's get out of here before the Graziers come down to collect their guns. We don't need a firefight." As we were walking back to the rigs, I said, "Busting a pot farm on private land is beyond our authority. All we can do is report what we saw along with reporting Grazier for beating his wife and son."

"The man's a walking, talking clear and present danger," Loq said. "We can report it, but it'd be better to get them out of there right away."

"If we storm the place, somebody's sure to get shot. And there's no telling if Mrs. Grazier and Silas would go. If they're scared of living with Grazier, they're probably terrified of what he'd do if they tried to take off."

"I made a mistake leaving the mother and kid behind," Loq said. "I won't make it twice."

"Okay, let's say we get them out, then what? Where do we take them? Where do they go? They don't have any money, no jobs, no home. They have to be suffering from some kind of trauma from being abused too. Dealing with that takes a professional."

"Then we get help from people who know what they're doing."

"You mean, family welfare agency folks, counselor types. We'll need to do it in such a way where there's no blowback on Mrs. Grazier and Silas. Having Grazier arrested for beating them and growing pot would take him out of the picture long enough for the professionals to go in there and meet with them."

We walked alongside the ditch that was carrying water from the marsh to the pond with the waterwheel.

Loq said, "You haven't mentioned the oldest son. You don't think he's getting beat on?"

"He probably is or, at least, was, but I think his father has messed him up so much, Ebal would back his play no matter what. He didn't see anything wrong with shooting me if Grazier told him to. It's like he's been brainwashed, but that's for a head doctor to decide. All we can do for now is make sure he isn't the one doing the blowback on his mother and brother after Grazier is arrested."

"How old do you think Ebal is?"

"Eighteen or thereabouts."

"Then he's old enough to be arrested along with his old man. That'll put him in a place where counselors will be able to evaluate him to figure out how best to help him."

"Good idea. I can ask Pudge to contact the Klamath County sheriff about making the arrest. Do you know anybody who works at the family welfare agency in Klamath Falls?"

"No, but my sister will. She works in a rehab clinic in town."

"You never told me you had a sister."

"You never asked."

We reached the end of the field. "What's her name?"

"Carrie Horse."

"How did she get it?"

"After a bareback race at a *C'waam* Ceremony." Loq meant

the long-nosed sucker fish that was sacred to the Klamath. "Her horse went down right before the finish line. The horse got up, but was hobbling. My sister ducked between his front legs and made him rear. Then she threw her arms around his cannons and started to run. They crossed the finish line first, but the judge disqualified her. The tribal elders gave her a new name to honor her feat. Woman Carries the Horse."

"Can you ask her to help us out?"

"I will, but once she hears what's happening, there's no guarantee she won't charge right up there. Carrie was married once. She doesn't tolerate bad men."

I climbed the embankment and turned the wheel to the grease screw to close the head gate. Water stopped pouring out of the marsh. "In about an hour, Grazier's waterwheel is going to grind to a stop and the generator will stop spinning."

"He'll come down and reopen the gate," Loq said.

"I'm counting on it. He was duly warned. Now when he violates again, our case to have him arrested will be even stronger."

12

S ince Pudge had already gone home by the time I reached Burns, I continued straight to No Mountain. The thought that Gemma might be there made the miles seem even longer. I finally reached the one-blink town and slowed as I passed through what accounted for Main Street, a block-long stretch lined with sagging false-fronted buildings that included Blackpowder Smith's tavern and dry goods store. Moments later I clattered over the metal cattle guard that marked the entrance to the Warbler ranch and pulled to a stop alongside Pudge's white pickup with the seven-point gold star on the door. Gemma's red Jeep was also parked in front of the house, but her single-engine airplane wasn't tied down alongside the dirt airstrip.

I found November sitting at the dining room table stitching bright ribbons around a length of dark fabric.

"What's that you're making?" I asked.

The old healer tsked. "What I hope to wear, but *tabah* and *muha* are rising and setting far apart instead of sharing the sky at the same time to let their light shine upon each other."

"Sun and moon," I said, recalling the *Numu* words from the

hours I spent learning the language. "You're talking about Gemma and me getting married."

"Hm. Perhaps my teachings have not fallen on ears that do not hear. This is no ordinary dress. This is a ribbon dress, special to us and many other peoples. Ojibway. Menominee. Meskwaki. My mother taught me how to make it as hers taught her. She wore a ribbon dress when Shoots While Running and I were married, but when our daughter Breathes Like Gentle Wind made the journey to the spirit world, I thought I would never wear one myself."

"You will soon," I said.

The old healer stood and draped the length of fabric in front of her. She began humming and swung the fabric to and fro, making the colorful ribbons ripple and flutter.

I left her to her reverie and found Sheriff Warbler in his home office. It still looked the same as when it doubled as a department substation the four years he was semi-retired and served as a deputy. He hung up the phone and swiveled his desk chair to face me.

"You sure stuck your nose in a hive that's got more bees than honey this time," he said.

"I didn't know Loq was going to call you," I said.

"And why would he, outside of the fact we're both leathernecks?"

"To tell you about what we found at Klamath Marsh."

"What's the marsh got anything to do with Catlow Valley and your archaeology friends?"

"Not a thing. It's a different problem."

Pudge sighed. "Why is it there's always more than one problem at a time with you, son? You're like a fellow who gets struck by lightning twice while standing in the same spot."

"Tell me about Catlow Valley and then I'll tell you about the marsh."

"And here it is already past supper time. I'd've eaten by now if November hadn't spent the entire day sewing. Okay, listen up."

Pudge had called the Eugene police department and University of Oregon campus security office about Flip Carson and the former assistant professor, Cecil Edwards Oliver. While Oliver's threat against Pax Sizemore didn't raise any concern with either law enforcement agency, Carson was another story. Campus security told Pudge they'd had their first run-in with him a few years prior when he got a job as a groundskeeper on campus. The resident assistant at a girls' dorm reported him for lurking outside ground-floor rooms. When confronted, Flip claimed he was only trimming hedges, but it turned out that Stephanie Buhl lived in one of the rooms he was peeping in. A month later, he was reported for barging into the girls' bathroom at MacArthur Court during a basketball game that Stephanie was at. He said it was all a big mistake, that he'd accidentally picked the wrong door. Later, he crashed an anthropology department party that Stephanie was attending and punched the boy she was talking to and threw him through a window.

That prompted the university to fire Carson and ban him from campus. He became the Eugene PD's responsibility after that, racking up a string of arrests that included drunk and disorderly, resisting arrest, and assault and battery. One victim, another classmate of Stephanie's, wound up in the ICU at Sacred Heart Hospital. That landed Carson in lockup for ninety days. He was placed on parole and ordered to check-in regularly with a parole officer.

"I spoke to a detective by name of Dallas Skinner," Pudge said. "Flip Carson's his pet project. Skinner says he's bad news and a headline in the Eugene *Register-Guard* waiting to happen."

"What did he say when he learned Stephanie and Sizemore were in Harney County?"

"That if I see Carson, to arrest him on the spot and hold him until he can come fetch him. He likes him for the unsolved homicide of a man found beaten to death behind a tavern."

"I radioed Orville on my way here. He said he didn't get a radio check-in from Sizemore today."

"Could be something, could be nothing. Your plan with the professor is to radio him first thing the next morning to make sure everything's jake, right?"

"It is, but I'll drive down and talk to him in person. I have to take Tuhudda his new tire anyway."

"Fair enough. Now, tell me about Klamath Marsh."

I was about to get into it when November came in. "Supper is ready," she said. "We eat now. I still have much sewing to do and need the table back."

Pudge bolted out of the swivel chair. "About time. I got an appetite for two."

She eyed his paunch, but didn't say anything. We followed her to the dining room. The table was set for four.

"Is Gemma on her way?" I said.

"I always set a place for her. It is bad luck not to. After she gives birth, I will always set a place for the baby also."

We sat down and Pudge lifted the lid to a cast-iron Dutch oven. He breathed in the steam. "Ah. Chicken and dumplings with pounded wada root added to the flour." The local *Numu* were known as *Wadadökadö*, the "wada root and grass-seed eaters."

We passed plates and ate family style. November listened as I told Pudge about the Graziers and the marijuana farm. He all but spit out a forkful of dumpling when I said Grazier beat his wife and son and mentioned the deaths of the daughter and uncle.

"There's a special place in hell for men who strike their wife and kids," the lawman said. "I know the Klamath sheriff all right, but there could be a hitch if I call him straight out."

"What kind of hitch?"

"The Bust'em Burton kind. When they organized the county sheriff's departments by region, they put a bunch of make-work protocols in place. Mostly they're there to put us sheriffs in our place so Bust'em can lord over us."

"Every day that's lost to red tape is another day of hell for Mrs. Grazier and Silas."

Pudge bristled. "I know that and I'm not about to let Bust'em and a bunch of new how-to's stand in the way of me doing the job I was elected to do. I'll go as far as giving him a heads-up before I call the Klamath sheriff. In the meantime, get on the horn with Orville and give him the names of that family. Let's see what kind of magic he can work with all his new-fangled computing machines. See if he can find any info on how the little girl died, like a death certificate or coroner's report. The same with the uncle."

November looked up from her plate. "Gemma is close."

I cocked my head. "I don't hear anything."

"You will," the old healer said.

Sure enough, a small plane buzzed a few minutes later.

"Well, go on, son," Pudge said. "If you're not there to greet my daughter when she lands, it could be a whole lot longer before I get to see her in a wedding dress."

When Gemma and I returned to the ranch house after tying down her plane and chocking the wheels, November and Pudge had retreated to their respective bedrooms. A log had been added to the fire crackling in the fireplace and the fourth setting had been moved from the dining table and placed on the coffee table in front of the sofa. A covered plate was set between a napkin and the cutlery.

The horse doctor kicked off her boots, plopped down, and lifted the cover. "My favorite, chicken and dumplings made with wada root."

"That's exactly what your father said."

Gemma gave me a mock look of annoyance and then patted her bulging stomach. "You haven't seen me for days and the first thing you do is compare me to Pudge?"

"He should be so lucky."

"Nice try. Sit down and tell me what you've been up to while I eat. I'm famished."

I gave her a quick rundown on the dig at Catlow Valley and the marsh. "Grazier sounds insane," she said. "You need to help that woman and her son get out of there as quickly as possible."

"Loq and I are working on it."

Gemma finished eating and pushed away the plate. She leaned back and rested her head on my shoulder. "March twentieth marks the first day of spring this year. Not the twenty-first or twenty-second or twenty-third like it is in other years."

"The vernal equinox," I said. "It always seems to be the busiest migration day of the year at the refuges, especially Malheur and the ones in the Klamath drainage."

"That's the day," she said.

"I know. It's like all the birds have a built-in clock telling them the exact date when day and night are equal length."

"I mean, *the* day." When I looked at her questioningly, she added, "For our wedding, hotshot."

A mixture of surprise, relief, and unease washed over me. "That soon?"

"Don't tell me you're going to back out now."

"I meant, well, it's coming up pretty fast. Right around the corner. Be here before you know it. Not a moment to waste."

"You're running out of clichés." She tugged on my arm so it was tighter around her shoulder and then placed my hand on her stomach. "And the baby's running out of days in here."

"Then the vernal equinox it is. I'll be ready."

"Me too." Gemma squeezed my hand. "There's something else we need to plan."

"What?"

"A name."

"Isn't that something you do afterward, when you know if it's a boy or a girl?"

"Do you have a preference?"

"For a name?"

Gemma squeezed my hand again. "Whether it's a boy or a girl."

"All I want is healthy."

"Me too, but I've been thinking of names for both sexes."

"Such as?"

"I keep going back to family names."

"You mean your mother's. It'd be a good way to honor her memory."

"She went by Hattie, short for Henrietta. Do you like it?"

"I do. Does that mean if it's a boy, you want to name him Pudge?"

Gemma squeezed my hand even harder. "That's a heck of a name to saddle a baby with, and if we called him Pudge's birth name, he'd surely disown us as parents."

I didn't say anything. Gemma let it go for a while and then nudged me. "You don't know what it is, do you?"

"What?"

"You know what. All this time and you still don't know what Pudge's real first name is." She laughed. "Some son-in-law you're going to be."

"Okay, what is it?"

"Let's see how the marriage goes first. Maybe if you play your cards right, I'll tell you someday."

"Funny," I said.

Gemma's breathing slowed and soon she was asleep. I sunk

deeper into the sofa and thought about the changes that were coming. There was much to do before March 20. Get Mrs. Grazier and Silas to safety. Fix the broken levees at the marsh. Take the tire to Tuhudda and make sure all was well at the dig site. Check on the elk at Malheur.

The long day was catching up. My eyelids grew heavy. I decided to rest them for a few seconds before rousing Gemma so she could go sleep in her own bed instead of curled up on the sofa next to me.

13

THE FIRE

G emma doesn't move all night on the bed of pine boughs inside the wickiup while my thoughts keep spinning about what I need to do to get us home.

"The plane crashed," I say out loud, hoping she can hear me. "You're injured, but safe. I'm going to get your medical bag and some other things. I'll be right back." I put my ear to her lips in case she answers. All I hear is her breath. It's slow and shallow, but speaks volumes.

I draw the hanging duffle bags apart and slip through the wickiup's opening, closing them behind me. Dawn is breaking and the condensation from my own breath matches the liquid color of the sky. The storm let up during the night and a fresh white blanket now covers the wickiup. The snow will be good insulation until it melts and tests the water-tightness of my pine branch weaving.

I break a new trail to the wrecked plane. While I'm grateful a spark didn't ignite the leaking fuel and destroy the emergency kit and medical bag, I chide myself for not capturing some of it to use for signal torches.

The broken propeller blade does its job again prying apart

metal. I jam it under the passenger seat and free it from its tracks. I wrestle it through the door and let it fall to the snow before crawling into the rear of the crumpled fuselage. Everything is tossed around. I paw through the clutter. The frost coating the bags and boxes reminds me of November's fry bread. I give a shout when I locate Gemma's medical bag, and when I put my hands on the emergency kit, I entertain a brief moment of hope.

I dig some more and locate the kit bag where I store my service weapon. The Smith and Wesson is still in its holster with the belt wrapped around it. A box of magnum cartridges is in there too. I keep rooting around the plane and come up with some aeronautical charts, an Oregon highway map, and a thermos of coffee and two sandwiches wrapped in wax paper that November had packed for the flight. I take everything outside and place it on the passenger seat sitting upright in the snow. Using the seat belt as a towline, I drag the makeshift sled back to the wickiup. Along the way I strike gold when I stumble on a metal object. It's the spinner dome, the cone-shaped housing that covers the propeller hub to streamline airflow. It'll make a good cook pot for turning snow into drinking water.

Gemma is still unconscious. I comb the undersides of the trees for dried twigs and branches and pile them near the wickiup. Using the spinner dome as a scoop, I dig a shallow hole just inside the entrance and line the bottom with rocks. A handful of moss placed on top catches the spark of a waterproof match from the emergency kit. I blow on the curl of smoke and add twigs until the tongue of flame licks high enough to feed bigger sticks. Smoke rises up and out of an angled gap I left at the top of the wickiup. The fire takes the chill off.

While snow melts in the metal spinning dome placed near the fire, I take stock of the plunder. In addition to matches, the emergency kit contains a silver space blanket—the kind developed for the Apollo missions that put men on the moon twice the prior year with a third attempt coming next month. I flick on the flashlight. The beam is strong. The compass is similar to the one I used in Vietnam. It fits in my palm as welcome as the handshake of an old friend.

The feeling of hope tingles again when I see the flare gun. I break it open and check the single chamber. It's empty, but I spot a box containing three flare rounds that resemble shotgun shells. I picture the Browning shotgun Pudge gave me as a wedding gift. I'll never be able to face him again if I don't bring his daughter back alive.

Gemma's veterinarian bag contains welcomed items too. A stethoscope, scalpel, forceps, scissors, and an assortment of rolls and squares of gauze along with elastic wraps and adhesive tapes. The labels on the medicine bottles run the gamut from topical antiseptic to isopropyl alcohol to lidocaine to saline solution. I doubt I'll have a need for the farriers rasp or hoof dressing, but I don't throw anything out.

The melted snow starts to boil. I set it aside to cool. I twist open the stopper to the thermos. The coffee is lukewarm, but I've never tasted better. November's sandwiches are made with leftovers from the wedding reception. I lift the top piece of bread. The slices of roast beef came from a dressed steer hand-cranked on a spit over an open flame in the field where we said our vows. I can hear the laughter and chatter as people eat, drink, and dance. Blackpowder Smith plays the fiddle and sings Bob Wills and Hank Williams tunes. Lucy Lorriaga squeals with delight while she sits on Orville's lap as he spins them around in his wheelchair. After the father-daughter dance, Pudge takes a turn with Bonnie LaRue, the formidable editor and publisher of the Burns *Herald*. Tongues wag as guests watch the once romantically linked couple Texas two-step.

I close the sandwich and rewrap it. I'll use the slices to make broth. Gemma will need all the protein she can get when she comes to.

The water in the metal dome is still too hot to drink. While I wait for it to cool, I stand outside and hold up the compass. The red needle spins inside the housing, wobbles, and then settles. North is to my right. West is straight ahead. What the compass doesn't tell me is, north and west of where? The taste of defeat rises like bile and I try to choke it back, knowing that being cold is one thing, hungry another, but feeling beaten is cancer to the soul.

I think of the call and response I taught my squad. "Stay in the fight, men," I shout. "Never give up. Never give in."

The call echoes across the clearing and into the forest. Pine boughs rustle and something moans. A cold wind is trying to drown me out and so I shout the men's response in defiance. "Still in the fight, Sarge. Won't give up. Won't give in."

I wait for the wind to dare me again. The rustling and moaning returns, but nothing blows in my face.

And that's when it hits me.

The sounds aren't coming from in front of me, they're coming from behind.

"Gemma!" I shout, and rush back inside the wickiup to be by her side as she wakes...

14

A leg cramp woke Gemma in the middle of the night and she abandoned the sofa for her bed. I continued to doze in front of the fireplace until roused by noises coming from the kitchen. November was up before first light as was her custom. I found her making fry bread. The coffee pot was already on.

"Tell Tuhudda I will come give blessings for the Ancient One," she said before I could say good morning.

I couldn't remember having told her about the bones in Catlow Valley, much less planning to drive there that morning. She might've overhead Pudge and me talking, but then again not.

"Will do, though I'm not sure what Professor Sizemore's plans for them are yet."

November brandished the wooden spatula she was using to turn patties of dough sizzling in a cast iron skillet. "It is not for him to decide. The Ancient One's bones are not something to put on display or sold. He used them to walk in the brown world and showed the way for *Numu* to follow. Tuhudda and I will honor the Ancient One with songs and blessings so his journey continues in the spirit world."

"Tuhudda told me about nowhere bones and his grandparents, Bear and Yellow Moon. Maybe the Ancient One was like them and never started the journey because his bones were never found until now."

November sighed. "It was a time of great sorrow for *Numu*. *Padooa* was a brave warrior and hunter. *Ohalune* was a singer and healer. My grandfather and father searched for them also, but nowhere bones are not always found." She went back to tending the fry bread. "Tuhudda and I will honor the Ancient One no matter if there was a ceremony or not."

"I'm sure the professor will be fine with that," I said. "He made a point of telling Tuhudda and me he's not like other scientists who treat artifacts as buried treasure."

November harrumphed. "But still he digs up the dead."

"In order to learn more about people who lived here thousands and thousands of years ago so all people can learn from them."

She tsked. "Are the dead of long ago different than the dead of today? Did they not have families who loved and mourned their passing also?" She flipped the patties of dough over. The oil in the skillet sizzled. "*Numu* have had so much taken from us. Our land, our ways, our lives, and even our dead."

I couldn't argue with her there, and so I said nothing, but she wasn't about to let me off that easily. "Would you want someone to dig up Gemma or your child whether it was tomorrow or next year or a thousand years from now?"

"I'll make sure the professor understands about the blessing," I said quickly. "You can count on it."

"I already did. Here, take some fry bread and go."

I left the Warbler ranch and headed south. As I chewed the cooked dough she'd dusted with powdered sugar, I thought about her reaction to the discovery of the old bones. I'd been to a *Numu* mourning ceremony once before. Wyanet Lulu, a friend of November's, invited me because I'd been present at the hospital when her husband was readying to start his journey to the spirit world. There was both sorrow and joy to the ceremony —sorrow that a beloved had died, but joy that his journey with his ancestors would continue forever. I wondered what the mourning and blessing rituals had been like thousands of years ago and if they'd changed much. One thing hadn't, I knew. Honoring the dead was as much for the living.

I finished the fry bread and washed it down with black coffee as I passed the turnoff to the Malheur refuge. I'd already decided to check on the elk herd on the way back since the light would be better later in the day for sketching the pregnant cow with the cougar scars.

The white clapboard-sided wayfarer's inn at Frenchglen was still closed for winter as I passed by. The two-lane climbed up and over the steep face of a basalt-capped butte before dropping down into a seemingly endless sea of sagebrush rendered first silver and then gold by the rays of the rising sun. A herd of pronghorn looked up from grazing. They didn't bound away from the sound of my pickup. Perhaps they recognized it from my frequent patrols at Hart Mountain National Antelope Refuge that lay to the west.

Before turning onto the road that led to the dig site, I radioed Pax Sizemore to tell him I was en route and he needn't bother making a daily check-in call. The paleoanthropologist didn't pick up. Neither did either of his two student assistants. I checked the channel he'd given me and tried again. Still no answer. I was easily within range. Maybe the channel was wrong. Maybe his radio was on the fritz.

I stomped the gas pedal. Marines weren't the only ones who didn't do maybe.

The snow did little to smooth out the bumps and potholes on the rough-and-ready track. Tuhudda's spare tire bounced in the back of the pickup. The sound was like a kettle drum's. I drove with my teeth gritted to keep from biting my tongue. When I neared the dig site, I slowed. No smoke curled from a cookfire. No throb echoed from the generator. I counted vehicles. The Wills' junker without a trunk lid and the pickup and Land Cruiser with U of O emblems on their doors were all still there.

I left my rig and proceeded on foot, keeping my hand on the butt of my holstered service weapon. The Wills' lean-to was nearest. I passed my hand over the fire ring they'd built in front of it. The ashes were cold. I drew my revolver.

The big basecamp tent that served as mess hall, office, and storage room was quiet. So were the three smaller backpacking tents that housed the professor, Stephanie Buhl, and Jelly Welch. No sounds of snoring came from the other side of the nylon walls. No grunts were made as the occupants pulled on their jackets and boots readying for a hard day's work in the rockshelter. I moved my finger from alongside the trigger guard to inside it.

I sidled up to the big tent where we'd eaten Scottish biscuits in the warmth of the propane heater. The wall was as cold as the Wills' campfire. I raised the gun in a two-handed grip and moved to take a look inside.

I smelled him before I heard him. I wheeled around with my finger on the trigger. Jelly Welch stumbled toward me. One side of his beard was matted with blood. A gouge above his ear furrowed his scalp.

"Help me. I've been shot." He fell to his knees.

I checked his neck for a pulse without looking down as I swept the perimeter for targets. "Who shot you?"

"I need a doctor," Jelly wheezed.

"Where are the others?"

"I don't know."

"What happened?"

"Someone shot me."

"When?"

"Last night. I heard voices. I went outside. Someone fired at me. I shot back and then got hit. I need to go to the hospital."

"How many shooters?"

"I don't know. It was dark." He started whining. "Come on, let's get out of here before they come back."

"Did you see them leave?"

"I didn't see anything. I was knocked out."

"Where are the others?"

"What others?"

"Tuhudda and Nagah. Sizemore and Stephanie."

"They're probably hiding. Come on, let's go."

I grabbed him by the jacket. He squealed. I hauled him to the basecamp tent. The door was unzipped. I looked in. The tent had been tossed. Boxes were turned upside down. The camp chairs were upended. I dragged Jelly in behind me.

He took one look and whimpered. "You see why we have to get out of here? It was badass looters, I tell you. They could still be here."

"Where's your gun?"

"I don't know."

"You said you fired it."

"I think I hit one too. I must've dropped it when I got shot."

"Where was that?"

"Outside my tent."

I found what was left of the radio. It'd been smashed.

"Stay in here. Don't come out until I tell you to."

Jelly moaned. "I want to go to the hospital. You have to take me."

"And the fastest way to get there is if I radio the sheriff."

"Then I'll drive myself."

"No, you won't. You're staying put until the sheriff gets here."

"But I'm hurt. I need a doctor."

"You'll live."

"How do you know?"

"I've seen more than my share of bullet wounds." I moved toward the tent flap.

"Don't leave me here alone to die."

"I have to look for the others."

"Ah, jeez. Why do you have to go do that?"

I ran to my pickup and got Orville Nelson on the radio. "The dig team's been attacked. Jelly Welch's been shot, but he's alive. I don't know where the others are."

"Ten-four," he said. "Is the shooter active?"

"Unknown."

"Any casualties beside the one GSW?"

"Unknown."

"Any description of suspects or vehicles?"

"Unknown."

The young deputy's voice revealed neither frustration nor excitement as he asked questions. It was a far cry from when he was an overeager college intern handling emergency calls. "I will alert the sheriff and ask state police to set up roadblocks in and out of Catlow Valley. We might get lucky."

I grabbed the Winchester, chambered a round, and went hunting. First up was checking the inside of the three smaller tents. Jelly's was identifiable by the smell of his BO that seemed baked into the nylon. Pax Sizemore and Stephanie Buhl weren't hiding in theirs nor lying dead in their sleeping bags. There weren't any bullet holes or scorch marks from gunfire on the walls either.

The snow around the campsite had been trampled over the

past few days. It made distinguishing one set of footprints from another difficult, but blood splatter on a patch of snow near Jelly's tent was hard to miss. I searched for ejected cartridges. No brass gleamed in the snow or atop bare patches. When I couldn't find Jelly's Colt Python, I had to assume the shooter had at least two weapons. Another blood stain darkened a spot ten yards away.

I followed a trail that led from it to an outdoor privy, a white toilet seat set atop a five-gallon metal bucket with a roll of TP stored in a coffee can with a plastic snap lid placed within arm's reach. I walked back to the blood splatter and tried other trails that extended from the camp like spokes from a hub. One led back to the vehicles, another to a cluster of used and unused propane tanks that were for the main tent's heater and cooktop, and, finally, the trail to the generator and rockshelter beyond.

As I walked it, I spotted a less-traveled path branching off. It led away from camp. I followed it. In about a hundred yards, the ground on the left-hand side dropped away and I found myself walking on the top of a basalt postpile that rose from a low spot in the desert floor. The vantage point provided a view of the rough road that led to the camp. A set of tire tracks veered off it and ran in my direction. I looked down. There was no vehicle at the base of the postpile, only the shape of a human-sized crucifix darkening the snow.

I hurried down the path to reach it, careful to avoid stepping in three sets of footprints as I went. One set traveled up. Two sets traveled down. One of the downhill prints was about the same size as the one coming up, but was set deeper as if the person who'd made them was weighted down by something. The set of boot prints that only went down left a distinctive tread pattern.

By the time I reached the bottom, I knew who'd made those. Leather hiking boots with rubber lug soles called *Carramato*— Italian for "tank treads"—pointed toes up. The red laces confirmed it. Professor Paxton Sizemore lay on his back with his arms flung out. His mountaineer-handsome face was disfigured by an open-mouth cry that was frozen in place. Bloody goose down stuck to the edges of a jagged hole in the front of his vest. I could tell by the tire tracks that the vehicle that made them had come and gone.

There was nothing I could do for Sizemore and so I hiked back up the trail and cut over to the rockshelter to look for Stephanie and the Wills. It was the most likely place for someone to hide. I stayed low as I ran toward the entrance in case a gunman was hiding there too.

As I entered the gapped-tooth frown, I recalled a skinny nineteen-year-old who'd been my squad's tunnel rat. He'd crawl into the passageways to underground bunkers armed only with a handgun. "No room for an M-16 down there, Sarge," he'd say. "This be up close and personal work, you hear what I'm saying?" I stashed my rifle near the box of flashlights, grabbed one, and held it alongside my .357 as I began silently ticking off steps remembered from my previous trip.

The cave floor was fairly level and any wrinkles in the walls that could provide cover were far and few between. My heartbeat echoed like thunder. Sweat dripped beneath my shirt. I kicked a rock that pinballed off the wall and immediately ducked. A thousand fluttering wings responded as a colony of big brown bats whorled overhead amid a storm of high-pitched clicking. I braced for balls of rattlesnakes rolling toward me next.

I reached the fork. To the left lay the Ancient One's bones, to the right the spot where Stephanie had discovered the Clovis point. I'd seen few places to hide in that section of the cavern, but the left fork was an unknown. I chose it and started counting a new set of steps while treading lightly, still clutching the flashlight and revolver with both hands. The walls closed in and the ceiling dropped. Stalactites forced me to duck while stalagmites made me dance around them.

No gunman popped out when I entered a large chamber, nor did Stephanie, Tuhudda, and Nagah reveal themselves when I called their names. I swept the walls with my flashlight. The only grotto was about the size of a sleeping berth on a Pullman car. The ledge had to be where the ancient bones had reposed for two thousand years. I drew closer to take a look, but it was empty. The ledge was coated with crystals that sparkled in the flashlight's beam. I touched them. They were as rough as coarse sandpaper. I wondered if they'd formed when the soft tissues of the now missing Ancient One decomposed. It was a question for a paleoanthropologist, but the answer I wanted right then and there was the identity of the person who took the bones. Was it the same person who killed Sizemore?

The echoes from three rapidly fired gunshots reached the chamber and sent me racing back to the gap-toothed entrance. When I reached daylight, I scooped up my Winchester and looked toward the camp. Emergency lights flashed from atop a pair of sheriff's vehicles. A third was speeding up the rough road. Sheriff Warbler stood in front of his pickup aiming his .45 at the sky, readying to discharge another volley.

I waved my rifle to get his attention and then fast-stepped to give him the news. The Ancient One would have to remain nowhere bones until the missing trio and Sizemore's killer were found.

15

The old lawman told one of his deputies to drive to the postpile and prevent turkey vultures from scavenging Pax Sizemore's corpse and ordered the other pair to scour the campsite for clues.

"Where's the one who got shot?" he asked me.

"Jelly Welch," I said and pointed to the main tent. "I left him in there."

"Let's go have a chat."

I held the tent flap open for Pudge. The bearded student was hiding behind a wall of boxes.

"Come on out, Jelly," I said. "I have the sheriff with me."

"How do I know that's not a badass looter and he's holding a gun on you?" he said.

Pudge gave me a you got to be kidding me look before saying, "Son, I'm Harney County Sheriff Pudge Warbler. I understand you got shot."

"I did and it hurts real bad," Jelly whined from behind the boxes. "He wouldn't take me to the hospital."

"I got an ambulance on the way. Come on out and let me have a looksee."

Jelly crawled out on all fours and poked his head in Pudge's direction. "It's bad, isn't? Tell me the truth. Am I going to die?"

The sheriff peered at the wound. "Appears the blood's already clotted. That's good. So is where you got hit. Another inch it would've drilled a hole clean through your skull. Half inch the other way, taken the top of your ear off." Pudge righted two of the overturned camp chairs so they were facing each other. "Here, take a load off while we wait for the ambulance. Let's see if you can help me find your teammates."

Jelly plopped down. Pudge sat across from him and began asking about the hours leading up to the shooting. While they spoke, I poked around the tent and examined the contents that had been dumped out of the boxes. The Clovis point was missing. So were the buffalo-bone handle knife, sandals, and fire-starter kit.

Jelly told Pudge yesterday had been like any other day. They woke up, ate breakfast, and then spent the day working in the rockshelter. Jelly and Stephanie started off by sifting through their assigned quadrants in the righthand fork while Sizemore and the Wills worked in the one on the left. At one point, Sizemore asked Jelly and Stephanie to join them.

"I thought maybe they'd found another set of old bones, but it wasn't anything like that," Jelly said. "Sizemore wanted me to help Nagah move this honking big rock. It was a total putdown because that's not my job and also he knows I got a bad back." Jelly patted his shoulder and winced.

"Were they able to move it anyway?" Pudge asked.

"Yeah."

"How?"

"Stephanie helped. She's a lot stronger than she looks. Plus, she's a woman's libber. She doesn't like anybody telling her she can't do things. It turned out to be a waste of time like I knew it

would. There wasn't anything behind it, not another tunnel or
more old bones."

"Tell me what happened after that," Pudge said.

"It was nearly quitting time. I knocked off and went back to
my tent to rest my back. The others came down a little later. Uh,
let's see. It was Stephanie's turn to cook. We rotate. One night
cooking, one night washing dishes. She's terrible at it, by the
way. Even burns canned chili. Of course, listening to Sizemore
oohing and ahing, you'd think whatever she made was filet
mignon at a fancy restaurant."

"What happened after dinner?"

"Stephanie wrote up her notes in the logbook and Sizemore
worked on the textbook he's writing. All the professors do that.
They make their students buy them. It's another scheme they
have to get rich."

"What did you do?"

"I went to bed early. My back was still acting up. I fell asleep,
but then sometime in the middle of the night loud voices woke
me up."

"Did you recognize them?"

"Not at first. I was asleep, remember? But then I could tell
one was Sizemore's. I didn't recognize the other guy's."

"You could tell Sizemore was talking with another man?"
When Jelly nodded, Pudge said, "Did you hear Miss Buhl speak?
How about the Wills?"

Jelly shook his head. "Only Sizemore and the other guy, only
they weren't talking so much as yelling."

"What about?"

"I don't know. Everything was muffled. I was in my
tent."

"Could you tell if they were exchanging punches?"

"They could've been, but I didn't see it. I got out of bed,
grabbed my gun in case it was looters, and went outside. It was

dark. Then someone took a shot at me and I fired right back. I'm pretty sure I hit him."

"If it was dark, how do you know that?"

"I'm a good shot."

"How long after you fired your weapon did you get shot?"

"Right away. He must've rushed me. I got hit and it knocked me out cold."

"What happened when you came too?" Pudge asked.

"It was daylight. I heard someone moving around. I went to take a look and it was him." Jelly pointed at me.

"Lucky you didn't freeze to death laying in the snow all night. Where was Professor Sizemore during the shooting?"

"I don't know."

"What about the Wills?"

Jelly scratched his beard. "I never saw them."

"When you fired your gun, how did you know you wouldn't hit the professor?"

"I fired at who shot at me, that's how."

"And you don't know where the professor went or where Miss Buhl and the Wills were during all this?"

"You already asked me and I told you. I never saw them," Jelly said.

"You sure?"

"Sure, I'm sure. I told you, I didn't. You sound like you don't believe me."

"Son, it's my business to ask questions. You said it was dark, right? They could've been close by and you didn't see them."

"I suppose, but, well, I didn't. Okay? I didn't see them and I didn't see Sizemore or who I shot or who shot me. I didn't see anybody, I tell you."

Pudge nodded slowly, as if thinking on something. "What did you shoot the person with?"

"My Colt Python."

"Where's it now?"

"I don't know. I blacked out when I got hit. When I came to, it was gone. The guy who shot me must've taken it."

The old lawman kept nodding, and then without preamble said, "Professor Sizemore's dead. Murdered."

"What!" Jelly's jaw went slack. "Was he shot too?"

"No. Drake here found his body. Says it looks like he was stabbed. In the heart."

Jelly slumped. "Oh my god, that's horrible. I can't believe the professor's dead." The sheriff didn't say anything. Neither did I. "It was badass looters. You have to catch them and throw them in prison for life. Better yet, hang them. That's what you do out here, isn't it?"

"Why are you so sure the person you heard arguing with the professor was a grave robber?" Pudge said.

"Who else would've it been? Look at this place." He waved his hand. "I bet if we took inventory right now, we'd find they stole everything we found up in the rockshelter."

The sheriff squinted at him. "Such as?"

"Let me think. A Clovis point, a stone knife, and bark sandals. Some animal bones too. Real old animals like giant sloths."

"What's a Clovis point?"

"A spearhead made out of rock."

"Is something like that worth money?"

"Can be. Clovis points are really old and rare and—"

"How much is the one found here worth?" Pudge said.

"I don't know. Depends." Jelly eyed him. "Why do you ask?"

"Because if it's over a certain dollar amount, that makes it a felony robbery, not a misdemeanor. And the fact you were shot makes it an armed robbery. Another felony. Those will add a lot more years to go along with the murder of Professor Sizemore I'm gonna charge the killer with."

"And what about me? Shooting me has to be worth something more than armed robbery."

"You're right. Assault with intent," Pudge said.

Jelly almost looked pleased by that. He touched the injured side of his head. "I have a huge headache. Where's that ambulance?"

"It's coming." Pudge kept his gaze on him. "You haven't asked about Miss Buhl or Tuhudda Will and his grandson."

"Getting shot in the head's got me turned upside down. Are they okay?"

"They're missing."

"They probably ran off when they heard the shooting and are staying out of sight until the coast is clear." Jelly paused. "I sure hope the looter didn't take them as hostages."

"Do you have reason to believe they might've been taken?"

"How am I supposed to know what a badass is thinking when he raids a dig site?"

"Maybe you heard something when Sizemore and the other man were arguing. Maybe the other man threatened Sizemore, told him he'd already rounded up the others and would hurt them if he didn't turn over what you all found."

"I told you I didn't hear any words, only loud voices."

"So you said."

Jelly frowned again. "I mean, it's not like I think Stephanie was working with the looter, how he knew where we were and what we found." He paused for a long moment. "You don't think that about her, do you?"

The old lawman stood. "You best stay put until the ambulance arrives. It won't be long now. They'll take you to the hospital in Burns. I'll drop by and check up on you there. You take care."

Pudge headed out of the tent. I followed and caught up to

him as he was getting behind the wheel of his pickup. He said, "Come on, son, time to show me the professor."

He backed out of the camp using only the side mirrors, straightened out when we hit the road, and then drove one-handed.

"What did you make of Jelly Welch?" I said.

"For a college boy, he's dumb as the rocks he's digging in to let someone come right up to him and shoot him during a gunfight. Either he's lucky or he's got reflexes like a cat to be able to jerk his head in time so all he'll have to show for it is a scar like an inchworm crawling across his scalp."

"From what I've seen, the only time Jelly moves fast is to dodge work."

"The old bad back excuse," Pudge said. "I had a deputy like that once. The only thing he did with any speed was cashing his paycheck. Jelly sure doesn't hold Miss Buhl in high regard, pushing her in front of a speeding train like he did."

"When I was here earlier, the two were always trading insults. She treated him like a moron. He called her teacher's pet."

"Sounds like a couple of kids vying for their pappy's attention, the pappy in this case being the professor. Still, since Miss Buhl's missing, I can't rule anything out, either her as a willing or unwilling participant. Maybe she needed money. Maybe she didn't have a choice but go along because the robber turned killer was threatening her family or holds a secret over her, something from her past she doesn't want anybody to know."

He pushed the brim of his Stetson up. "But whether she was in on it or not, it doesn't change my opinion on who I think is the most likely killer, and that being her caveman ex-boyfriend who might or might not be so ex."

"Flip Carson," I said. "But none of that answers where she and the Wills are."

"I haven't forgotten about old Tuhudda and his grandson. He knows this land better than anyone. Tuhudda has a habit of disappearing and showing back up when you least expect it."

"One thing that doesn't add up for me is where was Sizemore when Jelly and the gunman were trading shots? If Sizemore was still there, how come the gunman didn't shoot him too? If Sizemore had already chased whoever killed him out of camp and down the hill, then who shot Jelly? A second gunman?"

"Second gunman, huh? Sounds like what some folks think that home movie taken during the Kennedy assassination shows. A shooter on the grassy knoll."

"The Zapruder film," I said.

"People see in that what they want to see. Seven years later and no one can prove there was anyone but Lee Harvey Oswald pulling the trigger. The killing here? Well, I'll keep an open mind about two suspects, but I also know that sometimes you can't always tie up a murder investigation with a nice, neat bow. A loose string or two goes with the territory of being a lawman."

The tracks that veered from the rough road to the base of the postpile came up and Pudge steered onto them. They were cut deeper now because of the deputy who'd driven ahead of us. We pulled behind the other rig. Pudge walked in a wide circle around the professor's body and examined it from every angle before approaching.

"Well, Professor Sizemore, you may not be from Harney County, but you can be darn sure I'm going to treat you as if you were. I won't rest until I bring the person or persons who did this to you to justice. On that, you have my word."

The sheriff reached down and opened Sizemore's down vest and flannel shirt. The stab wound in the chest was a couple of inches long and had jagged edges.

"Doesn't look like a jack knife or hunting knife did that," he said.

I took a close look. "It wasn't a knife. It was the Clovis point."

"The sharpened rock Jelly Welch said was missing from the tent and worth a lot of money?"

"The same."

"Now, don't that beat all. Since it's not sticking in him or laying around, the killer must've taken it with him. Find the Clovis, find the killer."

We spent the next half hour searching for evidence, but none was to be found except for the boot prints and vehicle tread marks, which were already starting to melt. Pudge ordered his deputy to photograph them since we didn't have the means to make plaster casts. I showed Pudge the trail the killer had used to go up to the campsite and back down with Sizemore hot on his heels.

"You're onto something about the set of boot prints that went up are deeper coming down," Pudge said. "See here, he was putting his weight back on his heels to keep from slipping or pitching forward while the professor's fancy Italian boots were coming down on their toes, meaning he was light on his feet and running fast."

"The killer's prints could be deep because he was weighted down coming back."

"With the loot he stole."

"But all that wouldn't weigh more than several pounds at most."

"You think he was carrying Miss Buhl?"

"It could explain where she went."

"That it could." A siren sounded in the distance. "Here comes the ambulance. I'd like it if they could pick up the professor while they're here but that wouldn't sit well with Jelly who'd have to ride alongside him. Besides, the body's got to stay put until Doc has his looksee." He meant the coroner.

"Are you going to wait for him?" I said.

"I'm heading back to Burns straightaway. I got a manhunt to launch and talk with that detective in Eugene some more. Dallas Skinner. My deputy will stay put with the professor here while the other two finish up searching the site and collecting blood samples from the two spots and whatever else they can find."

"Have you had a chance to think about the family living above the marsh, the Graziers, and the best way to approach the Klamath sheriff for getting an arrest warrant?"

"Not yet. I'll do it when I get back to the office."

We were both looking at Pax Sizemore's frozen corpse. The grotesque tableau was a stark contrast to the beauty of the multi-sided columns of wind-polished basalt that resembled the pipes on a church organ. His death started to weigh. Though I'd only known him a short time, I realized I'd missing learning from him. The professor was a natural born teacher and the world needed more like him. Like Pudge had done, I made a vow to find his killer, even if it meant delaying my own marriage vows.

16

B lackpowder Smith was behind the bar when I returned to No Mountain. He poured me a tall glass of water with no ice and pushed it across. "Your regular, young fella." He paused while I drank. "Gemma was in a little bit ago and gave me the news. About time she picked a date. There's lots of planning to do and little time to get it done since all of Harney County will be there."

I nearly choked. "Gemma invited everybody?"

"She couldn't keep 'em away even if she wanted to. It's the way it's done in these parts, especially when the father of the bride happens to be the sheriff." The old codger cocked his shoulders and beamed. "'Course, when they learn yours truly is tying the knot for you two, neither a blizzard nor a dust storm would stop 'em from coming. I got a reputation for being right handy with the words."

"But that's why I'm here. I was going to ask you to officiate."

"Gemma beat you to the punch, young fella. You still got a lot to learn about women. Now, what I typically do is mix in a special passage from the Good Book that matches the particular couple and then throw in some poetry. Did I ever tell you I write a little verse myself? I've been called the Bard of the High Lonesome. I'll also be playing the fiddle when the dancing starts. I'm partial to Charlie Daniels and the like. People will want to kick up their heels."

"Did Gemma happen to mention where it is we're getting married?"

"You don't know? Well, then, maybe I'm not supposed to say. Could be she wants to surprise you. She did mention Loq's goin' stand up there with you to catch you in case you faint." He cackled. "Now remember, there's only two things you need to do. First is tell the bride she's the most beautiful woman in the whole world and you're the luckiest SOB on the planet. Second is XYZ."

"What's that mean?"

"Examine Your Zipper. You don't want to forget to pull it up when you're putting on your new suit trousers. You'd never hear the end of it for ruining all the photos." Blackpowder's new round of cackling filled the tavern.

I finished the water. "There's another reason I dropped by." I gave him the lowdown on Catlow Valley. "Driving home, I started thinking that Tuhudda and Nagah's disappearance along with the bones gone missing isn't a coincidence."

He stroked his white goatee. "Knowing old Tuhudda, I tend to agree with you. Him and his grandson could've taken the bones to give 'em a proper burial out at some sacred spot in the desert only the Paiute know about before the bad guy ever showed up. Or they could've ducked and covered during the gunfire and when all the commotion was over and seeing the professor was dead and Jelly Welch was goin' live, they grabbed the bones and skedaddled."

"Not in their car, they didn't. It's still there."

Blackpowder's black cowboy hat with a snakeskin band bobbed up and down. "Paiute are born walkers. They've been walking all over this land for thousands of years, summer, winter, spring, and fall. They were walking it long before cars were invented, clothes too for that matter. Little cold at night and snow on the ground ain't goin' stop a Paiute, no sirree."

"I hope you're right. Thanks for agreeing to marry Gemma and me."

"No problem. One more thing. Don't forget ABC on the big day." When I gave him a questioning look, he cackled. "Always Be Charming."

A ringing telephone greeted me when I got home to the old lineman's shack.

"Ranger Drake, this is Regional Director F.D. Powers. I didn't hear back from you as I expected I would."

"Sorry, some things came up that required my presence in the field. The weather has been pretty tough on wildlife and a herd of Rocky Mountain elk became stranded at Malheur. There's also a situation at Klamath Marsh."

"What kind of situation?"

"The criminal kind. Someone breached a series of levees in order to redirect water for their own purposes." I paused. Going into specifics with the little bureaucrat would only complicate matters. "Loq and I have tracked down the culprit and are working with local law enforcement authorities to file charges."

"Make sure I see a complete report on the matter. It's important I know about interagency cooperation throughout the Western Region." He paused. "There's still the outstanding matter of the district supervisor position. While there are other candidates who have extensive management experience, my charge from President Nixon is to shake the dust off the agency. New blood, not old thinking, is my recipe for doing just that. You're that new blood, Ranger Drake. I'm willing to stake my reputation on it."

It was time to bite the bullet, even if it meant getting lead poisoning. "Sir, while I appreciate your confidence in me, there's something of a personal nature you should know. You see, I'm engaged. As a matter of fact, I'm getting married on March 20."

"That soon? Why, congratulations. Who's the lucky girl?"

"Gemma Warbler. She's a large animal veterinarian."

"Is that a fact? I've never had time to contemplate marriage myself, what with the president depending on me, but being married won't be any impediment for your Fish and Wildlife career. Far from it."

"Wait, sir, there's more. We're expecting a child pretty soon too."

F.D. Powers didn't answer right away. I could hear him clicking a ballpoint pen as he thought. "Even more reason for congratulations. And it's even more reason why you need to take the job in Portland. Not only does it come with a modest increase in salary, but the agency provides housing for district supervisors. I'm told the house in Portland is located in a very nice neighborhood and has a big backyard. I'm sure your bride will be very pleased."

"I'll let her know," I said as a way to keep from making a commitment.

"Show, don't tell," he said. "Why don't you and your bride plan on spending your honeymoon in Portland. I'll have my secretary make all the arrangements. She'll book you into the honeymoon suite at The Benson. Consider it my wedding gift. While you're there, you can take a look at the house, meet the personnel you'll be supervising, and see the city sights."

"You don't need to do that."

"Think nothing of it, District Supervisor Drake. Now, tell me that doesn't have a nice ring to it?"

Powers clicked off before I could protest. As I thought about how I was going to tell Gemma about the honeymoon proposal, the phone rang again. I picked it up, hoping it was my boss telling me he'd changed his mind about offering me the job.

"We got a SNAFU," Loq grunted.

"It's been a long day. Should I be sitting down?"

"As long as it's behind the wheel while you're breaking the speed limit getting over here. I'll call you back on your rig's radio in five."

The way Loq told it to me, he'd gone straight to Chiloquin after we left the marsh and stopped by his sister's to ask her to talk to someone at the family welfare agency about Mrs. Grazier and Silas.

"Let me guess," I said into my radio's mike. "Carrie Horse did exactly what you thought she might. She galloped off to the Graziers right then and there."

"No, she didn't," he said.

"Good."

"We went the next morning."

I blew out air and then asked him what happened when they got there.

"I was betting on Grazier and Ebal being down at the marsh reopening the head gate or getting the waterwheel restarted. I turned on the same logging road you and I took, but instead of staying on the west side of the ridge, I cut over to the east side where their cabin is. I found a road leading straight to it."

Loq went on to describe entering a thick part of the pine forest. A locked gate hung with Keep Out signs blocked the way and a barbed-wire fence ran from both sides of the gate. He and Carrie hopped the gate and continued on foot. Two hundred yards in, they saw the ramshackle cabin and broken-down school bus. They circled the compound, keeping a line of trees between them and the clearing, but didn't see anyone.

Carrie said, "You wait here. I'll go knock on the door."

"Grazier and Ebal could be inside," Loq warned.

"I'll tell them I was out picking huckleberries and got lost."

"It's too early in the year for berries."

"Then you better be faster than you are strong, little brother."

Carrie marched off, leaving Loq no choice but to cover the door with his Winchester. She knocked, but no one answered. She knocked again. Still getting no response, she backed up a few paces.

"Mrs. Grazier," she called. "My name is Carrie Horse. I'm here with my brother who you saw with the other ranger. We're here to help you."

No one answered.

"Please, Mrs. Grazier, we want to help you, but we can't if you don't want to help yourself."

A minute later, the door opened a crack. "Go away. You'll make things worse." The voice was timid, shaky.

"We can protect you and Silas. Is your son with you right now? Come with us. There's others who will help you too. You'll have a safe place to stay."

"Go away. My husband will be back any minute. He'll be angry." The voice turned frantic.

Loq walked out of the woods to show himself. "Is Ebal with him?"

A loud gasp came through the crack in the door. "My husband swore he'd kill you if he ever saw you again. Go. Run." The door closed.

Carrie gave no warning. She rushed forward and pushed it open. The woman shrieked and threw her hands up to cover her face. Her hair was a fright and a faded pioneer dress hung on her like a collapsed tent.

Gently taking hold of her bony wrists, Carrie shushed, "Shh, it's okay. We're not going to hurt you. We're here to help."

"Go away." Mrs. Grazier was shaking, but didn't lower her hands. "You can't help me. Nobody can."

"Your husband came home and beat you after my brother and the other ranger talked to him, didn't he? Let me see what he did to you."

"I deserved it. I broke the rules."

"You're hurt. Let me help you."

"I don't need your help. I'm fine. Go away."

"I'm not going anywhere. I'm not going to let him hurt you again."

"You don't know him."

"Oh, yes I do."

"How could you?"

"Because I was married to a man like him. He hit me too."

The woman started trembling. "I'm... I'm so ashamed."

"So was I. I'd tell people I'd fallen down or got kicked by a horse."

The woman peeked between her fingers. Her eyeballs were bloodshot. "You have a man who beats you?"

"Had. I told you my name, what's yours?"

"It's... it's Ruth."

"That's a beautiful name. Come on, Ruth. Let me take a look. I want to make sure you don't have a broken nose like I got."

Carrie gently pulled Ruth's hands away from her face. Bruises the color of crows circled her swollen eye sockets.

"It's all my fault," Ruth whimpered. "I shouldn't have left the cabin. I shouldn't have let your brother follow me back here."

"This isn't your fault." Carrie's tone went from gentle to resolve. "Nothing you could ever do deserves this. Nothing, you hear me? I know, because I was where you're at now and I used to blame myself too. But I'm not there anymore and you don't have to be either."

"But I could never leave. I love my husband."

"You love the man you fell in love with, but your husband's not that man anymore. If he was, he wouldn't do this to you. He wouldn't strike Silas either."

"He'll hit him even harder if I was to try to leave. I need to stay to protect my baby boy."

"He can't hurt Silas if Silas comes with you. My brother and I won't leave without you both. We can take you to a safe place where your husband can't get to you because he won't know where it is."

Ruth shook even harder. Her baggy dress billowed. "I can't leave. I'm too scared. I've never been on my own before."

"How old were you when you got married?"

"Seventeen. We eloped."

"Because you were pregnant with Ebal?"

Ruth bowed her head. Loq could see scabs in her scalp.

"I would've married him anyway. I loved him. He was the best-looking man I'd ever seen. Smartest too. Graduated from college. Had a salaried job. Wore a tie. He took real good care of us. He had to move us up here to keep us safe from the bomb. He knows all about them from his work."

"But you're not safe," Carrie said. "Not from him, you're not."

"I can't leave my husband. I can't. I can't be on my own. I don't know how." She gulped.

"You won't be on your own. You'll have Silas with you. Ebal too, if he'll let us help him. That might take some time, but there are people who can help him see that he's in danger living with his father."

"My husband will come after us," Ruth said. "He'll think we were taken by the people who are out to get him."

"Is that what you think, that there are people who want to do you harm?"

"Yes, I guess, well, no. But it doesn't matter what I think. It's what he thinks and they're real to him."

Carrie hadn't let go of Ruth's bony wrists. "You're husband's mentally unwell. You know that, don't you? He needs help too."

"He'll never allow anyone to help him. He won't let them get close."

"He won't have a choice if he's been arrested."

"For what?"

"Hitting you and your children is against the law."

"But he's my husband."

"It doesn't give him the right," Carrie said.

"I won't press charges. I can't. I need him. My boys need him."

"He's making them criminals by forcing them to help him grow and sell marijuana. Do you want them to be arrested and go to jail too?"

"Of course not."

"Then you have to get them out of here and to safety. He's endangering them. He's a danger to you all."

"I can't leave him. I can't." Ruth's sobs grew even louder.

Carrie pulled her close. "Do it for Silas and Ebal. Do it for Rebekah. She'd want you to be safe."

Ruth pushed away. "You know about Rebekah?"

"He hit her too, didn't he?"

"My poor, poor little girl!" she cried. "I couldn't keep her safe. She wanted to go back to our old life. She was always running away, but my husband would catch her and bring her back."

"How did she die?" Loq said.

"One time he was chasing her through the woods and she tripped and fell and hit her head."

Loq started to ask if she saw it happen or if Grazier only told her about it, but Carrie warned him off with a look. She said to Ruth, "But you can keep Rebekah's memory safe by helping yourself and Silas right now."

"You don't understand. I can't leave, because I can't leave her.

My husband buried her somewhere in the forest. He won't tell me where because he doesn't want people to take her. My Uncle Jim is buried somewhere out there too. I might not be able to put flowers on their graves, but at least I'm close by so I can talk to them."

"My brother will find them," Carrie said. "He can find anything. You'll be able to come back and visit them anytime you want because your husband won't be living here to stop you. The sheriff is going to arrest him."

"He is?"

"Yes. That's why you and Silas need to come with us right now so you won't be arrested too."

Loq said, "Clock's ticking, sister."

Carrie nodded. "Where's Silas, Ruth? Is he with your husband?"

"He's down at the marsh. My husband told him to check on the other levees and make sure the breaks didn't get filled. If they did, he's to open them up."

"I know where he's at," Loq said. "We can pick him up on the way."

Ruth looked around the dingy cabin frantically.

Carrie said, "Leave everything. We'll get you new clothes and such to start off with and you can come back later to get what you want when your husband's no longer here."

"My photograph! I can't leave the picture of my little girl. It's all I got."

Carrie went to help her find it. Loq kept watch on the tree line, expecting Grazier and Ebal to show any second. The minutes dragged by. Finally, Carrie and Mrs. Grazier emerged. The woman was clutching a brown paper sack. They double-timed back to Loq's pickup.

I asked him if driving away with Mrs. Grazier was the SNAFU, but my gut told me there was more—a lot more.

"I'm in the middle of something right now," Loq said. "It's why I'm radioing you from my pickup. I'll tell you when you get to Chiloquin. Radio me back when you're ten miles north of town and I'll direct you to Carrie's. If you don't reach me, get patched through to her." He gave me a telephone number.

Silver Lake Road dead-ended at Highway 97, a scenic two-lane that ran the length of the state along the eastern flank of the Cascades. I turned on it and headed south. Most of the other vehicles were big rigs. Some had teamed up in convoys to take advantage of the slipstream created by the tractor-trailer in front. It was the same thing V's of waterfowl did. Thinking of the murder and disappearances in Catlow Valley and Grazier beating his wife and kids made me long to see the life-reaffirming act of millions of birds flying thousands of miles to raise their young.

The highway crossed Spring Creek, a noisy feeder stream that crashed over boulders in a steep canyon lined with jagged cliffs. A mile past the bridge I radioed Loq. Static and crackle filled the cab. I adjusted the knob and tried again, but the static grew louder. I switched over to a familiar channel.

"Harney County Sheriff's," Orville Nelson answered.

"Don't you ever sleep?" I said.

"Good evening, Ranger Drake. No one in the department will be sleeping tonight, what with the murder in Catlow Valley and three missing persons. Are you in No Mountain?"

"I'm near Chiloquin. It has to do with the stolen water in Klamath Marsh."

"I apologize, but I have not been able to locate very much information on the Grazier family."

"There's been a development I can fill you in on later, but right now I need to get patched through to Loq's sister. Here's her phone number."

"Hold while I try it. If I lose you, I will radio you right back."

Orville didn't need to. The radio-to-telephone connection worked and a woman answered with a blunt, "Who's this?"

"Nick Drake. Your brother said to ask for directions to your place. He's going to meet me there."

"I don't have a street number. Look for a raven and bear totem on the river side of the road. Take the dirt drive. I'm a quarter mile in."

"Where's Loq?"

"Trying to fix things."

"Fix what?"

Carrie Horse snorted. "My brother said you'd ask that."

17

My headlights shined on two modular homes. Their vinyl siding told a tale of bitter winters and scorching summers. A swing set and a listing tetherball pole were set between them. As I got out of my rig, a scruffy dog with pointy ears and a white patch that reminded me of the pregnant elk yapped ferociously.

"*Wac'aak*, enough," Carrie Horse commanded from the front porch of the house on the left. The mutt stopped barking and then circled my pickup. "She usually doesn't bite."

"Usually? What's her name in English?"

"Dog. She's my mom's, but spends most of her time over here because she likes to play with my kids and sleep on their bed."

"Where does your mother live?"

Carrie pointed at the other house. "She's asleep. At least she's supposed to be. Sometimes she sneaks out to play Bingo with the other *weeleeqs*." She sighed. "Old women are trickier than little kids."

"Has Loq ever mentioned a *Numu* healer named November?"

"My little brother, the big, brave Marine. He told me Girl Born in Snow scares him."

Carrie came down from the porch. She had Loq's eyes and high cheekbones, but her nose was crooked from having been broken and a scar bisected her upper lip. A glass-bead barrette with a carved hairstick rode at the top of her long, swinging braid. Porcupine quills dangled from hoop earrings and turquoise rings encircled the fingers on her right hand like a colorful pair of brass knuckles.

"We need to get something straight before we go inside," she said.

"What's that?"

Carrie cocked her head. "Do you hear that?"

The steady drumbeat of water breaking itself against rocks filled the darkness. "The Williamson," I said. "Loq told me it comes from Crater Lake and is sacred to the Klamath Nation."

"The river gives my people strength and teaches us important lessons. One is when you commit yourself to something, you never back down. We're taught that life is like the river, if we wade into the fastest and strongest current, we'd better be prepared to get swept all the way downstream if that's what it takes to finish what needs to be done."

"I'm already wet up to my hips and not about to turn around," I said. "Tell me what happened."

"The river also teaches us patience," she said. "Did Loq tell you how *Gii-was* was formed? One day, great spirits pushed ice up through a hole in the sky and created *Moyaina*, what white men call Mount Mazama. The spirits climbed back to earth and created all that you see, the lakes, rivers, and marshes. When they were finished, they returned to the spirit world, except for *Gmo'Kamc*, the spirit chief. He stayed and created the *Maklak* people and gave us a home. Life was beautiful for everyone."

Carrie stared in the direction of the river. "But the spirit of the underworld, *Monadalkni*, grew envious of the world *Gmo'Kamc* created. One day he came up and spied a beautiful maiden. He told her parents he would marry her in exchange for giving them eternal life. The maiden didn't want to marry *Monadalkni* and so her family refused him. The spirit of the underworld grew angry. He ran back and forth beneath *Moyaina*, making it rumble and shake violently. He threw lightning bolts into the sky and caused lava to rain down.

"The people called for *Gmo'Kamc* to save them. The two spirits met atop *Moyaina* and waged a ferocious battle. *Gmo'Kamc* beat *Monadalkni*. He forced him back underground and collapsed the mountain onto the entrance of the underworld to keep him there. This created a vast crater that raged with fires. *Maklak* medicine men sang songs for the rain to come and put them out. Their songs were answered and the rains filled the crater. This is how *Gii-was* became a holy place."

"Why do I see Loq and Grazier's faces when you're telling me about the spirits fighting each other?" I said.

"My brother also told me you'd ask questions you already know the answers to." Carrie brushed a fingertip across her lip as if it could erase the scar. "The people I treat at the rehab clinic are addicted to alcohol and drugs. I met my husband there. I thought I could save him, fix him, and I did for a while, but then I couldn't help him anymore. I thought I'd seen the worst of people who are devoured by self-hatred until I saw Mr. Grazier. I thought I'd seen every kind of hopelessness there is until I met Ruth Grazier."

"And Silas?"

"Youth has resiliency, but there's a limit to everything."

"What happened?"

"We found Silas on a levee like his mother said we would," Carrie began. "He was shoveling dirt. When he saw the pickup, he grew frightened and started to run away. Loq sped after him.

He stuck his head out the window and told him to stop, that we had his mother with us."

"Did Silas stop?"

"Finally, but he was as skittish as a wild pony put into a corral. He wouldn't come any closer than this yard is wide. I got out with Ruth and told her to tell her son that everything would be okay, that we were there to help them. As soon as she started to speak, she broke into tears and started gasping for breath. She was crying so hard, I had to put my arm around her to keep her from collapsing."

Carrie went on to say that Silas thought his mother was being held against her will and charged Loq with the shovel, swinging it wildly. Loq easily sidestepped him and snatched the tool away. Silas then rushed at Carrie. She let go of Ruth, who fell to the ground. Used to warding off blows from her husband, Carrie grabbed Silas by the wrist and spun him around, pinning his arm to his back. Then she threw her arms around him and clutched him to her breast.

"Shh, sweetie, shh. I'm not your father. I'm not going to hurt you. Your mother asked us to help you and her get away from your father so he can't hurt you anymore."

"You're lying," Silas cried. "You're the ones Daddy warned us about. You're them. You're here to get us."

"No, we're not, sweetie. We're here to help. You need to trust us."

"Carrie's telling the truth," Ruth sobbed from the ground. "They can help us. I can't protect you on my own. You know that." She pulled herself up and went to Silas. Tears streaked her bruised and battered face. She held her arms out.

Carrie let go of Silas. He rushed into his mother's arms and they clung to each other like a pair of exhausted swimmers trying to stay afloat. Their desperate embrace was short-lived.

The roar of a pickup speeding down the levee drowned the sound of their crying. Gunshots rang out across the marsh.

"Get off the levee," Loq barked. "Keep your heads down."

Carrie pushed Mrs. Grazier and Silas down the embankment and followed them. Loq jumped in his rig and mashed the gas pedal. The rear tires shot up a spray of clods and the pickup fishtailed, nearly sending the back wheels off the narrow track. Loq aimed straight for the oncoming pickup. It was a mortal's version of *Gmo'Kamc* versus *Monadalkni*, and Loq had every intention of sending Grazier deep into the underworld.

As his father drove, Ebal stood in the bed braced against the cab and fired his rifle. Most of his shots went wild, but one grazed Loq's rig. He didn't duck. He didn't step on the brake pedal either.

"Men who smack their wives and children have something in common," Carrie Horse said as she described the events while we stood in the chill of the night. "Besides hating themselves, they're cowards. Grazier cranked the wheel before my brother smashed into him head-on. His pickup sailed off the levee and plunged into the marsh."

"Did Grazier go headfirst through the windshield or drown?" I said.

"Neither. He wore a seatbelt yet made his son stand in the back."

"Ebal must have flown right over the cab."

"He did. I was sure he'd broken his neck, but he skipped across the water like a flat stone and came to rest in a bed of lily pads."

Carrie told me how Loq waded into the marsh and yanked Grazier out of the pickup. He hauled him onto the levee and left him spitting up water while he went back to fish out Ebal. By the time he reached the lily pads, the teenager was nowhere to be seen. Loq plunged his hands into the water and felt around for him while shuffling his feet in case he was lying on the bottom. Hearing Carrie's shout, he looked over his shoulder. Ebal had swum back to the levee. He still had his deer rifle and was pointing it at Carrie who stood several feet away with her arms outstretched as Ruth and Silas cowered behind her.

"I'm here to help you," Carrie said to Ebal.

"I don't need your stinking help!" he cried. "Let 'em go."

"I know you don't like doing what your father tells you to," she continued in an even voice. "I know you know, deep down inside you, that he's unwell. You know he's trying to turn you into a version of himself because if you act like him, it'll let him think he's normal, and how he treats you, your brother, and mother is normal too. But it's not normal. You know that."

"Shut up!" Ebal shouted. "You don't know nothing."

"I know he tells you you'll go to prison for growing marijuana if you don't do what he wants. I know he hits your mother and little brother. And I know he beats you too."

"Not anymore, he don't."

"Because you do what he wants." Carrie raised her crooked nose at him. "Is that what you want to do too, hurt people to make yourself feel better about yourself?"

As they spoke, Loq stepped quietly out of the marsh and began climbing up the embankment. He drew his service weapon. Carrie could see him out of the corner of her eye. With her hand still at her side, she extended her index finger with a turquoise ring on it and made a slash. Loq froze.

Ebal sighted down the gun barrel at her. "I'll hurt whoever's trying to get us."

"No one is trying to get you, only help you," Carrie said, her voice still calm and even.

"Looks to me like you're trying to hurt 'em by taking them away. Let 'em go or I'll shoot you right between the eyes."

"Stop it, Ebal," Ruth said. "Stop it, right now. I asked Carrie

to help us. She's going to take us to a place where we can be safe.
All of us. You too. Come with Silas and me. Please, I love you."

"Funny way of showing it, trying to run off."

"We have to," Silas said. "Daddy's gonna kill us."

"Shut your mouth, Sissy Silas. You don't know what you're
talking about."

"Do too. Come on, Ebal. Come with us. Please. I want you to.
Want you to real bad. Ma too. We need you. You're the biggest,
the strongest. You've always been. We can't do it without you."

Ebal didn't say anything, but the deer rifle's barrel started to
waver as if it had suddenly grown too heavy.

A wracking cough sounded from up the levee. Grazier was
now standing upright. He shook the water out of his ears and
then turned to face them. Blood dribbled from his mouth where
he'd struck the steering wheel. He spit out a tooth.

"Don't listen to them," Grazier wheezed. "Can't you see? The
man's got them."

Carrie made the slashing finger motion at Loq again when
he started to raise his weapon. Once again he halted.

"What do you want me to do, Daddy?" Ebal cried without
taking his eyes off Carrie.

Grazier's soggy beard dripped like moss hanging from a pine
limb in the rain. His eyelids blinked rapidly and his eyeballs
skittered. "Don't be fooled by her. She's the *man*. You got to stop
her from getting us."

Ebal hesitated. "What are you gonna do to Ma and Silas?"

"Nothing if they come home."

Ebal's bottom lip quivered. "I don't want you to hurt them."

"Hurt?" Grazier said. "Everything I do is so you all don't get
hurt. Haven't I always protected you? Kept you safe when the
world was going to blow itself up. Kept you safe from the *man*."

Ebal said to Ruth, "Come on, Ma. You heard Daddy. We gotta
go home. You and Silas can't leave. You'll get hurt if you do."

"And we'll get hurt if we stay," Silas cried. "We're not going home. We're not!"

"You're my son. You're not going anywhere," Grazier shouted. And then he glared at Ruth. "And you're my wife. You're not going anywhere either. Didn't I marry you when no one else would have you? Didn't I give you children? Move you out of the filthy city. Keep us from getting blown up. I gave us everything we ever wanted or needed."

Ruth's lips puckered. "Except for Rebekah and Uncle Jim. I'm not going to let the boys end up like them. I'm not."

"You don't know what you're talking about!" he screamed.

"Don't I? Rebekah slipped and hit her head? A girl who could run through the forest like a deer." With each word, her voice grew stronger, louder, and she stood taller, brandishing her bruised face like a weapon. "And you expect me to believe Uncle Jim had a heart attack the night he told us we had to move out because you'd agreed to grow marijuana for those men you met in Medford? I saw you hit him. An old man who took us in when we had nothing. You kept hitting him after he ran out of the cabin to save himself. You killed him and buried him."

Grazier lurched forward. Loq had given Carrie her chance, but he could see the man was drawing the pistol with the walnut grip from his waistband. Loq raised his sidearm, trying to decide in a split second who to shoot first, Grazier or Ebal.

"Wait, brother. Look!" Carrie shouted.

Grazier wasn't pointing the gun at them. He'd placed the barrel against his temple.

"I'll kill myself, I swear I will! You come home with me right now or you'll have my blood on your hands. All of you. You won't have anyone to protect you anymore. Save you from the missiles that are pointed right at us. The ones with the nukes. I swear I will."

Silas clutched at his mother. "Ma, what are we gonna do? We can't go back. You'll know what he'll do."

"I'm warning you," Grazier said. "If you don't come, I'll do it. I swear I'll do it!"

"Don't, Daddy. Don't," Ebal begged. "We'll come. I'll make them come."

Carrie didn't move. Loq either. Ruth reached out and pushed the barrel of Ebal's rifle down until it was pointing at the ground. She stepped around him and faced her husband. She was so skinny inside her baggy dress, a breeze would've blown her off the levee and sailed her across the water.

"If you love us, like you say, then you'll let us go," she said, the strength in her voice surprising Carrie.

"I won't let you," Grazier said.

"All right, then we'll come if you promise me one thing."

"What?"

"Show me where you buried your daughter after you killed her. Show me Uncle Jim too."

Her voice had a razor's edge that cut straight through the power he held over her. The pistol shot's echo rolled over the marsh and Grazier dropped to the levee, blood spurting from the hole in his temple. Carrie Horse spun and pulled Ebal and Silas to her so they couldn't see him while Ruth watched stone-faced as her husband twitched one last time.

18

The timeless current of *Gii-was* sacred water running past us couldn't dilute the potency and portent of what happened upriver. "Ebal's not inside your house with his mother and brother," I said to Carrie Horse.

Her long black braid swished back and forth. "He walked away without saying a word. He never looked down at his father's body as he passed nor did he ever look back at Ruth and Silas."

"And Loq didn't stop him right then because it would've turned everything upside down. After he brought you and the Graziers here, he drove back to get Ebal. That's where he's at now, the cabin above the marsh."

"My brother thinks Ebal will be better off if he goes with the rest of the family to K Falls to tell the sheriff what happened rather than wait for the sheriff to come looking for him."

"He's right. If Ebal feels like his father's death is somehow his fault, someone is sure to get hurt if the law shows up."

"Loq wants you to smooth the way by talking with the sheriff in Harney County."

"I'll call Pudge Warbler right away. Does Mrs. Grazier know Loq went back to get Ebal?"

"I told her."

"We should also tell her she'll have to explain to the Klamath County sheriff why there was a delay reporting Grazier's suicide."

Carrie led the way. The front door had stuck from the cold and she gave it a hard bump with her hip. It opened into the living room. Two posters of men were pinned on the wall above a worn sofa that faced a TV set.

"Have you heard of them?" she asked. "They're modern day warriors. That's Dennis Banks on the left. He's Objiwe. The man on the right is Russell Means. He's Oglala Sioux. They're leaders in the American Indian Movement."

"I've heard of AIM. They focus on poverty and police brutality in the big cities."

"They did that in the beginning, yes, but the more of us who join, the more we can do to protect people living on tribal lands and reservations. I started an AIM chapter for the Klamath Nation, but it's probably best I don't tell that to the sheriff when I see him." When she smiled, it tugged the scar on her lip.

I smiled back. "Probably."

"The Graziers are waiting in my children's bedroom. They don't want to come out here because of the front windows. They're scared of being seen because they've been living in isolation for so long. Their bruises from being hit will heal, but not all the ones inside them. That's the real hurt Grazier did. He was trying to kill their spirit. Only time will tell if he succeeded."

Ruth Grazier was hunched on the edge of one of the twin beds with her hands clasped on her lap. Silas was curled on the other bed with his face turned toward the wall.

"Hello, Silas, Mrs. Grazier," I said. "I'm here to help."

Silas didn't respond. Ruth put her hands to her face to hide the bruises, but then abruptly let them fall. "My older boy blames himself for his father's death."

"Carrie told me what happened. I'll take you to see the sheriff in Klamath Falls in the morning. You'll want to tell him how you and the boys were mistreated, what happened to Rebekah and Uncle Jim too."

Ruth hung her head. I could see bruises around her neck from having been choked. "Won't he arrest us for the marijuana garden?"

"Not if you tell him it was your husband's doing, that he forced you to go along. There could be a hearing, but once you talk with people from the family welfare agency, I can't believe anyone would choose to prosecute."

"I'll go to jail if it means keeping my sons from being blamed," she said.

Carrie put her hand on Mrs. Grazier's shoulder. "No one's going to jail once we explain everything. I'll introduce you to the folks who can get you and your boys the help you need. Now, you and Silas should get some rest. This room's yours. My kids are already asleep in mine."

"Do you think your brother will bring Ebal here tonight?"

"If he does, I'll come wake you."

Carrie motioned me with her eyes and I stepped out of the bedroom. We went into the living room. While I could call Pudge on her phone, I wanted to talk to him in private.

"I'll go radio Sheriff Warbler," I said. "Once he's onboard, I'll try contacting Loq again so we can synchronize meeting in Klamath Falls. I'll keep trying all night long."

"You're going to spend the night in your pickup truck? It's only going to get colder. You can sleep on the sofa here."

I glanced at my watch. It was less than twenty-four hours since I was asleep on the sofa at the Warbler ranch. It seemed a lot longer. "I have a sleeping bag with me. It won't be the first time I slept in my rig."

"If it helps, I built a sweat lodge near the river. I always keep dry kindling and wood inside it along with a pail of water for steam and tied bunches of sage. After a day like this, a sweat will make sleep easier."

"I'll keep it in mind, but I'm pretty bushed. I'll be lucky if I don't fall asleep making my calls."

"Then may the sound of *Gii-was* give you powerful dreams."

"And you," I said.

I got in the front seat and wrapped the sleeping bag around my shoulders. Frost coated the windshield. I picked up the radio's mike and got Orville Nelson on the line. "I need to talk with Pudge. Is he available?"

"He should be. His extension is unlit. I will transfer you."

Orville stayed on after the old lawman picked up. His reaction was about what I expected, the reason why I didn't want Mrs. Grazier and Silas to hear his roar.

"You think he beat his little girl to death and now that sorry sonofabitch is dead before I can get my hands on him?" Pudge's voice all but caused the frost on the pickup's windshield to melt.

"Mrs. Grazier said Rebekah could run like a deer and didn't believe it possible she'd lose her footing like Grazier said. His hold on his temper was a lot slipperier that a wet forest floor."

"A pathologist would likely be able to confirm cause of death for both the girl and the uncle depending on the state of decomposition," the young deputy said.

"We'll have to find the graves first," I said. "Only Grazier knew where he buried them."

The radio hummed as Orville and Pudge took that in. I could picture their faces. Pudge's jowls would be turning bright red. Orville's forehead would furrow as he tried to think up a way to use one of his machines to find a solution.

"The FBI has been testing ground-penetrating radar to locate clandestine graves," the young deputy said. "The testing is still very much in the preliminary stage. I also recall reading that the Army was experimenting with training military canines to search for cadavers to help locate MIAs in Vietnam. I will make some calls."

"Until then, it'll have to be done the old-fashioned way," Pudge said. "Boots on the ground. I'll let the Klamath County sheriff know when I speak to him."

I knew finding the graves would do more than help explain why the family was terrified of Mr. Grazier. It would also give them peace of mind knowing where the bones of their loved ones lay.

"Before you call the sheriff, we should coordinate timing as soon as I know Loq and Ebal's ETA."

"Assuming Loq talks him into coming with him," Pudge said.

"He will."

"All right, I'll wait until I hear you're on your way."

"I'll try radioing Loq now."

"Hold your horses. Seeing as you're gonna be in Klamath tomorrow and that being a three-hour drive to Eugene as opposed to me sending a deputy on a ten-hour round tripper from Burns, you could do me a big favor by stopping by the police department there on your way home. That detective, Dallas Skinner, told me he has something he wants to give me that's a possible connection to Sizemore's murder as well as a new homicide he's tangling with."

"Who's the new victim?"

"A man who runs a pawnshop in Eugene. He has a record for fencing stolen goods."

"What is it he wants you to see?"

"Skinner was a little vague about that. Said he didn't want to influence my reaction ahead of time."

"I've never been to Eugene, but I'm sure I can find the police department."

"Thanks, son."

I tried radioing Loq again, but only reached static. Part of me wanted to race up to the marsh and help him, but I knew that would likely do more harm than good. The last thing Loq needed was for me to spook Ebal. I tried shutting my eyes, but my head started spinning with a kaleidoscope of faces that included the Graziers, Pax Sizemore, Stephanie Buhl, Jelly Welch, and the Wills. I didn't know what Flip Carson or Assistant Professor Cecil Edwards Oliver looked like, but their shadowy figures were also part of the whirligig. Too many questions and too few answers made me wired. Where were Tuhudda, Nagah, and Stephanie? What did Detective Skinner find? Who took the Ancient One's bones and why?

The questions made my head spin, and any thought I had of reading the copy of *Baby and Child Care* I'd brought along before falling asleep went out the window. Remembering Carrie's prescription, I grabbed a flashlight from the glovebox and found a well-trod trail that led to the sound of the river.

A low, dome-like structure covered with canvas tarps stood on the bank. I pulled back the flap and shined the light inside. A ring of stones next to a pile of wood and a pail of ice-covered water beckoned. I crawled in and started a fire. When the flames licked and I could feel their warmth, I backed out, undressed, and hung my clothes on a tree. Back inside, I sat cross-legged with the fire between me and the door. I fed more wood and sweat began to bead on my face. I ladled water from the pail and flicked it on the flames. They spit and hissed and the air grew heavy with steam.

I breathed in deeply and felt the tension in my muscles and mind loosen. Thoughts of murder and abuse evaporated with every drop of perspiration that ran down my skin. I closed my eyes and felt as if I were being borne away with the smoky steam as it rose toward the ceiling.

The flames flickered to life again from a draft of fresh air. I opened my eyes. The door flap closed quickly. Carrie Horse stood on the other side of the fire ring. Her hair was unbraided and cascaded over her shoulders and down her breasts in a thick, black wave. She'd even taken off her turquoise rings and porcupine hoop earrings.

"I see you took my advice about a sweat being good medicine," she said. "I couldn't fall asleep either."

Carrie knelt and sat back on her heels. She picked up a small bundle of sage from a basket, lit the end, and then quickly blew out the flame so that the stalks smoldered. Holding it close to her face, she made a cup with her hand and swept the smoke toward her. Her eyes were closed as she breathed in through her crooked nose. After she did this a couple of times, she passed the smoldering bunch to me.

"The smoke will purify you. It will allow you to see the truth. In the sanctity of the sweat lodge, all untruths must be cast into the flames."

I cupped my hand and waved the smoke toward my face. It smelled earthy and ancient and conjured up images of people dressed in animal skins and wearing sagebrush-bark sandals while they danced and chanted around a blazing fire at the mouth of a rockshelter. Spitting and hissing caused me to blink away the vision. Carrie was sprinkling water on the fire to produce even more steam. Her skin reflected the now glowing embers, making her toned body shine like a bronze statue. Beneath her beauty and strength I sensed something troubled her.

"What's wrong?" I said.

"A falsehood that consumes me. In the sanctity of the sweat lodge, only pure thoughts and deeds should be spoken about."

"Do you want to tell me what it is?"

"It's something I've never told anyone."

"Not even Loq?"

"Especially not him. Thankfully, it happened while he was in Vietnam. If he'd been here..." Her voice trailed off.

"If I told you something, would that make a difference?" I didn't give Carrie a chance to say no, but launched into talking about the mistakes I'd made in country, how I led my men into an ambush and was the only member of my squad who survived.

"Good people pulled me from the edge after I'd given up on myself. They worked hard so I'd have another shot at life. And now I have it. Living in No Mountain, being a wildlife ranger, and about to marry the woman I love and have a child."

"Yet you remain burdened by untruths," Carrie said.

I breathed in more of the sage smoke and closed my eyes. "I tell myself that danger seeks me out, and not the other way around." Sweat beaded. I waved more of the sage smoke at my face. "It's all a lie. I seek danger as surely as I sought heroin. I need it to remind myself that I'm alive, that not all of me died on the battlefield along with my buddies. I lie to myself that violence doesn't have to be part of danger, but the truth is, it is. I will never be free of violence as long as I need danger."

The embers glowed brighter. Carrie sprinkled more water on them to create more steam.

"Yours is a warrior's lament," she said. "You and Loq have that in common. Now that you have spoken of it, you can accept the truth and cast your self-deceit aside."

We stared into the steam for a while. I passed the bundle of sage to her. I knew better than to say it was her turn. After a while, Carrie Horse put fire to the sage bundle again. When she held it to her face, the smoke created a halo around her glistening skin.

"Growing up," she began, "I was proud that I could run faster, swim longer, and ride harder than the other girls and boys. I won many honors at *C'waam* Ceremonies and I took home prizes for the Klamath Nation every year at the All-Indian Rodeo. But my pride was my undoing."

She rocked back and forth on her knees. "The first time my husband struck me, I convinced myself it was an accident. The second time, I wouldn't allow myself to believe I'd made a terrible mistake marrying him. Each time after that, I convinced myself that being able to endure his blows confirmed my strength. I believed that until the day he struck our son."

Carrie picked up another bundle of sage, but did not light it. Instead, she rubbed the leafy end on her forearms and thighs. She took a breath and when she blew it out, it rose like steam.

"It was on a winter's evening much colder than tonight. My husband had been drinking as always. He used the back of his hand to try and silence our son's cries. I could no longer tell myself the blow was an accident. I grabbed my husband's arm to keep him from striking him again. He wrestled it away and punched me."

She touched her nose. "When he went to hit me again, I grabbed the liquor bottle and smashed it over his head. Then I picked up a kitchen table chair and hit him with it too. The children were crying. My mom heard them and ran over from her house. I told her to take them, that I needed to drive my husband to the hospital."

Carrie brushed her cheeks with the sage. "He was unconscious, either from the blows to his head or from the alcohol, I don't know which. I carried him to our car and put him in the backseat, but I didn't drive to the hospital. I drove to the lake instead. Some people take what we call the blue walk, people who believe they can walk across the lake when it's frozen in order to flee the demons that haunt them. It's where the ice grows thin that they find their freedom."

She added water to make more steam. It rose like an apparition. "I dragged my husband onto the ice in search of the nearest hole. But all was frozen and I couldn't find one. I left him lying there and went back to the car and got the emergency can of gasoline from the trunk. I poured the gas in a circle around him and lit a match. I watched the flames burn and waited for the ice to melt, but it was still too thick.

"*Gmo'Kamc* didn't want me to have my husband's death on my hands, and so when the flames went out, I dragged him back to the car and drove to the bus station. I bought a one-way ticket to Los Angeles. When the southbound bus arrived, I told the driver my husband was drunk, carried him onto the bus, and placed him in a seat in the back.

"When I got home, I told my children their father had gone on a trip. For two years I lived in fear that he'd return. One day I got a call from Los Angeles. It was a woman who worked for the coroner's office. She said my husband had been living on skid row and was stabbed to death fighting over a bottle of wine. She said someone needed to claim the body. I told her no one would. She said then he'd have to be buried in a potter's field. She started to tell me the address in case I wanted to come put flowers on his grave someday, but I hung up before she could say another word."

Carrie gazed through the steam and smoke. "Sometimes my children ask me when their father's coming home, but I tell them I don't know. A man like that, it's better he stays nowhere bones forever."

The embers continued to burn and we took turns sprinkling more water on them whenever the steam began to fade. I lit a bunch of sage and waved it around for both of us. Finally, as the last of the embers died, we called it a night. Carrie had hung a robe next to my clothes and put it on in the half-moon light while I pulled on my jeans and jacket.

"Tonight was a good night. A very good night," she said. "You know what it means, now that we've told each other our truths and cast out our lies in front of each other?"

"What?" I said.

"It makes us brother and sister."

"I've never had a sister," I said.

"You do now. Sweet dreams, little brother."

All the sweating left me rubber-legged as I walked back to my pickup. I crawled into the front seat and pulled the sleeping bag over me, thinking about the many forms that redemption can take. As the lullaby of water that came from a crater that was once a mountain began rocking me to sleep, I saw an endless sea of ice riddled with holes. I knew if it ever stood in the way of saving the ones I loved from danger, I'd run, walk, crawl, and scratch my way across, or die trying.

19

THE CHOICE

Hearing Gemma trying to speak is more heartbreaking than listening to "Moondance" alone. I crouch over the bed of pine boughs and brush her forehead with the back of my fingers. "Come on, you need to drink some water."

Her eyes blink rapidly. "Ca... ca... can't. Moo... moo... move."

"I'll help you. I don't want you to get dehydrated."

I palm the back of her neck and gently lift, careful to keep her head still. The cup from the thermos is filled with melted snow. "There you go. Come on. Tiny sip. Wet your lips. Good. Again."

What little color there is drains from Gemma's face from the exertion. She groans even louder as I ease her back onto the rolled sweater that serves as a pillow. Her eyes fix on me. The pupils are fully dilated, but I tell myself it's because the only light inside the wickiup comes from the gap between the hanging duffle bags that serve as the door.

"What's your name?" I say.

A look of confusion answers me. My stomach tightens. I can see the chalkboard in a first-aid class at basic training about concussions from explosions. Amnesia is a common symptom. Sometimes it's fleeting, other times permanent. I don't want to think about what life will be like if Gemma has forgotten who she is.

"What's your name?" I say again.

Her lips twitch and tongue darts as she struggles to form words. "Wh... why? Ha... have you already for... forgotten who... who you married?"

I want to laugh, but settle for a grin. "Not a chance. Here, take another sip of water."

She drinks some more, but I don't let her take too much. I know what aspirating looks like from the time a squad mate was hit and fell face down in a rice paddy.

"We're in a wickiup in the mountains," I say, launching into the mantra I repeated throughout the night. "The plane was struck by lightning. You saved our lives landing it, but you got knocked out. We're going to be okay. They'll send a search plane as soon as the weather lifts."

Gemma starts groaning again. She moves her arms beneath the space blanket and tries to pull up the multiple layers of clothes I've dressed her in.

"Don't worry. We're going to get out of this. Just stay calm until help gets here."

"My... my bay... baby," she gasps.

I think about truths and untruths. This isn't the time or place for telling it like it is. "The baby's okay. You're warm, out of the snow, and I'm going to make some beef broth that'll put hair on your chest and the baby's too." I grin stupidly, knowing how lame it sounds, wondering if she sees through the bravado.

"No... no." Gemma starts squirming. I can tell she's cradling her stomach. She tries to draw her knees up. Moving her feet triggers a chilling scream.

"Stay calm. Don't move. Your ankle's broken."

"No," Gemma cries again, this time louder. "I... I'm...ha... having con... contractions."

I nearly drop the cup of water.

Her cheeks puff as she purses her lips and mimics a bellows. Her face turns crimson. After a minute of huffing, she sinks into the pine boughs. "Ow. Tha... that real... really hurt."

There was nothing in combat first aid class about labor. Not a single word. "What should I do, boil water?"

The redness leaves Gemma's face, leaving her ashen. "Prob... probably Brax... Braxton Hicks." When I look at her quizzically, she says, "Fal... false labor."

As long as it's not false hope, I say to myself. I circle back to the broken ankle, tell her I had to cut off her right boot. "Sorry, I know you bought them especially for dancing at the wedding reception. Your ankle was really swollen. The boot was cutting off circulation."

"Pack... pack in ice," the horse doctor manages to say. "Re... reduce swell... swelling."

"We got plenty of that. Well, snow, anyway."

"Nee... need to set... set it when swell... swelling goes down."

"Fine, but you're staying put for now. I'll make you that broth."

Gemma tries to say something, but her eyelids flutter and then close. She falls asleep.

I listen to her breathing. It sounds steadier than before, but I don't let down my guard. The false labor hammers home a certain truth. The baby is coming and this is no place to have it. I need to get us out of here. I need to do something to attract a search party's attention. Broth can wait.

I crawl out of the wickiup and gather more dry wood. I break it into small pieces and stack it near the entrance so I'll have plenty to burn to keep us warm through another night if it comes to that. Then I make a return trip to the wrecked plane to see what I can salvage for making signal torches. I crawl into the back and rummage around, coming up with a couple of plastic bags. I shove them into my pocket and then slash open the back seat and cut out squares of foam rubber.

The ruptured fuel tanks in what's left of the sheared wings are dry, but an engine's an engine, whether in a car or a small plane, and moving parts need lubrication. I wrestle the crumpled cowling off and locate the oil pan. The drain plug will take a wrench to open, but the closest thing to a tool I have is a broken propeller blade. I find the oil filter and give the canister a few whacks with a piece of wood to loosen it. Gripping and twisting it sends the hot blade stabbing me in the chest again. I wonder how many cracked ribs I have, if any are in danger of puncturing my lungs. The oil filter comes off and I hold it up to keep from spilling any of the precious liquid. I pull out one of the plastic bags and pour the oil into it and tie it shut. I find the fuel line and cut it. There's gas in it. Not much, but some, maybe a quart, maybe more. I drain that into the other plastic bag.

I crawl back into the plane for a final search for anything that can be useful. I scrounge around, digging through the clutter that litters the floor. A corner of some fabric pokes out from beneath the now chunked-up back seat. I tug at it. It's stuck. I reach under the seat and can feel the fabric is caught on a jagged edge. I unsnag it and pull. It's a shawl that belonged to Gemma's mother. Wrapped inside it is a short pine board swaddled in soft white buckskin with glass-bead designs at the head and foot, and shoulder straps on the backside. November made the traditional *Numu* cradleboard last fall. Gemma takes it with her everywhere as a good luck charm.

If ever good luck was needed, it's now. I rewrap the cradleboard in the shawl, tuck it under my arm, and crawl out of the plane. I return to the wickiup. Gemma is still asleep when I stick my head in to check on her. I spread her mother's shawl over her and prop the cradleboard against the bed of pine boughs so it will be the first thing she sees when she wakes up.

I lug the foam blocks and bags of fuel down to the clearing. I hack branches off pine trees and arrange them in the snowfield to spell out SOS in ten-foot letters. Then I cut four sturdy limbs and sharpen their ends. I spear a chunk of foam rubber on each one and then stab the other end into the snow to stand them upright around the three-letter call for help. If I hear a plane, I'll pour the oil and gas onto the wicks and light the equivalent of tiki torches. I'll shoot the flare gun as soon as the plane comes into view. With only three rounds, I'll have to make every shot count.

I've been gone an hour. I check on Gemma. She's still asleep. Her pulse is steady. I slide my hand under the shawl and space blanket and work it between the layers of clothes and bare skin. With my palm placed gently on her curved belly, I start to count. One one hundred. Two one hundred. Three one hundred. Thirty-five one hundreds later I feel a kick.

Relief floods through me. I rub Gemma's stomach and whisper, "Do me a favor, kid, and stay in there until we get home. I'll give you whatever you want. Toys, allowance, you name it." Something tells me Dr. Spock wouldn't approve of bribing my child the first time I speak to it.

I grab the compass and head back outside. The forest climbs on the north side of the clearing. If war taught me anything it's that commanding the high ground in a fight can mean the difference between living and dying. I may not be in a mountainous jungle, but I'm in a fight and I don't plan on losing.

The going is slow slogging through the snowy forest as the slope grows steeper. I reach a crest. The trees thin considerably. It's no clearcut like the ones on the ridge above Klamath Marsh, but the sight lines are unobstructed. I hold the compass out and turn in a slow circle. The silhouettes of distant mountains rise to the west. More mountains block the view to the north and east. Only the south, beyond the clearing where SOS is spelled out, do the trees run downhill toward the horizon.

South is where we flew from and south is where No Mountain is. If no search plane comes, it's where we'll head. Since Gemma's broken ankle rules out her walking, I'll make a travois —the two-pole sled *Numu* used for dragging belongings across the Great Basin—and fit it with a platform for her to ride on and a harness made of seatbelts and duffle bag straps for me. I'll fashion ski poles out of long sticks and snowshoes out of woven branches. I'll pull Gemma behind me. I'll carry her on my back if I have to. I'll get us off the mountainside and through the forest. I'll get us home and if I do—no, *when* I do—I'll never think of moving away again.

Having an escape plan feels good. Real good. It gives me a boost as I follow my tracks back to the wickiup. I hurry to tell Gemma about the SOS and signal torches, that I see a path of least resistance for reaching No Mountain. Panting and moaning comes from the wickiup. I scramble inside. Gemma is huffing and puffing. Her face is bright red from exertion. Sweat runs down her forehead.

"Don't worry, I'm here."

She turns toward me. She keeps sucking in and blowing out air through pursed lips. A minute goes by. And then another. And another. Finally, her breathing eases.

"More false labor pains?" I say.

"No," she gasps.

"Pain from the broken ankle? I'll get some snow for the swelling."

"Not my... my ankle." She gasps again.

I look into her eyes and read what's there. The inside of the wickiup is warm, not as much as a sweat lodge, but the similarity between the two is impossible to ignore. I take a deep breath and let it out slowly. Time for self-deception is over. Falsehoods need to be cast into the flames once and for all.

"It's not Braxton Hicks," I say. "You're in labor for real. The baby is coming. Okay, let it come. You and me, we can do this. I'll get everything ready."

Gemma grips my forearm. Her face contorts as she struggles to form words. "I... I have a con... concussion. If I'm un...unconscious I won't be able to... to push. To deliver. The bay...baby will get stuck. Must come out or... or will die. Prom... promise. Promise me you'll deliver the baby."

"I promise. I've seen you deliver foals and calves plenty of times. I can do this."

Her grip tightens. "No! Prom... promise me you'll..." And she throws off the shawl and space blanket and takes my hand and guides it, dragging my fingertip in a straight line from her navel to her pubic bone. "Use... use the scalpel. Make incision. Straight cut... six... six inches long. Slice through ab... abdomen. Skin and fat... layer by layer. Quick... do it quick. Then slice through... through uterus. Careful. Bay... baby is in there. Suck... suction the amnio...the fluid. Lift... lift baby out head first. Clear... clear nose and mouth." Pain wracks her and she moans. "Umbil...umbilical cord. Don't forget. Got to cut it." Her rapid breathing starts up again.

"It won't come to a cesarean. We're having this baby. You and me. Together. Like the ancient ones did in rockshelters. Like the *Numu* did in wickiups. Like Girl Born in Snow's mother did in the middle of a blizzard. Nobody's cutting anybody open." I hold the white buckskin cradleboard up. "See? Good luck is with us. You'll see. You'll be carrying our baby around Harney County in no time."

Gemma's eyelids flutter. "Promise," she says. "Promise me... you'll save the baby no matter what."

Her eyes roll back and her head lolls to the side. Her body

goes limp. I shake her, but she doesn't come to. I pinch her. Nothing. I pinch again, harder this time. Still nothing. I take hold of her hand and close my eyes. I clamp them as hard as I can until all I see are two black dots.

"Choose one now," a voice says as the black dots become the mouths of two forks in a long, dark cavern.

"I can't."

"You can only choose one. Choose now."

"I won't. I know what lies at the end of each."

"Choose."

"If I save the baby, Gemma dies. If I save Gemma, the baby dies and Gemma will never forgive me. I lose her either way."

"Time's up," shouts the voice I know is my own. "Choose."

And so I do...

20

There were two ways to go, but I chose the fastest. Upon leaving Klamath Falls after the sheriff heard and accepted Ruth Grazier and her sons' story, I drove north on Highway 97 and turned west on Highway 58 toward Eugene. The drive took me through three national forests, along countless rushing creeks and shimmering lakes, and over the Cascade Mountains. While the wild beauty helped salve the still-raw wound of knowing how evil from within could beset a family, it didn't silence Carrie Horse's warning that the Graziers would bear emotional scars for life.

While at the sheriff's office, Loq told me about his journey to get Ebal. His first stop was at the marsh to collect Grazier's body from the levee. Loq wrapped the dead man in a tarp and put him in the back of his pickup. Then he drove to the gloomy cabin next to the old school bus. He found Ebal sitting at the kitchen table. The teen hadn't bothered to start a fire in the woodstove or light a kerosene lantern. He didn't run when the *Maklak* came in and sat across from him.

"What did you say to him?" I asked.

"I started off by talking about things that had nothing to do with death. I described the waterwheels the villagers in Vietnam used and the beauty of rice paddies and how water buffalos look different than cows and oxen. I asked him how come they never ran electricity up to the cabin or used the pumps to send water there too."

Loq's long mohawk shook back and forth. "He said his father reserved all the power for the pot farm. Grazier was growing it for a middleman to a big West Coast drug dealer. He didn't want any lights in the cabin because he wanted to keep his family in the dark about everything. He forbade the children to read or write. Ebal says he never learned how."

Ebal, not Loq, finally brought up his father's suicide and asked if his mother and brother were safe. When Loq told him they were spending the night at his sister's, he asked if his mother would ever forgive him. "I'm the reason Daddy killed himself."

"No, that was all on him," Loq said. "No one put that pistol in his hand. No one made him pull the trigger but himself. There is something you can do for your mother, and that's to go to the sheriff's office with her and tell him what happened. You'll need to tell the sheriff about the marijuana too, how your father made you help him."

When Loq told Ebal the family wouldn't be arrested, it was like watching a big wind on Klamath Lake quit blowing. All the chop and churn in the water, both what can be seen on top and what can't be seen underneath, suddenly stilled.

"I told him I'd take him to his mother in the morning and he fell asleep. Around midnight, I heard something outside. I thought it might be an animal after Grazier's body, and so I went to take a look. In the moonlight, I saw something moving across the clearing and into the woods."

"Was it a coyote, cougar, or bear?" I asked.

Loq shrugged. "I checked the back of the pickup. Sure

enough, the tarp had been pulled open, enough to show Grazier's face. His eyes, well, at least the one on the other side of his head from where'd shot himself, was wide open. Gave me a start, seeing it like that, because it was closed when I wrapped his body up."

He let that sit before continuing. "I saw movement again at the entrance to the woods and followed it. Snow covered the ground. A white hare saw me, but didn't run off. I ducked under a low branch. A spotted owl was perched there. His yellow eyes didn't blink. The forest grew thicker. Not a single tree had been cut in there. I kept walking. No snow was crunching ahead of me and no branches rustled either, but something was ahead of me, leading me on.

"I didn't think it was a big cat or a bear fresh from hibernation luring me into a kill zone. I didn't think about turning back. I couldn't have even if I wanted to. After a while, I don't know how long it was, the forest opened up some and I came into a little clearing, no bigger around than a pickup. The moonbeam shining on it fluttered like wind was blowing it.

"The thin blanket of snow was humped. I counted two mounds. One long, one short. The crowns of the trees circling the clearing were bowed toward them. The spotted owl flew over me. I knew why I'd been led there and so I sang a song for little Rebekah and Uncle Jim. They're somewhere bones now."

The turnoff from the highway into Eugene came quick. I rolled my window down and the air was thick with the smell of fresh bread and pulp mills. A commercial bakery with a billboard advertising tasty and convenient sliced white bread stood right next to a cluster of red-brick buildings that housed university classrooms and dormitories.

I stopped at a red light while a herd of students crossed. Most of the boys sported long hair and beards and had on expensive hiking boots like the kind Pax Sizemore wore. The girls were dressed in denim skirts and peasant blouses. Many favored light brown, calf-high leather boots with square toes.

One boy flashed me the peace symbol and nodded at the duck and fish emblem on my pickup's door. "Far out, man. I'm into nature too. Having a soak at Cougar Hot Springs up on the McKenzie is, like, totally Zen."

The coed walking alongside him had on a knit alpaca cap that made me think of Stephanie Buhl. I wondered if she was still alive. The girl peered over tinted granny glasses. "You look like you could use a soak yourself. You'll have to leave your uniform behind. Everyone goes naked." She tittered.

"I'll bear that in mind," I said.

She tittered again. "I get it. *Bare* it."

"Can you tell me where the police department is?" I asked.

She looked at the other students to see if they were watching what she'd do and then wrinkled her nose. It made her granny glasses slip down. "I don't know where the pigsty is." That earned her a round of laughter.

Another coed walking behind stopped. "Keep heading straight. You'll see a sign for it in a few blocks. You can't miss it."

"Thanks," I said.

She took a few more steps, and then glanced over her shoulder. Her eyes danced and her smile dazzled. "People go to Mick's after classes for a beer. It's a lot of fun."

I found parking on the street near the police department and went inside. The desk sergeant had a brush moustache that reminded me of Bust'em Burton's. When he was Harney County's sheriff, he always kept it neatly trimmed. Now that he was a regional sheriff, he probably paid a barber to do it for him.

"What do you want?" the desk sergeant said.

"My name's Nick Drake. I'm here to pick up an item from Detective Dallas Skinner."

The sergeant looked at his logbook. He used a ruler to read across each entry line. "Let me see some ID."

I fished my driver's license out and slid it across the desk. He studied it. "Can't be too careful. Last year Eugene got hit by bombers. They dynamited a bank, the newspaper office, and a store near the state trooper's HQ. Hippie war protestor types. Either that or Black Panthers."

"Where can I find Detective Skinner?"

"Sit yourself in one of those chairs over there and I'll let him know you're here. Smoke 'em if you got 'em, but use the ashtray. The City Council is in another budget fight. This one's a doozy. They're holding up our paychecks, and forget about them giving us any housekeeping money. They told us if we want a clean office to bring mops from home and swab the floors ourselves."

The detective didn't keep me waiting long. He was in his mid-thirties, wore a jeans shirt, and his dirty-blond hair fell past his ears. It looked like he hadn't shaved for a week. A black semi-automatic rode in a brown leather shoulder rig.

"You're no deputy," he said, pulling up short and not offering to shake hands.

"I'm a Fish and Wildlife ranger. I was nearby and agreed to pick up the item you have for Sheriff Warbler."

"That's a bit irregular. Is that the way things are done out in the sticks?"

"I'm the one who found Professor Sizemore's body. Two friends of mine were working at the dig site and now they're missing. I offered to help the sheriff any way I could."

The detective thought about it and then said, "When you say two friends, you mean the Indians?"

"They're Paiute. Tuhudda Will and his grandson, Nagah."

He squinted. "Their disappearance makes them either suspects or victims."

"If you knew the Wills, you'd know they didn't have anything to do with the professor's murder." I paused. "You don't sound like you're from Texas."

"My first name, yeah, I get that from outsiders. My parents named me after Dallas, Oregon, where I was born. It's a pretty little town near Salem. Your sheriff tell you what it is I got for him?"

"Only that it might be connected to Sizemore's murder. If you don't want to give it to me, fine. Mail it or take it yourself."

"Hold on. No need to get pissed off. It's a very important piece of evidence and I can't have it getting lost."

"It won't with me."

The detective rolled his shoulders. "Seeing that we're short-handed around here because of the budget shortfall, plus they suspended per diem for out-of-town travel, I could use some help delivering it. Come on, follow me."

He led me to the squad room. It didn't smell like fresh baked bread in there, more like a locker room. Styrofoam cups crowded the desks. The floor around the trash cans was littered with pieces of balled-up paper. I hoped the Eugene cops were better at aiming their guns than they were shooting baskets.

Dallas Skinner's desk was gunmetal gray and had a blotter on it that may have been the color of a pool table at one time. One armrest of his chair was lower than the other. A public service ad torn from a magazine was taped to the wall between wanted posters. It showed a clown smoking a joint and read, "Why do you think they call it dope?" Someone had inked a Hitler moustache on the clown.

"Grab a chair," he said, gesturing at the empty desk next to his. "My partner got lucky and took a job in a city that doesn't balance its books on the backs of cops."

I tried wheeling the chair over. One of the casters was stuck. I picked it up and carried it. "Sheriff Warbler told me you're working the homicide of a pawnbroker."

"The sheriff tells you a lot of things. What is he, a—"

"About to become my father-in-law."

Skinner's dirty-blond eyebrows rose. "Hope you have better luck with marriage than I did. Mine only lasted two years. She got fed up being a cop's wife. Can't say I blame her. I was assigned to narcotics then and worked undercover before I came over to Robbery Homicide. Spending time with drug dealers and hypes can sour you on people in general. Chasing down killers is outright poison."

The detective reached into a desk drawer and took out a package wrapped in brown paper and tied with kite string. He dug into his pocket, pulled out a switchblade, and thumbed the button. The silver blade flicked open with the menace of a rattler's tongue and he started slicing strings. "Souvenir from a doper who tried to shank me," he said.

He took his time unfolding the brown paper. When he was finished, a spherical piece of dark obsidian between four and five inches long and about an inch across rested on the faded green desk blotter. Serrated edges shined in the harsh whiteness of the overhead fluorescent lights.

"I assume it's already been dusted for prints. May I?" I picked it up and ran my finger down the front and back sides, feeling for the grooves called flutes that were used for attaching the projectile to a wooden shaft for throwing or lancing. I ran my thumb along an edge and could hear Sizemore describing how Paleo-Indians shaped stone tools by striking a rock with another rock and then fine tuning them by pressure flaking with a stick.

"It looks like the Clovis point Professor Sizemore's team uncovered at the dig site in Catlow Valley. Where did you find it?"

"Sticking between the shoulder blades of the dead pawnbroker. Name of Harry Silver." The detective leaned back and watched how I'd react.

If he was expecting shock, I disappointed him. "Can you tell me about him? I'll relay it to the sheriff."

"Harry runs a pawnshop down on Pearl Street. Ran, I should say. He has a reputation for being able to buy and sell anything anybody brings him, no questions asked."

"He's a fence."

Skinner nodded. "Harry's been arrested for it more than once. Every time he gets thrown in Muni, he makes bail and beats the charge thanks to a brother-in-law who bills himself as a criminal defense lawyer but is really a low-rent bagman for shylocks and a motorcycle gang running a protection racket and dealing speed."

I hefted the Clovis point and thought about the strange bends history could take, how short time really was when measured against the history of Earth and the infinity of the universe, how something once made by a man living in a cave to bring down woolly mammoths could be used to murder two men fourteen thousand years later.

"You still with me?" Detective Skinner said.

"Just thinking. Are you sending it to Pudge so he can have the coroner match it to the hole in Sizemore's chest?"

"That's right." He squinted at me. "Pudge, that's his nickname, huh? I've only spoken to him on the phone, but pictured him more like James Arness or John Wayne."

"Pudge acts on instinct, not in front of a camera. I'm sure he told you Flip Carson is his number one suspect for killing Sizemore."

"I tend to agree with him. I also like him for Harry's murder. The fact this murder weapon came from the archaeological dig over there and wound up here is the next best thing to a smoking gun. Line up all the other connections and it's hard to think of another suspect. Carson knew Stephanie Buhl. He would've known an artifact like this is worth a lot of money. Goes on and on and on."

I said, "If Carson stole it to sell it, and Harry Silver was the most likely fence, why did he kill him?"

Skinner played with the switchblade. "Either Harry balked because an antiquity of this sort was way out of his league or Carson disagreed with the price he offered."

I gave the Clovis point a heft. "If he thought it was valuable enough to kill for, why would he leave it behind?"

"Could be he got scared off. Someone may have knocked on the door or passed by the front window when he was trying to yank it out. See, it was plunged in at an angle. The coroner had to use a bone saw to free it since the blade was wedged between a rib and the scapula. That's the big one in the shoulder blade."

He eyed me. "What do you make of the girl, Stephanie Buhl?"

"I only met her one time, at the dig when she discovered this." I hefted the point again. "She seemed very serious about her work, her studies."

Skinner's eyes narrowed. "Was she and the professor engaging in extracurricular activities?"

"I don't know. Sizemore swore they weren't. Did Stephanie have a crush on him? Maybe. He was her mentor, probably her idol, but, even so, I can't see her setting him up so Carson could steal this."

"And a lot of people couldn't believe it was girls who butchered Sharon Tate and the others in LA last year."

"You sound like you think Flip Carson is some kind of Charlie Manson."

"You don't know anything about him, do you?"

"Only what Sizemore told me from his personal experience and what Harney County sheriff's has learned."

"Carson is the baddest bad boyfriend a girl could have. Most of the charges against him have something to do with Stephanie. Stalking her. Making her life miserable. Beating up would-be boyfriends." Skinner reached into his desk drawer again and extracted a file. "Take a look for yourself."

A photograph of Philip "Flip" Carson sneered back. Beady eyes stared beneath a jutting brow. He wore his hair in a mullet. A series of mugshots followed. The one with a height chart showed he stood six-five. His weight was noted as two-forty.

Skinner watched as I thumbed through the folder. "Carson's big and strong, but also quick. And not just his temper. He grew up in a rough and tough town where fathers raise their sons to be the same. Most of the men either work at the Weyerhaeuser mill or cutting down trees to feed it. Carson's a choker setter for a gyppo outfit."

"What's that?" I said

"The scut work they give newbies. It's the most dangerous job in the forest and pays the least. Carson never graduated from it. The setter takes this heavy-as-hell steel cable called a choker and nooses a felled log. Then he hooks the choker to an even bigger cable that gets winched uphill to a landing where the log is put on a truck. A setter has to be fast on his feet and very strong. He's out there scrambling over downed logs, making sure the choker and winch cables don't whip back and slice him in half, and dodging logs that bust loose and steamroll back down the mountainside."

"He gets off on the danger," I said.

"Same could be said about a lot of people."

"Including homicide detectives who like chasing killers?"

"I was thinking about wildlife rangers who forget their real job is watching out for Bambi."

We exchanged hard stares for a bit, but then he grinned.

I said, "Pudge told me Flip Carson is a suspect in a previous murder."

"He is. A known associate was found beaten to death behind a tavern a few months back." Skinner's lips disappeared when he grimaced. "My guess is, the guy said something about Stephanie that Carson took offense to. Most beatings at a tavern are done with a pool cue. This one was by fists. Big fists that threw punches hard enough to knock a block off. And that's exactly what they did. Every bone in the victim's face was crushed. His skull was separated from the top bone in the neck." He reached behind and patted himself. "This one."

"It's called the atlas bone, named after the Titan in Greek mythology who held up the world on his shoulders."

"They teach you that at wildlife school?"

"The woman I'm marrying told me. She's a veterinarian. Cows and horses have them too. What's stopping you from pinning that murder on Carson?"

"I'll bust him for it. Count on it. It's only a matter of time until I crack one of the witnesses. So far they've been too frightened of Carson to say anything or they're still clinging to the logger's oath of what happens in the forest, stays in the forest."

"Was the tavern Mick's?"

Skinner shook his head. "The Lumberjack. It's a dive across the border in Springfield. Why, do you know Mick's?"

"Someone mentioned it to me."

"It's Eugene's oldest watering hole. If you go, they'll try to talk you into eating one of the pickled eggs swimming in a big glass jar on the bar. Don't. Trust me."

"Do professors drink there?"

"Sure, it's only a few blocks from campus. So do students, though half that do have fake IDs."

I told him about a student overhearing former Assistant Professor Cecil Edwards Oliver making threats against Sizemore at a tavern. "Have you questioned Oliver?"

"What for? When I spoke with campus police about Sizemore's murder, which, by the way, they're keeping on the QT, they mentioned Sizemore and Oliver had a tiff, but said it's par for the course for competing scholars. In their opinion, Oliver is a disgruntled former employee."

Skinner ran his fingers through his dirty-blond hair in an attempt to push it behind his ears. "Listen, I appreciate you helping out Sheriff Warbler because Sizemore was murdered in his jurisdiction, but the fact is, we like Flip Carson for two murders committed right here in Eugene. Harry Silver's and the guy behind the tavern. I'm going to nail him for those, and when I do, he'll spend the rest of his life in max security. That saves your future father-in-law all the trouble and expense of an investigation to achieve the same thing."

"Good luck trying to convince Pudge to stand down hunting for someone who committed a murder in Harney County."

"I wasn't going to. I was hoping you would. Tell the sheriff I'm very good at my job. In fact, my track record of catching killers stands right alongside Steve Prefontaine's for running the mile."

"I'll tell him, but it won't change his mind. And, just so you know, his record is one hundred percent. He's been at it a long time and has always gotten his man, though not all of them lived to see the inside of a jail."

I closed the folder and pushed it toward him. "Do you have a problem if I talk to Professor Oliver?"

"The only problem I'll have is if you get between me and Carson. The last thing I need is somebody riding in from the back of beyond trying to cowboy this."

"High lonesome," I said.

"What?"

"Harney County isn't back of anything."

"I get it, you were born and raised there."

"No, but it feels like it more every day."

The detective took the Clovis point back, rewrapped the brown paper, and retied the kite string. He put the package back in his desk drawer. "I'll keep it here for safekeeping. You can pick it up on your way out of town after talking to Oliver."

The stuck caster screeched as I got out of the chair. "I might be a while. It's my first time in Eugene. I thought I'd take a look around since I drove all this way."

Skinner sighed. "I had a feeling you were going to say that. Remember what I said about pickled eggs. Careful what you sink your teeth into."

"I'll try to remember, Detective."

21

I bought a turkey and alfalfa sprouts sandwich at the food counter inside Erb Memorial Union. The crowded student activity center was nicknamed "The Fishbowl" for its curved wall of glass that overlooked the center of campus. I found a seat by the window. While the wheatberries in the whole grain bread threatened to crack a tooth, I wasted little time chowing down. It'd been a long time since breakfast at Carrie Horse's.

A copy of the student newspaper had been left on the table. The front page of the *Daily Emerald* was devoted to coverage of Professor Paxton Sizemore's death. It featured two photographs of him. He was wearing a coat and tie and standing at a lectern in one. The other showed him grinning in front of Paisley Caves. He was in the same garb I remembered him wearing, a down vest over a flannel shirt and a carpenter's belt hanging with the tools of his trade.

The article was short on facts and vague about the cause of death. The head of campus security called it an unfortunate incident that was being investigated by local authorities. Neither Stephanie Buhl nor Jelly Welch was mentioned by name, only as two graduate students who'd been assisting Professor Sizemore at the time; one suffered a non-life-threatening injury and the other's condition was unknown. The quote from the university's president extolled Sizemore as one of the world's foremost paleoanthropologists and popular among student. The professor's wife was unavailable for comment.

I pushed the paper aside. The article wouldn't make it any easier to question Professor Oliver without raising his suspicions. That is, if I could locate him. He no longer had an office on campus and wasn't listed in the Eugene telephone book. Stephanie had an unlisted number too. I was swallowing the last bite of turkey and sprouts when the girl in the alpaca knit cap and granny glasses slid into the seat across from me.

"When I saw you sitting here all alone, I started feeling bad," she said. "You know, in the crosswalk, about cops? It wasn't very mellow of me. I—"

"Apology accepted," I said.

"Oh." She halted for a moment while she pushed up her granny glasses. "Were you able to find the police department?"

"I was."

"And everything's cool?"

"As a winter's morning."

"Well, see you later, I guess."

I said, "Is your cap from Peru?"

She put her hand to it. "Do you like it? It's alpaca. They're related to llamas only softer and cuter. They live in the Andes."

"Did you buy it down there?"

"I wish. I got it here. I've never been to Peru, but I really want to go. Like, hiking the Inca Trail and visiting Machu Picchu? They're these really cool temples built really high up on the side of a mountain. I hear the village of Cuzco is supposed to be groovy too. Backpackers from all over the world go there. A bed in a hostel only costs fifty cents a night."

"I met another student from here who wears a cap like yours. Maybe you know her. Stephanie Buhl?"

"What's her major?"

"She's a graduate student in the anthropology department."

"Oh my god! Did you read the paper? Everybody's talking about it. An anthro professor was working at a dig site and died. Some of the kids are saying it wasn't an accident like the university is trying to make it out to be. Like, maybe he was robbed or got in a fight with some Indians who didn't want him digging up their graves."

She frowned. "It's such a bummer because anthro is the coolest department and the archaeology classes are said to be the most fun because of the field trips. You know, getting out of a stuffy old classroom. I've thought about switching from sociology to anthro so I could go on a dig at Machu Picchu. That would be so cool."

"Do you know Stephanie or not?"

"If she's in grad school, we wouldn't have any of the same classes unless she was a TA. You know, teacher's assistant."

"What's the name of the shop where you bought your hat?" It was a longshot, but maybe they'd sold Stephanie hers too and could tell me where she lived.

"I didn't buy it at a shop. I got it at Saturday Market. It's this really cool outdoor crafts market downtown that happens every, well, Saturday. People set up stalls and sell all sorts of stuff they make. I bought this really cool backpack there for carrying books that's sewn from old blue jeans. See?" She held it up.

"Do you remember the name on the stall where you bought the cap?"

She scrunched her face. It made her granny glasses slip. "It was one of those rhymey names like Wavy Gravy or Mellow Yellow or Funky Monkey. Cat's Hats! That's it. Cat's Hats. The knitter's name is Cat." She tittered. "If you think that's funny, I know a guy named Jelly Welch. No fooling, that's his real name. It's not made up."

I didn't blink. "You don't say."

"I know. Crazy, huh? His parents must have a sick sense of humor to name him that. It's like that song 'A Boy Named Sue.' Johnny Cash made it famous, but he didn't write it. Shel Silverstein did. He's, like, this funny poet. I saw him perform at Mick's one time."

"At the tavern?"

"Uh huh. They have live music and readings. It's so cool."

"How do you know Jelly Welch?"

"I know of him, more than I really know him, know him. You know what I mean? He's always hanging out at Mick's. He can really down the beer. Probably why he's fat. The first time I met him I was there with a bunch of friends. Jelly came over and tried to pick us up. Tim Hardin was playing that night. He's so cute. Tim Hardin, not Jelly. He's from Eugene and even played at Woodstock and everything. He's, like, super famous now because of his big hit 'If I Were a Carpenter.' I love that song. But Tim Hardin hasn't forgotten where he came from. He still comes back home to play. He's super sexy for an old guy. He's, like, thirty."

"You sound like you know a lot about music."

"I do. I really dig it. I mean, I wanted to be a singer, but my parents freaked out and made me go to college instead. School's kind of a bummer, but I still want to be a singer." She started right in. "*If I were a carpenter, and you were a lady, would you marry me anyway, would you have my baby.* I love that song. It's so romantic."

"You're pretty good."

"Thanks. Hey, I just remembered. Jelly's in anthro too. I wonder if he took any classes from the professor who died?"

"How do you know he's studying that?"

"Because one time when my friends and I were at Mick's, Jelly was having a beer with a professor. Afterward, he came over to our table to brag about it. How he and this anthro professor were on a first-name basis and would chug-a-lug together. Like, we were supposed to be impressed, which we weren't. Believe me."

I pushed the *Daily Emerald* toward her. "Was this the professor?"

She aimed her granny glasses at Pax Sizemore's photograph. "Oh, my god, that's the one who died. What a bummer. I mean, I didn't know him, never took one of his classes, but, still, being dead, it's, like, forever. No, Jelly was with another professor. I don't know his name because I'm not in anthro, but he was really short. Like, I'm five-four, which is totally average for a girl —not that I'm average." She tittered. "And this professor wasn't any taller than me. He smoked a pipe too. It was super foul. They shouldn't let them smoke pipes in Mick's. Cigarettes are cool, but pipes stink."

I balled up the sandwich wrapper and napkin. "It was nice talking to you."

"Oh, okay. Hey, if you're not doing anything, you should check out Mick's tonight. Truth is playing. They're a local garage band that's starting to make it big. Sometimes they invite me up on stage. Maybe they'll let me do 'If I Were a Carpenter.'" She launched into the song again.

I felt like a salmon swimming upstream as I pushed through the crowd of students pouring into The Fishbowl. I found a campus map and made my way to Condon Hall. A student with a wispy goatee and purple turtleneck was manning the desk at the Anthropology Department's office. He barely looked up from a textbook he was highlighting in DayGlo yellow.

"I hope you can help me," I said. "I work on wildlife refuges on the other side of the mountains. A while back a man flagged

me down to ask for directions. He said he was an anthropology
professor here. I don't remember his name." I stuck my hand
out. "He was about this tall and smoked a pipe. I showed him
the route on a map and he thanked me and drove off. Thing of it
is, while he was looking at the map, he set his pipe on the roof of
my pickup and forgot about it. When I drove off, the pipe fell
into the bed. I only found it recently. I wanted to return it to
him."

Turtleneck was looking at me like I was a lecturer droning
on and on in an overheated classroom on a Friday afternoon.
"Short like a jockey? Sounds like Professor Oliver, but he doesn't
teach here anymore. There's a lost and found at The Fishbowl.
You can leave his pipe there."

"But if he's not here anymore, then he wouldn't look there,
would he?"

Turtleneck frowned as if trying to work out the answer to a
test.

I asked if he had a forwarding addressing for him. "I'll mail it
to him."

"You sure you don't want to leave it at lost and found?"

"Positive."

Turtleneck sighed, pushed away from the desk, and trudged
over to a filing cabinet. He flipped through folders, extracted
one, and leafed through it. "Nothing in here about what college
Professor Oliver is teaching at now or anything about a new
address."

"Maybe he's still living in Eugene. What's his address here?"

"I'm not supposed to give that out. Professors don't like
students to know where they live because some kids try to
deliver their take-home finals really late at night to make the
deadline instead of submitting them in class like they're
supposed to."

"All I want to do is mail him his pipe, not turn in a test. If he's moved, the post office will forward it to him."

"I told you, I can't give you his address."

"Okay, I'll leave it with you to box up and mail yourself. I doubt the postage will cost you very much."

"Hey man, I'm cramming for an exam here. I don't have time for that. Says here he lives on Eighteenth." Turtleneck read off a number and returned to wielding his yellow highlighter.

According to the campus map, 18th Avenue bordered the south side of campus. I began walking up University Street that intersected with it. The route took me past MacArthur Court, the basketball arena where Carson had once barged into the girls' bathroom while stalking Stephanie. Directly across the street was a park. Tall evergreens, grassy glades, and gravel paths beckoned, but as soon as I entered, I saw it was a graveyard called the Eugene Pioneer Cemetery. At the center stood a statue of a Union Army soldier. A bronze plaque said 145 veterans from the Civil War were buried there. I saluted it. At least those men weren't nowhere bones like so many other soldiers were, including more than two thousand GIs who were still missing in Vietnam.

The cemetery ended at 18th. I turned west and in a few blocks reached a brown-shingle house with double-hung windows trimmed in red and a front door painted to match. The brass numbers on it were the same ones Turtleneck had given me. I was about to knock when the door swung open. A white-haired woman's eyes grew wide behind horn-rimmed glasses.

"You certainly gave me a fright," she said. "I wasn't expecting anyone to be standing there."

"Sorry," I said. "I'm looking for Professor Oliver. Are you Mrs. Oliver?"

"My goodness, no. I'm his landlady. I rent out three rooms.

To professors only, mind you. No students. I tried that once before. My goodness, the noise and the clutter. Live and learn."

"Is the professor in?"

She glanced at her watch. "You missed him by a couple of minutes. Our Professor Oliver is a stickler about schedules. Every day, rain or shine, he takes his constitutional. Up Willamette Avenue to Spenser's Butte and back again. On nice days, he tramps all the way to the top. It's a steep hike, but our Professor Oliver is quite the alpinist."

She was looking south and I followed her gaze. A rocky summit rose above the tops of the trees. "I'll try him again when he gets back. How long is he usually gone?"

"There's no telling. Our Professor Oliver has quite the busy professional and social calendar, what with teaching classes, dinners with other professors, lectures, and so on. It's a rare night that I'm still awake when he gets home. I'm off to bridge club, but if you jot down your name and number, I can slip a note under his door before I leave."

I took a scrap of paper and wrote, "I'm back. I'll meet you at Mick's." And signed it, "Jelly Welch." I folded it and handed it to her. "Thank you."

"You're perfectly welcome, but it's no bother at all. There's nothing I wouldn't do for our Professor Oliver."

22

Eugene averaged four feet of rain a year and a sudden downpour seemed bent on reaching that level all in one night. I watched it come down from inside a telephone booth on a corner across from Mick's. I dialed the Warbler ranch and November answered.

"Are you at a drum ceremony? I cannot hear you," the old healer said.

"I'm in a rainstorm. Is Gemma there?"

"It is too cold to rain. It might snow, but snow falls as silently as butterfly wings."

"I'm not in No Mountain. I'm on the other side of the Cascades."

November tsked. "Did you forget Gemma is with child? All that I have tried to teach you and still you have not learned that only in the dream world and the spirit world can you be in two places at once. You need to be here to welcome your child with a song so the child will always know your voice whenever you speak, no matter which world you are in."

"I'll be back tomorrow. I called to see how Gemma's visit with the doctor in Burns went today."

"She is tired and went to bed early. The doctor told her what I already told her. Good night."

"Wait, don't hang up. What did you tell her?"

"The baby will come when the baby wants to be in this world and not in the world before it."

"But that's still weeks away, right? After I finish what I'm doing here. After the wedding on the first day of spring. After—"

November cut me off with another tsk. "The sound of the rain makes more sense than you. I will go see if Gemma is awake."

"Hold on. Remember, you asked me to tell Tuhudda you'd join him to give a blessing to the Ancient One's bones? Well, the bones were taken from the cave and Tuhudda and Nagah are missing."

"The blessing will still take place when it is time to do so."

"You're not worried that no one knows where Tuhudda and Nagah are?"

"Rain soaks into the ground. Snow blows off mountaintops. Those things are no more gone than the sun is at night."

I blew out air, but before I could ask her another question, she put down the phone. People were hurrying past. Many wore hooded rain parkas made out of a new wonder material called Gore-Tex. A few had on Sou'wester hats. Eugenians dressed like they were very accustomed to rain. There wasn't an umbrella in sight. Thunder rocked the telephone booth. Water streamed under the folding door and rose past the soles of my boots. I looked up. The roof was made of metal. I was a sitting University of Oregon mascot in a lightning storm.

"November says you're all wet," is how Gemma greeted me.

"I feel like I'm back in the Central Highlands during monsoon season, only without all the bullets flying. Tell me how your visit with the doctor went."

"He said everything was fine and progressing nicely. The

baby's heartbeat is strong. He told me to stop riding, though. When I said I'd miss being out on the trail with Sarah, he suggested I harness her to a buggy instead."

"Has she ever pulled one before?"

"No, but I'm going to teach her and Wovoka. Lyle Rides Alone has an old-fashioned double buggy he's willing to lend me. I can't wait to see how fast it'll go." She let out a yippee ki-yay. "When are you coming home?"

"I have a couple of things to finish up here tonight and then pick up a piece of evidence in the morning that the cops are holding for your father. I should be back by ten."

"What's the evidence?"

"A Clovis point. It could be the missing murder weapon from Catlow Valley. Has Pudge said anything more about the investigation?"

"Only that it's frustrating. They weren't able to uncover much in the way of solid evidence at the dig site beyond matching one of the blood splatters to Jelly Welch. The other splatter is a mystery."

"Jelly said he shot the intruder."

"Orville sent it off to a friend at the FBI lab to see what they can turn up. He said they have new techniques. Another big unknown is what else was taken from the main tent. Jelly isn't being very helpful. He said he lost his memory from being shot in the head. All the nurses at the hospital want him discharged because he's such a pain in the neck, but Pudge talked Doctor Goldman into keeping him there as long as possible. He doesn't want Jelly to take off while there's so many unanswered questions."

"I know of at least three items the dig team found in addition to the Clovis point and the Ancient One's bones." I described the stone knife, sandals, and contents of the fire-starter kit. "They haven't turned up?"

"Not according to Pudge."

"I saw them the first day I was there. So did the Wills. Tuhudda identified them for Professor Sizemore. He said his grandfather and grandmother had objects just like them, Bear and Yellow Moon. Tuhudda told us about them. They left on a journey and were never seen again."

"I know all about *Padooa* and *Ohalune*. November told me. She said the entire tribe felt lost after they disappeared. I think you and I should keep locks of hair too. That way we'll always carry the other person with us when we're away from home." Gemma grew silent. The raindrops grew louder. "You do know I plan on going back to work after the baby's born. My patients need me. It'll mean a lot of travel again."

."I know," I said.

"And you're okay with that?"

"We both travel for our jobs. We'll work out something."

"Where are you going to spend the night?"

"The same place as last night, wrapped in a sleeping bag in the front seat of my pickup."

"I wish you were spending it with me."

"Me too." I hesitated, and then charged right in. "Have you given any thought about honeymooning in Portland? I should get back to F.D. Powers and let him know our decision."

I listened to the rain pound for a good minute or more. Gemma finally said, "Does that mean you want to take the job there?"

"It means he's my boss and made me an offer and I owe it to him to at least check it out."

"You're not in the Army anymore, Nick. You don't always have to do whatever a superior officer orders."

"I know, but I should at least take a look at it. Powers brought up a good point about having another mouth to feed and a bigger salary will make that easier. And don't forget about the house."

"I don't care about having a big house. I'd be happy living in your old lineman's shack. It's not the house, it's who's inside that matters." More rain pounded. "What am I going to do in Portland anyway, treat cats and dogs? I'm a large animal veterinarian. It's what I went to school for. It's what I built my practice on. I like spending time on ranches. I like ranchers and farmers. I like working with cows and horses. I wouldn't know what to do in a big city."

"I haven't forgotten who you are."

The walls inside the telephone booth dripped with condensation. My socks soaked up more water. Gemma finally said, "That settles it. We'll go to Portland for our honeymoon and your looksee, but under one condition."

"What's that?"

"I fly us. No way I'm going on a long car ride and risk having our baby on the side of the highway where all the truckers passing by can catch a glimpse and honk their air horns. *Ahooga!*"

"Deal. See you in the morning."

I dashed across the street and ducked into Mick's. The rainstorm appeared good for business. I squeezed past a boisterous crowd of young people standing and clinking glasses. I made my way toward the restroom in the back and then turned around. I didn't see any men the size of a jockey.

A stool opened up at the far end of the bar. I took it and found myself staring at a big glass jar filled with eggs floating in a greenish-blue liquid. I couldn't tell if the color was natural or a reflection of the neon beer sign hanging above the cash register.

"What'll it be?" a bartender with muttonchop sideburns said.

"Draft. Whatever's on tap is fine."

"You want a pickled egg to go with that? House specialty."

"Maybe later."

He pulled the tap handle and filled a glass. "Let me know about the egg."

I left the glass sitting in front of me. I gave up drinking when I gave up heroin. I kept a lookout for Professor Oliver. People came, people went, but the professor wasn't among them. Muttonchops stopped asking if I wanted an egg.

A squelch of reverb coming from the back corner drowned out the buzz of voices. The woodpecker-like bap bap bap of someone tapping on a microphone sounded. "Check. Check one. Check two." An electric guitar strummed. A drum roll banged. The crowd surged toward the noise. "Hello, Mick's," an amplified voice rang out. We're the Truth and we're homegrown."

That elicited cheers and whistles. The band responded by kicking off with a lively cover of The Grateful Dead's "St. Stephen." The tune dialed up the energy level and people who'd been sitting at the bar abandoned their stools to join the crowd standing near the stage.

Truth followed with a composition of their own that reminded me of Blind Faith. The lead singer had a good voice that could hit the high notes without sounding whiny, and the lead and bass guitarists complemented rather than competed. I turned around to watch the musicians. Muttonchops said something, but I ignored him. When the song finished, I turned back. Muttonchops hadn't been talking to me; he'd been asking the man who took the stool next to mine if he wanted the usual, a man whose head barely reached my bicep.

Professor Cecil Edwards Oliver had very pale skin and thinning auburn hair. He'd placed a brown-tweed walking hat on the bar between us while I was looking at the band. A water ring now encircled it like a glass left on a varnished table too long.

"I trust you have no objection," he said with an affected tone. "Donegal needs to breathe. If I hung it on the coat rack, some scoundrel would make off with it. It is a favorite of mine. I bought it in Dublin while lecturing at Trinity."

The hat smelled like a wet dog, but I shrugged to let him know it was okay by me if he left it there to molder. "Excuse me, but are you Professor Oliver?"

"Indeed, I am," he said haughtily.

"I thought I recognized you. You gave a lecture on Paleo-Indians last year."

"I give quite a few lectures, my good man. So many, in fact, that I have lost count. I do hope you enjoyed it."

"It's a very interesting subject."

The little professor studied me more closely. "I do not take you for a student or a scholar."

"I'm neither. I didn't know much about Paleo-Indians, but after hearing about it from someone who does, the idea that our ancestors lived in rockshelters and made spearheads by chipping rocks, well, it sure makes you appreciate what you got."

"I am considered a bit more than *someone who does*," he said acidly and dismissed me with another, "Indeed."

Oliver glanced at the door and then twisted around to survey the crowd.

Muttonchops brought him a glass of beer and a saucer with a slice of orange on it. "Here you go, professor."

"Thank you, my good man. Rather a sizable gathering tonight."

"Truth always brings them out."

"Indeed," I said.

Oliver shot me a sideways glance, and then returned to Muttonchops. "Have you seen Mr. Welch tonight? With all these people in here, it is difficult to spot anyone."

Muttonchops placed his palms on the bar and raised himself

on his tiptoes. "I don't see him, professor. Come to think of it, I haven't seen Jelly for the past few days. Maybe he got onto that archaeological dig like he hoped he would."

Professor Oliver picked up the orange slice, wiped the rim of the glass with it, and then dropped it into his beer. It sank a couple of inches. When he took a sip, the lights from the neon beer sign gave the orange a penicillium hue.

I thought about Pax Sizemore sprawled in the snow with a gaping hole in his chest. I thought about Tuhudda, Nagah, and Stephanie running for their lives or lying dead in a similar snowbank. And then I thought about Vietnam. Sometimes we got tired of waiting for the enemy to show themselves. We'd launch a full-on, throw-everything-at-them, wake-up call with bombs dropped from B-52s, missiles launched from jets, 152 mm artillery rounds shot from howitzers, and full clips fired from handguns, M-16s, Hogs, and .50 caliber machine guns.

This was one of those times when patience wasn't a virtue. I leaned in close to the arrogant professor. "The someone who told me about ancient man wasn't you. It was Pax Sizemore. He was an expert and the tops in his field until someone plunged a Clovis point into his heart. I know Jelly Welch too. Last time I saw him, it was in Harney County and he was nursing a bullet wound to the head."

Oliver made a choking sound like he'd swallowed the citrus slice. He put the glass down and coughed. Once, twice. When he caught his breath, he said, "I have no idea what you are talking about."

"Sure you do. Your old rival who exposed you as a cheat was murdered, Jelly was shot, and Stephanie Buhl is nowhere to be found. None of that rings a bell, professor? Or should I say, disgraced former assistant professor."

Oliver glanced around to see if anybody was listening, but

everyone seemed focused on the music as the band burned through a hard-driving rendition of "Sea of Joy."

"What is the meaning of this?" he demanded.

"It means I have a pretty good idea of what happened. It goes something like this. When Jelly was accepted to go on the dig, you got him to tell you where the site was. He didn't like Sizemore any more than you did. Jelly blamed him for not accepting his transfer credits from Matchbook U. The two of you hatched some scheme to sabotage the dig to tarnish Sizemore's reputation. Trouble is, the spirit of ancient man was against you. Someone else raided the camp before you could launch your attack. You and Jelly were driven by revenge, but this other guy? Jealousy. And nothing is more dangerous and unpredictable than that."

Oliver's pale face turned crimson. "Rubbish. Whoever you are, whatever you think you know, you are most decidedly wrong. I did no such thing."

"But here you are, asking about Jelly Welch. Running down here as soon as you got a note that he was back in town."

"You? You left that?"

"Are you denying you know him?"

"Of course not. I was his graduate school advisor. After I left the university's employ, I continue to counsel him."

"For money."

He sniffed. "There is no crime in receiving a fee for knowledge."

"That still doesn't mean you didn't plan something to screw over Sizemore."

"I did no such thing."

"Prove it."

"How? Since I have done nothing, there is nothing to disprove."

"Then maybe I got it wrong," I said.

"I can assure you, you do."

"There wasn't someone else. It was you who was there. Hiking up the trail to the top of the postpile was a snap compared to Spenser's Butte, wasn't it? You blame Sizemore for costing you your university job and the salary that went with it. You weren't there to sabotage anything, you were there to steal artifacts to sell on the black market because you need money. Pax caught you in the act and so you killed him. You tried selling them at a local pawnshop and when the owner balked, you killed him too."

"You are insane!"

"No, I'm only greedy. I'll keep my mouth shut for a cut of the sale of the artifacts. Do we have a deal?"

"I refuse to listen to another word of your twaddle. Do not approach me again or I shall call the authorities. I shall sue you for slander. Good night!"

The professor clapped the soggy Donegal tweed hat back on his thinning hair.

"Everything okay, professor?" Muttonchops asked.

Oliver stabbed his finger at me. "I shall no longer frequent this establishment if management allows scalawags like him in here." He harrumphed and stormed out.

Muttonchops glared at me. I shrugged. "I told him I saw you take the orange slice out of the pickled egg jar."

As I went out the door, the lead guitarist for Truth was channeling Eric Clapton on his Fender.

23

The rain was still coming down hard as I hit the sidewalk and followed Professor Oliver. He'd been in such a hurry to leave that he grabbed the wrong parka from the coat rack. The shoulders drooped nearly to his elbows and the sleeves hung below his fingertips. He never looked back as he sloshed across the streets nor did he hurdle the overflowing gutters. Oliver appeared to be heading home, but I tailed him to be sure.

When the professor hit 18th, he turned left. By the time I reached the intersection, Oliver had opened the red door to the brown shingle house. He stepped inside and closed it behind him. An upstairs light turned on. My rig was still parked near the police station. I jogged back to get it, sticking to the street rather than the sidewalk to avoid curbs and overflowing gutters.

Halfway to my pickup I heard feet slapping and heavy breathing behind me. A lot of feet. A lot of breathing. I didn't waste time looking over my shoulder to see who was giving chase as I kicked it into high gear, but I was no match for this pack of hounds. The two options of fight or flight halved. I stopped abruptly and wheeled to face my pursuers.

The slapping feet never broke stride as a group of young men raced straight at me. They were all dressed the same: green shorts and matching windbreakers with a big yellow O and the word "Ducks" printed beneath it. Even their tennis shoes were identical, flimsy looking blue things with the outline of a yellow wing on the side. As I held my sides and sucked wind while they parted around me, I thought of the clunky P.F. Flyers I wore when running track in high school. Suddenly I felt my age.

I drove back to 18th and found a parking spot with a view of the red door. The water drumming on the pickup's roof ticked off the seconds. It was going to be a long, wet night, and for what purpose, I didn't know. Professor Cecil Edwards Oliver could be telling the truth. If I was wrong about him, could I also be wrong about Flip Carson? Could I be wrong about Stephanie not being in cahoots with Flip? Could I be wrong about Tuhudda and Nagah being alive and well? I needed answers and I needed them fast. Once the light turned off upstairs and nobody sneaked out the red front door, I fired up the rig and headed for the Springfield line.

The Lumberjack was a dismal outpost on a street where half the storefronts were boarded up and the ones that hadn't gone under weren't spending a penny on fresh paint. Broken glass crunched beneath my tires as I pulled into the vacant lot next door to the tavern and parked.

Despite the cold rain, the top half of the Dutch door was open. A cloud of cigarette smoke poured out. More swirled inside. No one was wasting nickels on the juke box. The wood floor was peppered with holes that looked as if someone had gone to work on it with an icepick. "No Caulks Inside" was lettered on a sign behind the bar. The men at the bar had ignored the rule. Along with the forbidden hobnailed logging boots, they wore red-and-black plaid flannel shirts, and oiled canvas pants held up by wide suspenders.

All eyes turned toward me. I nodded a hello to the closest logger. He had a burly build and a surly air. His lips curled into a sneer as he took in the khaki shirt beneath my open jacket. A spit of tobacco juice splattered at my feet.

"You took a wrong turn, bud, like you Forest Service fools always do on our haul roads. There's only one direction to go, same as where we tell you in the woods. Back the hell up!" He chugged a brown stubby dry to the sounds of laughter and then slammed it on the bar to join a row of empties.

I pulled aside my jacket to reveal the Fish and Wildlife emblem on my chest. "Next time you go hunting and fishing, thank me for all the game there is."

The logger next to him slapped the bar and guffawed. He leaned back so he could make eye contact with me. His cheeks were spidered with broken blood vessels. "I'll say one thing for ya, fella, ya got a big pair. Don't mind Twombly here. He had a bad day. Hell, every day he has is bad." He guffawed again. "Make yaself at home." He chinned at the barkeep. "Give this working stiff a Blitz and put it on Twombly's tab."

Twombly glowered for a bit longer, but his anger faded when the barkeep fished three stubbies out of the underbar icebox and set them in front of us. "Never gone a season without getting my buck," he muttered. "Twelve pointer last year, swear on a stack."

"Ya ain't a local," Guffaw said to me. "I can tell 'cause ya got a tan and no mold growing on ya like us." His heh-heh-heh was punctuated by a belch. "Ya live on the dry side, do ya?"

"Harney County," I said. "Near Burns."

"That a fact? I worked in all them forests over there. Ochoco to the north, Malheur to the east, Fremont south, and Deschutes west. Closer to Bend it was. Lotta good wood in them woods. 'Course, I'm partial to the Willamette forest right here because it's home. Ain't it the truth, Twombly?"

The burly man nodded. "Best damn wood in the world and no better town than Springfield. Only problem is having to live next door to Eugene with all that commie crap going on." He took a long quaff of his Blitz. "College kid couldn't lift an axe if he tried. I got my first double-bladed when I was five."

Guffaw guffawed. "Why Twombly's gotta stuff two rolls of socks in the right toe of his caulks, his swing was so piss poor." He pronounced the boots "corks."

The two men traded insults while I grinned and chuckled along with them in between miming taking gulps from the brown stubby. "A guy I pulled out of a snowbank told me if I ever got over to this side, The Lumberjack was the right place to get a beer. I can see he wasn't wrong."

"I'd say he was a smart fella 'cept for driving hisself into a snowbank," Guffaw said. "What was his name?"

"Let me think a sec. By the way, it wasn't his fault. He was going down a road only locals know where the black ice that never sees sun is. I bet it's the same over here."

"You got that right," Twombly said. "'Specially the two-lane going up the McKenzie. Lotta bad patches on it."

"Real bad one is on a curve right below the pass," Guffaw said. "Out-of-towners pulling a trailer always jackknife there. More than a few gone over the edge." He made a bomb dropping whistle.

I said, "Now I remember. His name was Flip. Don't recall him giving a last name. You know him?"

Guffaw and Twombly answered by immediately sucking on their beer bottles. The barkeep who'd been listening exchanged glances with them before looking down at the underbar icebox. "Looks like I'm running low. Better get some more from the back." He ambled to the end of the bar and pushed through a set of swinging doors.

Twombly put his bottle down first. "Can't say I know anybody named that."

Guffaw lowered his too. "Me neither and I know everybody. Ya musta heard him wrong. Maybe it was Chip or Kip or Rip. Lotta loggers named Chip. I knew a Chip once. Was a feller. Or was he a limber?"

The barkeep came back after being gone long enough to make a phone call. He had an armful of beers. "Reinforcements on the way," he said. He shoved them in the icebox and put three in front of us. "On the house." Twombly and Guffaw didn't thank him.

"A twelve pointer?" I said to the burly logger. "That's a good-sized buck. Do you ever hunt east of the Cascades? I know a place where the mule deer go four hundred pounds and more. That's a lot of venison for the back-porch freezer. Guy got a fourteen pointer there last season."

"Where?" he grunted.

"Base of Steens Mountain. It's a pretty rough track to the end, but there's good camp sites to be had. Plenty of firewood too." I paused. "Hang on, I got a map in my rig. I'll grab it and be right back."

"I'll go with you," Twombly said quickly. "Need a breath of fresh air from all the smoke in here. Coffin nails will kill you. Why I dip instead." He spit a mouthful on the floor to make his point.

"Ya shirt could use some fresh air too. When's the last time ya washed it?" Guffaw said without guffawing. "I'll walk out with ya. Wife's expecting me."

Guffaw following without paying his tab was confirmation enough for me that a call had been made and instructions relayed. I got ready for them when we were clear of the Dutch door, but the pair of loggers were surprisingly quick despite the beers they'd downed. Twombly grabbed me from the side,

Guffaw from the back. They fast-marched me to the vacant lot. A pickup with high suspension and oversized wheels roared in and braked. A menacing snowplow blade attached to the front bumper stopped inches from my hips. Flip Carson jumped out. He looked the same as the photo that had sneered from Detective Dallas Skinner's folder, right down to the mullet and sledgehammer fists that hung to his knees.

"I don't know you," he growled as Twombly and Guffaw pinned me. "I never seen you. And I sure as hell never drove into no snowbank, not with my blade." He reared back and threw a punch right into my solar plexus.

Twombly grabbed me by the hair and yanked my head up. "Playing me for a sucker, was you? I knew you was a cop."

He lifted his studded boot, but I pulled my foot back right when he stomped his down. Sparks flew as the hobnails struck pavement. Twombly yelped. I went limp, forcing Guffaw to readjust his grip. I grabbed his wrist, yanked him around, and spun him into Carson. The big man roared and shoved Guffaw aside, sending him careening into Twombly.

Carson charged, his long arms windmilling, his fists piledriving. I bobbed and weaved to keep away from his deadly knuckles. His reach was so long I couldn't get inside to land a decent punch. Twombly and Guffaw unknotted themselves and rushed in to join the fray. I ducked one of Carson's haymakers. It hit Guffaw square on the jaw and dropped him like a hangman's sandbag. Carson backed me up against my own pickup. He gripped my shoulder to hold me in place while he pulled his fist back to his ear.

"Wait, I talked with Stephanie!" I yelled.

Pit bull slobber dripped from the corners of his mouth. "What?"

"Stephanie. I spoke to her."

"You're lying."

"No, I'm not. She wears a cap with alpacas on it."

His fist quivered. "Where'd'ja talk to my Steffi?"

"Harney County."

"Bullshit."

"It's why I came looking for you."

"You're a cop."

"I'm Fish and Wildlife. Look at my badge, the emblem on the door."

His beady eyes darted between the two. "Same as a cop."

"Tell that to the deer and pronghorn. Do you want to know what Stephanie asked me to tell you or not?"

"I'm gonna bust your nose clean through the back of your head."

"Then you won't know what Stephanie said, will you?"

His brow ridge knotted. "I'll make you say it."

"I'm trying to tell it to you."

"How long ago d'ja talk to my Steffi?"

That he asked, made me wonder. It was make or break time. "This morning."

I braced myself, but the fist didn't launch. "In Harney County?"

"That's right."

His fist quivered some more. "You say this morning?"

"Bright and early."

"Why didn't Steffi come tell me herself?"

"You don't know?"

"If I did, I wouldn't ask you, would I. Who was she with?"

"She was alone. You want to know what she said or not?"

"Spill it."

"Okay, but," and I nodded at Twombly, "you don't want him to hear it."

"Why should I care?"

"Because it's personal. Real personal."

"Go on, spit it out."

"Okay, if you want the whole town to know."

"Know what?"

I glanced at Twombly again. "I can whisper if you want."

The big man hesitated. "Take a walk," he growled at Twombly.

"It's a trick, Flip. Don't listen to him."

"I said, take a walk and take him with you."

Twombly looked down at Guffaw. "He's out cold. He can't hear nothing."

"And I said drag his ass outta here."

Twombly slid his hands under the unconscious man's armpits and pulled him across the vacant lot. The heels of Guffaw's logging boots bumped and skidded. When Twombly reached the tavern, he propped him against the cinderblock wall. Then he kept a close watch on Carson and me.

"Okay, what'd my Steffi tell you?" Carson's beady eyes bugged beneath his jutting brow ridge.

"She said," and I switched to *Numu* and called him a murdering piece of cow flop.

"What'd'ja say?"

"I said," and I repeated the Paiute words.

"That don't make a lick of sense."

"Maybe there's something wrong with your hearing. All that noise from chainsaws."

Curiosity drew him in close until he was forced to bend the elbow of his long arm that was gripping me. I could smell his breath, feel the spray of his slobber as he growled, "Ain't nothing wrong with my ears. Now say it slow or I'll kill you."

"She said go to hell." And I headbutted him in the chin while driving my knee into his crotch. Lights flashed and my skull rang from the hard knock, but Carson let go as he doubled over and grabbed between his legs. I chopped him hard in the neck and yanked open my pickup's door and slammed it into him.

Twombly swore and rushed at me, his hobnailed boots sparking, but then halted mid-stride. Sirens screamed and red lights whirled as a patrol car and an unmarked black sedan with a stick-on gumball on the roof raced toward the vacant lot from opposite ends of the street.

Carson gritted his teeth. They were red with blood from the head butt. "I'm gonna kill you."

But instead of throwing a roundhouse, he lurched to his jacked-up pickup and shoved it into gear. The V8 roared and the oversized tires smoked as the rig shot forward. The patrol car was the first to enter the lot. Carson's snowplow blade slammed into it head-on, splitting the cop car's grill and puncturing its radiator. Steam hissed. He pushed it backward until it accordioned into a parked pickup.

Reversing, he cranked the wheel, and aimed at the fast-approaching unmarked sedan that had jumped the curb to reach the lot. I could make out the dirty-blond hair of the driver. Dallas Skinner swerved just in time and took the blow of the snowplow blade at an angle. The oversized tires of Carson's pickup climbed right up the detective's fender and landed on the hood. Metal scrunched, headlights popped, and the windshield shattered. Carson threw it in reverse, came off the detective's crippled car, and sped backward out of the vacant lot. When he hit the street, he cranked the wheel until his pickup was pointed east and shot forward. The engine screamed as he raced away.

I jumped into my pickup. The passenger door flung open as the ignition caught and Skinner got in. Blood was streaming from a slice above his left eye. "He's going up the McKenzie!" he shouted. "There's a thousand logging roads up there he can take. Go. Go."

I floored it, sailed off the curb, fishtailed onto the rain-slick-ened street, and sped after Carson. "My radio's police band," I said.

The detective wiped the blood from his eye and grabbed the mike. "This is Skinner, Badge Six Seven Niner. Officer in pursuit. Repeat. Officer in pursuit. East on Highway One Two Eight. Positive ID on Philip Flip Carson. Vehicle a late model Chevy C10 sidestep four-by. Color is mud. Request OSP set up roadblocks. Subject armed and dangerous. Repeat. Armed and dangerous."

We tore through Springfield. Floodlights bathed the towering pulp mills and illuminated the steam and smoke that swirled from their smokestacks like cyclones. I laid on the horn as we approached red lights, but didn't let off the gas. The rain continued to pound.

"There's a bandana in the glove box," I said.

Skinner retrieved it and pressed it to his forehead. "I warned you about biting into something that bites back."

"Did you have The Lumberjack staked out or were you tapping the phone?"

"Phone, but you didn't hear it from me."

"Carson must live close by. He was there in minutes."

"The call was too short to trace. We'll get the number in the morning when the phone company clocks in, but it won't do any good. He'll never go back."

The wipers clacked. The tires whined as we raced across Willamette Valley. The countryside turned more rural the farther we got from Springfield. Farms and filbert orchards gave way to forest. Carson was speeding on a road he'd driven hundreds of times while commuting back and forth to his job setting chokers. I had to rely on his tail lights to signal where the curves were.

Skinner glanced down at the bench seat between us and saw the Dr. Spock book. "Made the sheriff a granddaddy, did you?"

"Pretty soon," I said. "I tracked down Professor Oliver. He admitted to knowing Jelly Welch, but swore he had nothing to do with the raid on the dig site."

"Do you believe him?"

"It doesn't matter. He and Carson are the only trail markers I have. Tuhudda and Nagah Will are still missing."

"And you're beholden to find them."

"I served three years in 'Nam leading long reconnaissance patrols. Most of the time we were looking for the enemy, but sometimes it was missing GIs. You give up on your men, you might as well give up on yourself."

The detective pulled the makeshift compress from his forehead and examined it. The bandana showed plenty of blood, but the wound appeared to be clotting. "I thought OSP would've put up a roadblock by now. There's a state trooper based in Vida who patrols all the way up to the pass."

"Look. Carson's tapping the brakes."

The darkness flared red, bathing the thick tree trunks lining both sides of the narrow road in an eerie glow. I rolled down the window. A river's roar drowned the sound of raindrops.

"You're hearing the McKenzie. It's mostly whitewater," Skinner said.

"Is there a bridge up ahead?"

"At Blue River."

"A bridge is a good place to lay an ambush. Carson can stop at the far end and shoot us as we cross."

"But we can't back down now. We'll lose him to a logging road."

"Who said anything about backing down? There's a .30-30 in the rack behind you. Put a few shots into the pavement at the far end of the bridge. The sound and sparks might give Carson second thoughts if he's lying in wait."

"Good idea, but I prefer something I'm used to." He pulled

the semi-automatic from his shoulder rig and rolled down his window.

We rounded a slight curve. The buttresses of the bridge lay ahead. I sped up. Skinner placed his left palm against the dash to brace himself, stuck his gun out the window, and pulled the trigger. He kept on pulling it. Rounds ricocheted off the concrete and metal guardrails as we flew over the bridge. The mud-colored jacked-up pickup was nowhere to be seen.

"He didn't want to waste time stopping here with the Cougar Reservoir turnoff only a few miles ahead," the Eugene homicide detective said.

"Where the hot springs are?"

"Yeah, the one the naked hippies use. Carson can make time on the paved road that parallels the reservoir. Then it branches into gravel and dirt logging roads. This rain will turn to snow up there. Lots of the roads are plowed during winter time. Logging never stops, not even for snow."

After he finished reloading, Skinner got back on the radio. We learned the Oregon State Police trooper who normally patrolled the area was working a fatal traffic accident near the summit. I could see a camper towing a trailer going over the edge. The radio operator said Eugene PD had dispatched a couple of squad cars, but they were at least twenty minutes behind us."

"They're not four-bys. They'll get stuck in the snow," Skinner responded. "Have them stay on the highway and block the Cougar Reservoir road in case Carson doubles back." He signed off and then said to me, "That would be easy for him to do if we end up chasing blind alleys."

I took the turnoff faster than was safe, but that was the kind of mood I was in. I blamed myself for not stopping Carson back at the vacant lot. Rain turned to sleet as we followed the reservoir. I braked when we reached a junction with four logging roads. All were slushy.

"There," I said. "One o'clock. The tracks are fresh." We followed them for a half mile and reached another intersection. "There are more branches than on a fir tree."

The sleet turned to snow. Fresh tracks marred the middle road. We followed it. In another half mile we came to another junction with three more roads. Carson's tires tracks went down each one.

"He's doubling back on himself at each one," I said. "It's an old VC trick to make us chase our tails."

"One of these times he's going to be hiding in the woods and jump up shooting."

"It's what I'd do."

The homicide detective glanced at me. "Is that the way you fought in Vietnam?"

"Both sides did."

"And I thought working undercover narcotics was dangerous."

The road climbed. Snowfall grew heavier. We reached another junction. I stopped to inspect the tracks.

"Wait," Skinner said before I got out. "There's too many roads and too many choices. With that blade of his, he can build a berm we won't be able to bust through. We're not going to catch him out here tonight. It's his front and backyard."

"Do all these logging roads lead back to the main highway?"

"Most do, but not all. If you know what you're doing and have a good Forest Service map, not to mention if you're in your own snowplow, you could drive from here all the way to Harney County and never touch pavement."

"That's it. That's what Carson is doing. He's going back to Harney."

"Why?"

"Because he thinks Stephanie Buhl is still there. He doesn't have her. He doesn't know where she is." I told Skinner about the conversation in the vacant lot. "He let down his guard because he believed I'd talked to her this morning."

"But your sheriff said it looked like he'd carried her away from the dig site. Something about the depth of footprints in the snow."

"That's what it looked like to me too. She must've gotten away and hid, either when he was fighting with Pax Sizemore or later. Played possum and then jumped out of his rig."

"That's a lot of ground to search," he said.

"If she's out there, we'll find her."

"You and the sheriff?"

"And a fellow ranger. He's Klamath and served in the Marines."

"You could be wrong. Carson could've faked you out to throw you off. I've seen that lots of times, especially when I worked dope. Lying is like breathing to addicts. If the girl isn't in on it with him, then he's got her locked up somewhere."

"All the more reason we should search our own turf."

"You the high lonesome and me the big, bad city, is that it?"

"Sounds about right."

The detective thought it over. "So, what's it going to be? Give me a ride back to Eugene or make me walk?"

I gave it a few beats. "I guess I can take you."

"You guess? Well, that's awfully big of you."

"I got to go back anyway. The Clovis point is still in your desk drawer."

Skinner gave me a look and then laughed. "Next you're going to tell me you liked those damn eggs."

24

THE SONG

Melted snow boils in the crashed plane's spinner dome. I pull the scalpel out of the water with the forceps and place both newly sterilized surgical instruments on a clean piece of scrap metal. Other items from the horse doctor's medical bag are also laid out. The space blanket is now spread beneath Gemma while her mother's shawl is folded and placed under her neck to support her head.

I tick the boxes on a mental checklist. Disinfectant, check. Suction tube, check. Gauze, check. Scissors, check. Extra wood is stacked next to the camp fire. Sweaters and coats to serve as fresh blankets are placed out of the way to keep them from being sullied by blood. A stack of clean rags torn from flannel shirts stands ready. A strap made from an elastic waistband turns the flashlight into a headlamp.

The handmade white buckskin-covered cradleboard is close by. I run my fingers across the glass beads that decorate the head and feet, and call to November. "Girl Born in Snow, hear me in your dream world. See me too. Gemma needs you. She needs your healing, your medicine, the medicine of your mother who gave birth to you in a blizzard, the medicine of all *Numu* women. Help Gemma. Help me. Help us bring our child into this world."

I rock back and forth on my haunches, picturing the old healer, smelling the plants she gathers and dries, tasting the fry bread she cooks to perfection. I see her dancing, hear her chanting, see her soaring above the high lonesome on the back of an eagle as she dreams.

I follow with prayers that my mother taught me. I ask for help from *Mu naa'a*, the Paiute's great spirit, and *Gmo'Kamc*, the Klamath's. I call to the animals that give birth in the wild. Show me what to do, I ask the bears in dens, the pronghorn in the open desert, hawks in nests, and trout in their redds. I call to the Rocky Mountain elk cow with the white rump and cougar scars.

Last, I call to the rivers and forests, to the mountains and deserts. "Lend me your strength and resolve, your power and endurance, so that I can do what I must. Share with this baby the life that runs through your waters and branches, that exists in your plants and rocks. Let the beauty of a mountain waterfall and the grace of a desert sunrise shine on Gemma for eternity."

The wind blows. The trees groan. I scuttle to the foot of the pine-bough bed and check. The space blanket shimmers again. The first time was when Gemma's water broke. Now there is blood. I use torn-shirt rags to mop it up and then scuttle back to the head.

"Come back to me," I whisper against my wife's lips. "Come back and stay. You are strong. You have will. You have power. The baby needs you. I need you." I kiss her, but she doesn't kiss back.

I run my palms down her curved belly. The baby is lower than before. The contractions are coming closer together. Though Gemma is unconscious, I can see the impacts of labor as they make her body convulse. I've been timing them on my field watch. For several hours they came every fifteen minutes and lasted for nearly two minutes. Then they came every three to four minutes and went on for less than a minute. Now they are much closer together, but each contraction grows weaker than the one before as Gemma falls deeper into unconsciousness. If they stop before she fully dilates, the baby will be stuck.

I place rolled clothes under her knees, no longer careful to keep from moving her broken ankle, hoping the grating pain will wake her. I squat on my haunches and call to November again, repeat the prayers, and ask for help from all living things. I don't think about the past that led me to No Mountain where my life intersected with Gemma's or wonder if our meeting was a random act or destiny. I don't think about what might've happened if we'd taken off in the little plane five minutes earlier or five minutes later. And I don't think about tomorrow or the next day, or even the next hour. I focus only on the now as I summon the courage to do what I must.

Gemma's body reacts with a spontaneous jerk as a new contraction begins. I take a deep breath and then let it out in a roar. "Gemma, wake up!"

Tremors run up and down her. Her legs involuntarily clench then slacken. Her eyes remain shut. Her breathing stays the same during the contraction. When the spasms subside, I glance at the instrument tray. The headlamp makes the silver scalpel shine. I glance at my watch. I'll give her three more minutes before I cut, not a second longer.

I lean over Gemma's belly. "Listen up, kid. It's me again. I need your help. Wake your mother up. Whatever it takes, do it and don't stop. One more thing. No matter what. Stay in the fight. Never give up. Never give in."

The minute hand on my field watch moves once and then twice. Gemma's body jerks from the shock wave of another, more powerful contraction. A sudden downdraft from the angled gap at the top of the wickiup blows the smoke from the fire back down. It swirls around and settles over her as the convulsing continues. Then it spins, rises, and goes back up and out of the gap.

I blink away the sting in my eyes from the smoke and swat aside the momentary distraction. "Push!" I yell. "Push, Gemma, Push!"

Her face reddens and sweat beads. Maybe it's from inhaling smoke, I don't know, but it's the first change in her expression I've seen in a long time. "That's it!" I shout. "You're doing it! Push, babe, push!"

Gemma's back arches. Her chest heaves. She grabs at the space blanket and makes knots of the shiny fabric as her fingers lock. Her eyes flicker open and shut and then flicker open again. They glimmer in the flashlight's beam.

"You're doing it. Now short breaths. Breathe through the pain. Blow like you're blowing out a candle. Okay, let up. Let up!"

Gemma exhales and her cheeks dimple. The arch in her back collapses and she falls back on the covered pine boughs. Her eyes roll back.

"Gemma, can you hear me? Gemma?" No answer.

I can't tell if she was consciously pushing or her body was only spasming. I saw soldiers do it in the field, and I still see them in my nightmares, their hands twitching, their feet kicking in the final throes of living.

I give her another three minutes. Another contraction starts. It's as if the convulsions rocking her body create a downdraft, for again the column of rising smoke halts, turns, and spreads over her before spinning and rising again. I yell for her to push. After grunting and puffing, she falls back again when I tell her to let up and breathe.

I place pinches of snow in her mouth. I dry her brow. I ignore the cramps in my squatting haunches. I ignore the warning in my head that tells me it's already taken too long, she's grown too weak, she didn't fully dilate, the baby is stuck. I ignore the silver blade of the scalpel shining from the instrument tray and Gemma's instructions on where to cut and how many layers to slice. I ignore the lidocaine in the full bottle that if fully administered would end her suffering and make opening up her belly painless for her but a lifelong torture for me.

I take her hand. "Last time, babe. One more push. You're doing great. You're almost there." She utters a moan. "That's right," I say, willing her moans into words. "Only one more push, I promise."

I scuttle back to the foot of the pine boughs and grab her shins, keeping her knees up, her legs apart. I train the beam of the headlamp and count the seconds until the next contraction. A sudden noise makes me lose count. It's not the sound of my breath or the beat of my heart. It's not Gemma moaning or the space blanket rustling. It's not the wind blowing or the trees groaning.

It's an airplane. A twin engine from the sound of it.

Gemma's legs clench, her back arches, and she yelps. "Ahh. Ahhh."

The roar of the plane's engines grow louder. It's right on course to pass over the clearing and the wickiup.

"Ahh! Ahhh!" Gemma's yelps become cries.

The flare gun is hanging right at the entrance. All I have to do is let go of her shins, race outside, aim, and pull the trigger. I can run to the clearing and douse the signal torches with fuel and light them. I can shoot a second flare. And a third. They'll be seen. We'll be saved.

"Push!" I yell as loud as I can in hopes the pilot will hear me because it's the only signal I'll send. "Push!" I yell even louder.

The sound of the plane grows distant as Gemma's cries turn into a howl, a primal scream that rises from the depths of her lungs. I tighten my grip on her shins. She howls again, even louder, drawing deep from the recesses of her being, back to when her ancestors bore children out in the open, then in caves, then huts, then houses made of sod and buffalo chips.

The headlamp flickers, but it's not from batteries growing weak. The baby's head crowns and sends the light skittering in all directions. Everything happens fast now. A wrinkled face appears, followed by one shoulder and then another, and then in a rush with no time to think, I let go of Gemma's shins and scoop up the wet and shiny thing slipping and sliding toward me on the space blanket.

I hold the infant up, who greets the world with a sharp intake of air, a gasp, and then a wail. It's an ancient song of life, loud and strong, and more beautiful to my ears than "Moondance." I join in and sing a song of welcome, of joy, of love and gratitude...

25

Pudge Warbler beat me to the Burns hospital on my drive in from Eugene. I parked next to the pickup with the seven-point gold star on the door and went looking for him. He was jawing with a soap-opera-handsome doctor dressed in surgical scrubs next to the vending machines.

The sheriff gestured at me with a paper cup of coffee and said, "You remember Dr. Goldman from when he took the slug out of Orville's back."

I shook the surgeon's hand. "Good to see you again. Busy as usual?"

"Winter brings more than its share of slip 'n' falls," he replied. "Mr. Welch is the first GSW I've had in a while."

"Doctor Goldman was about to fill me in on Jelly's condition," Pudge said.

"I would've discharged him already, but the sheriff asked me to keep him here as long as possible." The surgeon winked. "For his own health and welfare, of course."

"How is he?" I said.

"The scalp wound is healing up fine. His hearing is another matter."

I asked him if the bang from the gunshot punctured Jelly's eardrum.

"There's no visible sign of damage, but we performed an audio test to be sure. While he appears unable to detect softer tones, there's no way of knowing if the condition predated the shooting or if it's temporary. Some impact to his hearing is to be expected given how close the gun was when it discharged."

"How close?" Pudge asked.

"In addition to the muzzle flash burning his hair, there was stippling to his skin from the impact of gunpowder particles. I'd say the tip of the barrel was only inches away."

I asked Dr. Goldman if the hearing loss went along with his faulty memory that Gemma had told me about.

"I'm of the opinion it's more the result of emotional trauma than a physical one. You and I both saw that when we were in country." The surgeon had done a tour at a MASH like the one I'd been medevacked to after being hit. "Now, if you gentleman will excuse me, I have a gallbladder to remove."

As he hurried down the waxed hallway, the old lawman said, "I can still see the photo of LBJ tugging up his shirttail and showing off the scar from having his gallbladder removed. First time in history Americans got a glimpse of their president's gut, and I guarantee you, it'll be the last." He made a sour lemon face. "Before we go in and chat with Jelly, why don't you tell me what you learned that got you so riled up you drove straight here without stopping off at the ranch to say hello to the mother-to-be of my first grandchild."

"Does Gemma know I did that?"

"Get used to it, son. It's called woman's intuition."

I plugged two bits into the vending machine and pushed the button for black coffee. A paper cup dropped down a chute, landed lopsided on the tray, and an oily liquid squirted into it. I took a sip and immediately wished I hadn't.

"I have a hunch Flip Carson is on his way to Harney County, if he isn't here already." I described the encounter at The Lumberjack and subsequent chase on the logging roads. "He didn't know where Stephanie Buhl is. If he grabbed her, she got away. Since the Wills have vanished, the only one who can tell us what happened is still Jelly."

"Tuhudda and Nagah aren't lying dead in a gully with bullets in their backs, if that's what you're worried about. We covered every square inch in and around the dig site. We also questioned Tuhudda's family back at his camp on the reservation, but if they know, they're not telling. I suspect November has a good idea of where they might be, but every time I ask her, she answers in riddles. Jelly? That boy's playing dumb, hearing loss or no hearing loss. The only thing I've been able to get out of him is he likes cherry-flavored Jell-O better than orange, laughs like a hyena when he's watching *The Beverly Hillbillies*, and wants a lawyer."

"What for, you haven't charged him with anything, have you?"

"Not that kind of lawyer. The suing kind. He thinks he's got a claim against the university for putting him in an unsafe situation. Willful negligence, he calls it. Jelly told me after he got to Catlow Valley, Miss Buhl told him about her ex and how he's crazy jealous and recently went after Sizemore with a caveman's axe. Jelly believes the university knew about it the whole time and never warned him beforehand nor did anything to protect him once he got out there."

"Did he mention Professor Cecil Edwards Oliver and the threat he was overheard making?"

"He didn't say a word about it. Why?"

I told Pudge about talking to the professor at Mick's. "Oliver is Jelly's grad school advisor. Jelly had to have known he tried and failed to torpedo Sizemore once before. Maybe Oliver said something to him about wanting to get back at Sizemore again."

"Let's go ask." Pudge dropped his paper cup in the trash can. It made quite a splash. I debated chucking mine too, but having driven all night and knowing it was going to be a long day, I chugged the rest of the foul brew instead.

Jelly's hospital bed was cranked up so he could eat breakfast from an overbed tray. The television set was tuned to a cartoon show. He was spooning oatmeal from a plastic bowl. When he saw us, he put the spoon down and sucked orange juice from a single-size waxed carton through a plastic straw. He smacked his lips. "Like the beauty queen says, a day without orange juice is like a day without sunshine."

"That'd be Anita Bryant," Pudge said, reaching over and turning off the TV. "How you feeling this morning?"

Jelly frowned. "My head hurts and I can't hear so good. It's something I'm going to be forced to live with for the rest of my life."

"The sheriff tells me you think you might have grounds for a lawsuit," I said.

"I don't think, I know. The university put me in a dangerous situation. I could've been murdered along with the professor. Being half deaf is going to hurt my chances of finishing my degree and landing a good job. You bet I'm going to make them pay. Big time."

The nurses must've stayed away from giving Jelly a sponge bath. His skunky BO was stronger than ever. "I just came from Eugene," I said.

"So?"

"Guess who I ran into?"

"Like I care."

"Your old pal and grad school advisor, Professor Oliver. He sends his regards."

Jelly's mouth fell open. Pudge ran his meaty fingers down the first few buttons of his uniform. "You're dribbling liquid sunshine on your hospital gown there, Jelly. Might want to put a napkin to it."

Jelly ignored him as he continued to stare at me. "How do you know the professor?"

"How doesn't matter as much as what we talked about."

Jelly pushed away the overbed tray. "And what's that?"

"You, the dig, everything. He was glad you didn't wind up dead like his old rival, Pax Sizemore." I gave it a couple of seconds. "You heard all the stories about them, how Oliver lost his job over it, why he had to take on paying students like you."

Jelly scratched at his beard like a dog going after a flea. "Professor Oliver's my advisor. I don't really know him."

"He certainly seems to know a lot about you. In fact, he was pretty anxious to meet up with you at Mick's last night."

"Why did he think I'd be there?"

"Maybe he misunderstood the note I left with his landlady."

"You went looking for him?"

Pudge cleared his throat. "Drake's been helping me out. Miss Buhl and the Wills are still missing and I need to find the professor's killer and whoever shot you. You're my only witness."

"But I've told you everything I know," he whined. "I've told you a hundred times. I don't know what happened. I heard shouting. I went out to look. Someone fired a shot. I fired back. And then I got shot in the head. That's it. There's nothing else. If you keep hassling me, I'm going to sue you too."

"I don't take kindly to being threatened, son. There's two ways to go here. Same as I told you before. Either you start remembering things right quick or I'm gonna arrest you for obstruction." Pudge pulled a set of shiny handcuffs from the back of his utility belt and held them out. "What's it gonna be, talk or the bracelets?"

Jelly whined again. "But I don't know anything. I swear."

I said, "Maybe we can help him remember, Sheriff."

The old lawman took my cue and hesitated as if thinking it over. "I suppose it can't hurt."

"Let's start with Professor Oliver, Jelly. What did you tell him about the field project?"

"That I applied for it and got accepted. He's been advising me to do fieldwork since day one. He said I needed to get my hands dirty despite my bad back, that it was a requirement for an advanced degree."

"You didn't tell him who was leading it and what you'd be looking for?"

"I didn't need to. Any dig in Oregon is going to involve Sizemore and looking for Paleo-Indians. He, like, owns the entire anthro department."

"Did you tell Oliver the location?"

"No way. They make you sign a letter promising to keep it top secret. You'd get kicked out of the department if you told anyone."

"Did he ask you where you were going?"

"In a roundabout way. I mean, he didn't come straight out and ask specific directions, but said stuff like it must be near Paisley Caves or Fort Rock or in the Alvord Desert. When I didn't answer, he dropped it."

"What else did he ask you?"

"The usual stuff. When did I leave, how long I'd be gone, when should we schedule our next meeting."

"Did he ask who else was on the team?"

"He already knew Stephanie was on it. He said something like, of course she was part of the team because Sizemore wouldn't go anywhere without her. See, Oliver thinks one of the reasons Sizemore got him fired was to make room for Stephanie so she'd get hired to fill his position. Once she got her PhD and with Sizemore's backing, she was a shoo-in."

"Did Professor Oliver tell you that?" Pudge said.

"Not in so many words, but, I mean, it's what everyone thinks. Nobody says anything to Sizemore's face about him and Stephanie because it'd be a total putdown and then he'd make your life miserable. Like I told you back in the rockshelter, she's teacher's pet. I mean, I'm sorry if something bad happened to her, but it wasn't fair she always got credit for everything because she was, well, I'm not going to say what she was doing to Sizemore out loud because she's missing and all."

"Isn't that big-hearted," Pudge muttered.

"I ran into someone else while I was over there," I said. "Stephanie's ex-boyfriend, Flip Carson."

"At Mick's?"

"Another tavern. The Lumberjack. It's in Springfield. Have you ever been there?"

"Never heard of it, but that's a whole different world over there."

"You don't seem very interested in the fact that I met up with Carson."

"Why should I be?"

Pudge groaned. "Because you just got done saying Miss Buhl told you about Carson going after Sizemore, that he's insanely jealous, and that the university knew all about it and that's the basis of your claim against them."

Jelly winced and touched the bandage on his head. "Right. I still have trouble remembering stuff. You know, because of getting shot in the head, which is the university's fault." He turned to me. "If you saw him in Springfield, does that mean he's not who attacked our camp?"

"What makes you say that?"

"Because if you killed somebody and stole a bunch of stuff,

you can't go around and act like nothing happened. Nobody can fake being innocent."

"Do you want to know what Carson and I talked about?"

Jelly scratched his beard again. "Not really, but okay, what?"

"He said he was going to kill me unless I told him where Stephanie was. Since I didn't know, he took off looking for her. He thinks she's here somewhere."

"In Harney County?"

"One other thing." I reached into my jacket pocket and pulled out the brown paper bundle tied with kite string. I unknotted it and held out the Clovis point. "Recognize it?"

Jelly peeked at it. "Should I?"

"Take a closer look." I handed it to him.

He felt the flaked edges with his thumb and then turned it over. "It looks and feels like a Clovis point. Where did it come from?"

"It's the one Stephanie found."

Jelly looked at it again. "I suppose it could be. I'd have to see the dig's logbook to be sure. Where did you get it?"

"A detective in Eugene by name of Dallas Skinner gave it to me."

"Where did he get it?"

"Pulled it out of a man's back. Someone stabbed him with it."

Jelly dropped the rock like it was freshly spewed from a volcano. "Whose back?"

"Harry Silver." I watched him as I said it. Pudge watched too. "You know him, don't you?"

Jelly touched the gauze bandage on his head. "Never heard of him, but my head is pounding from all these questions. I think I'm going to be sick." He reached for the call button and pushed it without letting up.

A nurse bustled in. "Quit your ringing. I heard it the first time."

"I feel like I'm going to barf and have the runs at the same time." His moans turned into gags.

The nurse had a mole on her chin. She aimed it at the door. "Unless you two want to hold the bucket or change the sheets—"

She didn't have to say another word. I plucked the Clovis point from the bed and followed Pudge out. He waited for me at the vending machines.

The old lawman said, "I've been thinking. Be worth our while to find out if this Professor Oliver and Miss Buhl have some history of a romantic nature, even if it was only one-sided on his part. Might be Flip Carson isn't the only one carrying a torch for her. Oliver's vendetta against Sizemore could be more about losing a girl than a job."

"Orville could check with the university and see if Stephanie's academic records show she took classes from him."

"I'll put him on it."

I handed Pudge the Clovis point. "For the coroner to match to Sizemore's wound. Skinner will want to know what the results are. When you talk to him, you might ask him to question the professor about Stephanie."

Pudge weighed the sharpened rock in his hand. "I've seen men who've been killed by a knife in a bar fight here at home and by a bayonet on Iwo Jima. A prehistoric spearhead is a first." He paused. "You gonna stop by the ranch and say hello to Gemma before you head to Catlow Valley?"

"What makes you think I'm going back to the dig site?"

"November's not the only one who knows things before they happen. Take it easy down there, but watch your back. The man who used this won't hesitate to make it three in a row."

26

The lineman shack's cockeyed stovepipe greeted me as I parked in front of the overhang that kept snow off my Triumph, trailered sixteen-foot skiff, and cord of split wood. I headed inside to take a shower, change my clothes, and call my boss. I needed to let F.D. Powers know Gemma and I would take him up on his offer to spend our honeymoon in Portland.

While the shack was heated by a woodstove, hot water came from a twenty-gallon heater connected to a propane tank. The shower was smaller than the telephone booth in Eugene, but at least I didn't have to worry about being struck by lightning. I trained the spray on aches and pains courtesy of Flip Carson, Twombly, and Guffaw. A bruise the shape and color of an eggplant darkened my stomach. More purple blotches stained my chest and shoulders. No way they'd fade before my wedding night. I could hear Gemma's tone when she saw them. It'd be half concern and half chiding, a habit she developed in childhood for dealing with a lawman for a father and how he went about doing his job.

As the shower helped ease the soreness, I thought about

Pudge's notion that Professor Oliver may have been jilted by Stephanie Buhl. It was as good a theory as any even though I couldn't see the short scholar having the gumption to carry a woman down a snowy trail, much less plunge a Clovis point into the chest of a man as fit as Pax Sizemore or the back of Harry Silver. Flip Carson was a better match for being the killer, and not only because of his strength, bad temper, and boot size. He struck me as fully capable of doing what Jelly had doubted possible: kill someone and then behave like nothing had happened. To do so was more than an act to throw off suspicion. It was the mark of a psychopath.

I was drying myself with a towel when bangs and rattles came from the other side of the bathroom's thin wall. My first thought was Carson had traced me to the lineman's shack and found the front door unlocked as I always left it. The second was my holstered Smith and Wesson was hanging on the back of a chair. He would've seen it and heard the shower running. There was no bathroom window to crawl out. The only weapons I had at hand were a comb and a safety razor. I tied the towel around my waist, held the comb like it was gun, and eased the door open. The hinges squeaked. I took a step. The floorboards creaked.

Loq glanced up from the stove where he was putting the kettle on. "That the first shower you had since sweating with my big sister?"

"For your information, she got in the sweat lodge after me," I said.

"She told me you were naked."

"That's how it's done, isn't it?"

"And was Carrie naked too?"

"I didn't notice."

His long mohawk waved as he shook his head. "See, that's the wrong answer. You say you didn't notice means either you did and you're feeling guilty about it or it means you didn't because you don't think my sister's pretty enough to warrant a look. Which one is it?"

"I didn't notice because of all the steam," I said quickly, "but I didn't need to notice because I already knew how beautiful she is from when we were talking to the Graziers. By the way, Carrie now considers me her little brother too."

Loq grunted, but it didn't cover up his chuckle for long. "Where do you keep your extra coffee grounds. The can on the shelf is filled with rocks. It's not the only one either."

The pebbles were how I marked the days I'd been straight. A new pebble for each morning and night. Fighting addiction was a day-to-day battle. "In the fridge. I keep all my valuables in there."

"Every white man I know does that," Loq said. "How do you keep things safe from each other?"

"Point taken."

By the time I'd finished pulling on my boots, Loq had the coffee made and we drank it while sitting on ladderback chairs at the rickety wooden table. Instead of answering his question, I asked him one.

"Where are the Graziers now?"

"Carrie found them a little house in K Falls through the clinic she works at. The county will pick up the rent for a couple of months while they settle in. A neighbor lady learned Mrs. Grazier is handy with a needle and thread and said she'd give her part-time work. Carrie lined up a tutor for Silas and the sheriff talked one of the mills in town into hiring Ebal." Loq drank some coffee. He seemed awfully pleased with what he'd brewed. "What did you find out in Eugene?"

"That Flip Carson has a thirty-seven-inch reach, a nasty right jab, and a mean left hook. He doesn't have Stephanie and he's coming here to find her."

"I saw the bruises when you marched out in your toga. I hope you landed a punch or two of your own. You want, I can teach you how to work a long-armed man inside."

"If you're there when I find Carson, you can show me on him."

Loq's eyes narrowed, no doubt seeing the combinations he'd use against the goliath choker setter. "What's your next move?"

"I need to head over to the Warbler ranch and say hello to Gemma. While I'm there, I'll ask November again about Tuhudda and Nagah. She knows something. After that, I'm going straight to Catlow Valley to take another look around the dig site."

Loq finished his coffee. "I'll go with you. While you're talking to Gemma, I'll ask November about the Wills for you."

"Why, do you think she'll tell you something she won't tell me?"

"No, but it gives me something to do while you're telling Gemma why you went to Burns first, here second, and then to see her third. And, brother, whatever you do, don't say anything about a sweat lodge and what you did or didn't see."

We drove convoy style and when I clattered over the cattle guard that marked the entrance to the ranch, I saw the horse doctor sitting in a double buggy next to the corral. She was wearing a tan cowgirl hat and a suede leather jacket lined with sheepskin. Her ponytail streamed down her back. Wovoka and Sarah were fitted with hangers, surcingles, and breast collars.

"Hop in," Gemma said, patting the bench seat next to her.

"Your training looks like it paid off," I said as I climbed up. "The horses seem pretty calm for being harnessed to a buggy."

"We'll see. This is our first outing." She tugged the brim of her hat down and clicked the reins. "Walk on." The pair of cutting horses hesitated for only a few seconds before beginning to pull. The buggy lurched forward. We'd barely rolled past the stable when Gemma said, "Trot on." Wovoka and Sarah were only too eager to pick up the pace. They trotted briskly along the trail that led from the house, across the dirt runway where Gemma's plane was parked, and toward a rise with a view of No Mountain.

"This is more fun than I thought it would be," she said gleefully.

"Because I'm sitting next to you," I said.

"That too, but you know me. I like riding, I like flying, and I like driving fast. This lets me do all three." She made a kissing noise, followed by, "Up, up, up."

The pair of horses responded immediately by breaking into a canter. Wovoka was hands taller than Sarah, but they'd shared a corral and trails for years and the sorrel mare effortlessly matched the big buckskin stallion's gait.

"Yeehaw," I said.

When we reached the top of the rise, Gemma called out, "Easy, easy." And finally, "Whoa." Wovoka snorted and Sarah whinnied after they came to a stop. When they shook, the harness hardware jingled a jaunty tune.

We sat in the buggy and looked out on the ranch below and the one-blink town of No Mountain beyond. Black basalt-capped buttes ringed the wide expanse of Harney Valley. Even with snow on the ground, we could make out the courses of the East and West Forks of the Silvies River as they flowed toward Malheur Lake. To the east ran the snow-dusted Stinkingwater Mountains and to the north rose the southern end of the Blue Mountains.

The little rise was a special place for us; it was where we finally let down our guards and let each other into our lives.

Gemma said, "I'm really excited about our wedding. I wasn't in the beginning because my first marriage didn't work out and I thought another big to-do would jinx it like last time. I told myself, okay, I love this man, we're going to have a baby, and we need to make it legal, so all we have to do is go to a justice of the peace. But then I realized that wouldn't be fair. Not for you or Pudge or November or all the people I'm lucky enough to have as friends. It's your wedding and theirs as much as mine."

"Blackpowder told me you've invited everyone in the county," I said.

"That's a slight exaggeration, but let me put it this way, it's going to be outside because there's no place with a roof big enough for everyone to gather under."

I looked up at the sky and the end-of-winter clouds that moseyed across it. It was bigger than anything and I couldn't think of a better roof to get married under, a roof that had sheltered the entire world since its beginning.

"I'm glad you've come around," I said.

"It's hard not to when I'm spending so much time working out all the details. The what, the where, the when, and the how."

"What about the why?"

Gemma leaned into me. "That's not a question that needs to be asked. Not now, not ever."

"By the way, I called F.D. Powers this morning and told him we're on for honeymooning in Portland. When I said you were going to fly us there, he said 'You let your wife fly?' I may take that job just so I can see the look on both of your faces the first time you meet."

Gemma grew quiet and I figured it was because we'd already talked the supervisor's job to death. The only thing now was to go to Portland, take a look, and then make a decision that was right for both of us. There was no reason we couldn't enjoy ourselves while doing it—have dinner at a fancy restaurant, take in a concert, and sleep in a big comfortable bed. With a baby coming, it'd be the last time we'd have a few moments together just the two of us.

"You've been in a fight," she finally said. "Your left ear is swollen and your eye is a little bloodshot. At least your nose isn't broken. Who slugged you?"

"Nothing gets past you. After we talked on the phone, I tracked down Professor Oliver and Flip Carson."

Gemma snorted. "Don't tell me the professor got the better of you. What did he do, slap you with a chalkboard eraser?"

"I ran into Flip Carson."

"You mean his fist. You went looking for him?"

"He's still the prime in Pax Sizemore's murder and Stephanie Buhl's disappearance. The Wills' too, for that matter." I told her about Detective Dallas Skinner, the Clovis point in Harry Silver's back, and the chase.

"You and Pudge are cut from the same scrap of leather," she said. "You're the son he always wanted."

"He never needed one. He had all he could handle with you."

Gemma smiled at that, but then turned serious again. "Remember, you're not a sheriff's deputy or a big city homicide cop like your new friend in Eugene. You need to be careful. The baby needs a father, not a photograph wrapped in black crepe."

"I will be, but I can't let what happened at the rockshelter go. I feel responsible. I could've stuck around and guarded them instead of leaving."

"To go do your real job, looking for whoever was stealing water from Klamath Marsh, a refuge you get paid to protect." Gemma paused. "Of course, look what you got involved in when you did. It's the story of your life."

"You wouldn't've wanted me to turn a blind eye to the Grazier family."

"Of course not. And for your information, I also don't want you to stop looking for Tuhudda and Nagah and Stephanie either. That's why I'm asking you to be careful, because I know when you leave today, you're going back to Catlow Valley."

"Woman's intuition," I said.

"Common sense," she said.

We looked at the view some more. Gemma leaned in closer. The buggy rocked with the shift in weight. Wovoka and Sarah nickered. I put my arm around her and hugged.

"You know I love the man who I fell in love with," she said, her lips close to my ear. "I'll never ask you to change, like you won't ask me to."

I hugged her tighter. "Never?"

"No, never." She snuggled in closer. The buggy rocked some more. The horses nickered some more. "Well, with one exception."

"I knew it," I said. "What do you want me to change?"

Gemma pushed away and looked me in the eye. Hers sparkled. "Diapers. You can bet the ranch you'll be changing a lot of those."

27

THE GOOSE

The scissors flash red as they catch the reflection of the campfire inside the wickiup. I cut another hourglass-shape out of the long linen skirt the color of sagebrush that Gemma had packed for our big night out in Portland and add it to the stack of homemade diapers. The baby suckles while the new mother hums. The sounds of contentment are sweet, but they can't drown out the danger warnings blaring in my head. I did the best I could to tend to Gemma after the delivery, but who knows if she escaped infection. The same is true for the baby. I see Dr. Goldman in his scrubs hustling down a waxed linoleum hallway toward the operating room at the Burns Hospital and wish he were hurrying through the woods outside instead.

"Try some more broth," I say.

"Did... did you have some?" Gemma says.

"It's pretty good," I hedge.

I put the scissors down and fill the thermos cup. Gemma is propped up on a pile of clothes atop the pine-bough bed. I squat next to her and hold the cup to her lips. "I let it cool in case it spills." I glance down at the nursing baby.

Gemma blows on the broth anyway and then takes a sip. "Another," I say. "Got to keep your strength up."

After the cup is empty, she says, "Thank... thank you."

"It's only broth."

"I mean... mean for keeping your promise. Delivering the baby."

"You did all the hard work. I was only there to catch it."

"You... you don't have to say it."

"Sure, I do. You did all the hard work. Clawing your way out of unconsciousness from a concussion—I don't know how you did that—pushing through the pain. Pushing the baby out, the afterbirth."

"I... I mean *it*. The baby's not an it."

My head cocks. "I know that, but after months of saying *it*, well, it's hard to switch gears." When Gemma tries a smile, I say, "Have you settled on a name?"

"Not yet. We have lots... lots of time for that." She pauses. "How... how long have we been here again?"

"This is the third day."

"Pudge... Pudge will be out of his mind with worry."

"Your father will be out looking for you, is what he'll be. So will Loq. Orville will be using his computing machine to figure out where the plane might've gone down based on the flight plan you filed, the time we went missing, radar, the weather, all of it. November, Blackpowder, and everyone in No Mountain? They'll be looking too. So will all the farmers and ranchers in Harney County. They don't want to lose the best horse doctor around."

Gemma kisses the top of the baby's head.

"Don't worry," I say. "We're getting out of here. I made a big SOS in the clearing and have signal torches ready to light when the next plane flies by. I have a flare gun too."

"It's my... my fault," she says. "I insisted we fly."

"And I insisted we go to Portland in the first place. Look, it's nobody's fault. It happened. We survived. We'll get home."

"You're so... so confident. How can you be sure?"

"Because I'm sure about you." I touch the top of the baby's head. "And I'm sure about her."

"Her." Gemma lingers on the word. "She's beautiful."

"She is. And she's strong and a fighter, like her mother."

"And father."

"She has your impatient streak too. She didn't want to miss out on all the excitement, had to rush her debut a couple of weeks to see what all the fuss was about."

Gemma readjusts cradling the baby. "You're... you're not disappointed?"

"About what?"

"That we didn't have a boy?"

"Not in the least."

"Because... because the next one will be, and if it isn't, we'll keep trying until we have one."

I put my palm up. "What's that you said to Wovoka and Sarah when you took me for the buggy ride?"

"Up, up, up!" A smile crosses her lips.

"Glad you haven't forgotten your sense of humor. I meant *Easy. Whoa!* Let's enjoy what we have for a while."

Gemma glances around the wickiup. "And what's that?"

"Us. The three of us. Now, come on, lie back down and get some rest. Both of you. I need to go out and check on some things. I won't be long."

I tuck the shawl around my wife and daughter to bind them even closer together and blanket them with Gemma's sheepskin coat. Then I grab the flare gun and my revolver and crawl out between the hanging duffle bags. The broth was the last of the boiled beef from the sandwiches November had packed. Gemma needs food to keep her milk production up.

After making sure there's ample firewood piled near the entrance, I hike to the clearing. Windblown snow covers portions of the letters. I pick up a branch and shake the snow off while I try to shake off the grim reality I hid from Gemma. The fact that I've only heard one plane fly overhead since we crashed tells me we're not below a regularly used flight path. If it was a search plane, chances are it was executing a grid pattern. Spotting nothing, the pilot would've checked the square off the search map and flown to the next.

Needing to conduct a search of my own, I walk along the southern edge of the clearing and look for animal tracks. As soon as I reach the western edge, I move several yards to the south and then walk east scanning the field in front of me. I continue the back-and-forth pattern the length of the clearing until I'm a couple of hundred yards below it.

I don't hold out hope for spotting hoof prints from a large mammal. It's too low for mountain goats and too high for deer. The same is probably true for the stronger and heartier elk. They'll stick to lower elevations until the snow melts and they can catch a scent of blue wildrye and pinegrass sprouting among the trees and in the meadows.

My best chance is to spot a squirrel or chipmunk venturing out of its nest to collect pinecones it buried last fall or mushrooms stashed in the crook of a tree. If I'm lucky, a hare emboldened by the camouflage of its winter coat might risk hawks to come out to nibble the undersides of bushes. I might not be the only one stalking them. Foxes, cougars, and lynx live in Oregon's mountains, no matter if the plane came down in the Cascades, Blues, Ochocos, or Wallowas.

I walk with my .357 held at my side. All six chambers are loaded. While hunting with a shotgun or rifle would be a better bet for bagging game, knowing hungry mouths are depending on my aim helps even the odds.

The forest continues to slope. There's no scolding from squirrels in the trees, no chittering from chipmunks, but I press on. I cross another clearing and search for tracks. The blanket of snow remains unblemished. As I'm about to enter the forest on the far side, something catches my ear. I freeze. There it is again coming through the trees. A groan? Maybe a croak? Is it a frog or only two branches rubbing together? I strain to listen.

It's a honk. It's a goose.

I silence my footsteps as I slink from tree to tree, avoiding stepping on fallen branches knocked down in the last wind. The honks grow closer. Sky shows at the tree line. I sneak toward it and look out, not on another snow-covered meadow, but a frozen pond with a dark spot in the center. It's dark from open water, and four, no five, six, seven, eight white spots float on it. They're not chunks of ice. They're snow geese.

Though spring is only a few days old, the birds on the pond are harbingers of what's to follow. Snow geese are the proverbial early birds of migration because their flight is among the longest. They must flap their wings all the way to the Arctic Circle.

That the eight were able to find such a tiny opening in a pond in the middle of a forest on the side of a mountain is testament to the species' ability to navigate thousands of miles of wilderness. I watch as the big birds rest in safety from prowling predators, protected by a clear field of vision across the ring of ice that surrounds the open water. In safety, that is, from all but one predator, the apex hunter who stands alone at the top of the food chain because of his ability to adapt a rock into a spearhead and a spearhead into a metal projectile that travels twenty-six hundred feet per second.

The geese are too far away to hit from where I am. I get down on all fours and crawl. When I'm thirty yards out, I drop to my belly and pull myself across the snow by my elbows. I get so close to the pond's edge I can hear the ice heave and the water splash from paddling webbed feet. It's all about timing now. Timing, marksmanship, strategy, and a little luck.

I slow my breath and steady my heartbeat. I jump up holding the revolver in a double-hand grip, aim, and pull the trigger, not at the geese, but at the ice on the other side of them, knowing the sound of it cracking behind them and the spraying of crystalline splinters will spook them to fly my way.

The strategy works. Water erupts and wingbeats drum as the geese take off instinctively. The flock rises at a steep angle and veers toward me. I take aim at the lead bird discounting the old adage that it has the toughest meat from breaking the wind for those that follow. I've watched too many V's darkening the sky over the refuges and seen too many birds in those formations take turns flying in front. I lead the snow goose by a few inches and pull. Bang! I miss.

The flock veers from the explosion. I aim at another bird and pull again. The flock veers at an even steeper angle as the bullet whistles past. They turn back over the pond. If I drop one now, it'll mean having to crawl across the ice to fetch it—ice that may support a goose or even a hungry coyote, but not a man of my size.

I don't hesitate. My family needs food. I aim, fire, aim, fire, aim, fire.

The geese fly on. I curse. I can't go back emptyhanded. How could I miss? I earned marksmanship ribbons for both pistol and rifle. Despair darkens. Then, when all seems lost, a bird in the middle of the flock abruptly plummets. It falls so fast it doesn't even have time to tuck its head. I watch a puff of snow rise from where it hits. Of course. Unlike a blast of BBs from a shotgun, when the high-velocity round from the pistol didn't strike bone or heart or lungs as it passed through the body, the goose kept flying until it bled out.

I trot to the dead bird and place my hand on its body. It's still warm and the eyes unglazed. I know if Tuhudda were with me, he'd light a handful of sage and wave smoke over the goose in gratitude for its sacrifice. Loq would do the same with tobacco. Since I have neither, I offer words instead. "While your journey in the sky world may be over, you'll live on in the lives you help save."

As I pick up the goose, I look across the pond and through the trees beyond. Something shimmers on the horizon. I can't make out exactly what's shining, but I can tell it's neither snow nor ice...

28

The pale sun was past its zenith when Loq and I arrived at the base of the basalt postpile where Pax Sizemore died. The snow had grown even patchier than the last time I was there. Loq stared at the dark towers that rose like totem poles. He squatted and held his palms over the ground without touching it.

"I'm *Maklak* and this side of the mountains is not my people's land, but I can feel these rocks have much power. It's a sacred place for my *Numu* brothers and sisters. The killing of the professor has dishonored it."

Loq lit some tobacco and blew smoke over the spot where Sizemore's life had ebbed away. "Tell me again what happened to bring such dishonor."

"I've been mulling it over for a while now," I said, "and the way I think it went down goes something like this."

Flip Carson, I began, discovered the location of the dig site. From whom, was still an open question. Motivated by jealousy and greed, he drove to the postpile in his high-suspension four-by with the snowplow blade clearing the way and waited until dark when everyone would be asleep. Then, he hiked up the trail and ransacked the main tent, grabbing relics he could sell to Harry Silver back in Eugene.

Sizemore woke up, either from the sound of Carson rummaging through the main tent or when he was yanking Stephanie Buhl out of hers. The professor shouted at Carson. That woke up Jelly Welch. Carson knocked down Sizemore. Jelly came out and Carson shot at him. Jelly fired back. Carson charged him and shot at his head. Then, he threw Stephanie over his shoulder and hightailed it back to his pickup. Sizemore gave chase. While Carson was putting Stephanie in his pickup, Sizemore tackled him. They grappled and Carson stabbed Sizemore with the Clovis point. He drove off and somehow Stephanie got away. Where Tuhudda and Nagah were during all this was another open question.

Loq remained squatting while he listened, his palms outstretched. "If she was able to get free, how come she ran instead of helping the professor fight off Carson?"

I thought of Carrie Horse before answering. "Not everyone is a warrior. Stephanie could've been tied up, scared to death, or knocked out from being manhandled. No tracks lead away from here except for Carson's going to the camp. That's why I think she made her escape later on."

"Could've she been in on it?"

"Dallas Skinner, the homicide cop in Eugene, wonders that too. He hasn't ruled it out. But if she was, how come Carson carried her down the trail? The deep boot prints, remember? They've melted by now, but Pudge and I both saw them."

Loq looked at the trail that led to the top of the postpile. "You told me Carson spent years hauling a choker through the woods. He probably digs his bootheels in when he's running downhill out of habit. You don't want to pitch face forward with a twenty-foot length of heavy-duty steel cable looped over your shoulder.

Do that, you'd be lucky if your arm was the only thing that snapped. Might be your neck."

"You say it like you have experience."

Loq grunted. "I set chokers in the Winema Forest to bulk up the summer before I walked into the Marine recruiting office in K Falls. Helped me pass for eighteen."

"If you're right about Stephanie working with Carson and he didn't carry her off, what happened to her?"

The Klamath thought for a few moments. "Could be she was supposed to play innocent and remain at the camp after Carson stole the goods and made his getaway, but she got cold feet after the professor chased Carson. When Sizemore didn't return, she knew Carson had killed him. Knowing he wouldn't want anyone to testify against him—girlfriend or no girlfriend—she took off to save her own skin. She knows if the law tries to arrest him, he won't be taken alive. Once he's dead, she can resurface and go about her business, no one the wiser." Loq let it sit and then said, "Could be Carson's not coming back to rescue her, but to silence her."

"That still doesn't answer where she is or how she got there. Stephanie wasn't in camp when I arrived in the morning. She didn't drive off either. Tuhudda's old junker was there and so were the two university vehicles. According to Pudge, they still are. He told me he left them so the university could come collect their property. Her tent was there too. So was her sleeping bag. It's too cold to sleep out in the open."

"She could've hiked across the desert to the main road and hitched a ride. A pretty girl wouldn't have to wait long with her thumb out. The two-lane runs straight to Nevada. That state is full of people who go there to get lost and stay lost."

"You have an answer for everything."

He nodded toward the postpile. "And you have more questions than they have years."

"I still don't see Stephanie turning her back on her academic career. Finding that Clovis point was her ticket out of Springfield and to a life as a tenured professor like her mentor, leading paleoanthropology digs around the world."

"Only way to know for sure is to find her. I'll give the killing ground fresh eyes. If there's a story here, I'll find it. If there are tracks, I'll follow them to wherever they lead, no matter how far. I'll meet up with you at the dig camp. If it takes longer, then at your place in No Mountain."

"Roger that. The camp is up the main road no more than a half mile. If I'm not around the tents, I'll be in the rockshelter. I want to make sure I didn't miss anything."

Loq slid the government-issued Winchester out of his rig's gunrack, levered a round, and moved out like he was on point leading a platoon of leathernecks in search of enemy. I got in my pickup and drove off.

Tuhudda's old sedan with the missing trunk lid was still parked alongside the university-owned pickup hooked to a cargo trailer and the Toyota Land Cruiser. All the vehicles bore storm clouds around the door handles from being dusted for fingerprints. I got in Tuhudda's car. The key was still in the ignition as was customary among the Paiute. They never wanted to prevent someone from using their vehicle who might need it more than them. I turned the key. The battery was dead. I got out and checked the two university vehicles. Their keys weren't in them.

I looked around the camp. The main tent and the three smaller backpacking tents had all sagged since their guy lines had gone days without being tightened. The interior of the big tent was still a jumble of boxes and camp furniture, only now they were speckled with fingerprint dust too. I poked around, but anything of value had already been removed to the sheriff's office in Burns as evidence.

Pudge had given me a copy of the crime scene report at the

hospital. I carried it to Jelly's tent. His skunky body odor still permeated the nylon. I stood next to the spot where he'd fallen after being shot and read the report. The blood sampled there was A positive, a match for a sample drawn from him at the hospital.

I walked over to the spot where I'd seen the second splatter of blood near the intersection of the main trail and the path that led to the white toilet seat set atop a five-gallon metal bucket. The report noted the blood sampled there was AB negative. I thumbed through the stapled pages and found the coroner's write-up on Professor Sizemore. It included a body outline with an X on the chest. The cause of death was traumatic blood loss resulting from a deep stab wound. Sizemore's blood type was listed as O positive.

The questions started flowing like the blood that had stained the snow. Who'd shed the AB negative blood? Was it Carson? Had Jelly's shot in the dark really hit the big logger? If so, it had to have been a superficial wound because Carson showed no signs of injury while wielding his fists at The Lumberjack. If Carson had exchanged shots with Jelly, why hadn't he shot Sizemore instead of stabbing him with the Clovis point? Had he wanted to make the killing up close and personal or did he put his gun down while loading Stephanie into his pickup before Sizemore tackled him?

Something wasn't adding up, but the now-deserted camp offered confusion, not a solution. I returned to my pickup to retrieve a flashlight and the 12 gauge before heading to the rock-shelter.

The radio squawked. "Ranger Drake? Do you read me?"

I clicked the mike. "Go ahead, Orville."

"I have a message from Sheriff Warbler regarding Jelly Welch." The radio reception had a bumblebee's buzz in it. "The hospital reported he discharged himself."

"Why'd they let him do that?"

"He was staying under doctor's advice, not orders. There was nothing they could do to prevent him from leaving once he signed a waiver releasing the hospital of all liability."

"Did Jelly give a reason?"

"He told the discharge nurse he felt fine and wanted to go home."

"The news about Flip Carson coming to Harney County must've spooked him."

"That is precisely what Sheriff Warbler said."

"Do you know how he planned to get to Eugene? I'm at the dig site now and both university vehicles are still here."

"The discharge nurse said he asked her to call him a taxi."

"And you've already called the cab company to see where they took him."

"Affirmative," Orville said. "I am waiting for a return call from the driver, but I suspect it was to the bus station. Greyhound operates a route along Highway 20. He could catch a bus to Bend and make a connection there to Eugene."

"What's Pudge doing about it?"

"Sheriff Warbler relayed the information to Detective Skinner when he called him to confirm the coroner matched the Clovis point to Professor Sizemore's fatal wound. The detective said they got a call list from the telephone company and were able locate the residence in Springfield where Flip Carson had been staying, but there was no sign of him or Miss Buhl."

"Carson's probably already here."

"We have issued a statewide APB and provided a vehicle description. Oregon State Police troopers are patrolling the highways and the Forest Service is keeping a watch on their roads."

"Is Skinner going to let Pudge know when Jelly arrives back home?"

"Affirmative."

"He should stake out the bus station in Eugene and tail Jelly to see where he goes."

"Detective Skinner is a step ahead of you. He has assigned an undercover detail to the bus station."

"It wouldn't surprise me if Jelly heads straight to Professor Oliver's. There's something going on between them, I know it."

"Speaking of Professor Oliver, I was able to ascertain from the university that Miss Buhl did take classes from him. An introductory course when she was an undergraduate and a seminar in graduate school."

"I wish I'd known that when I was talking to him. I'll finish scouting around the camp and rockshelter. Loq's here too. If we turn up anything, I'll radio you."

"Ten-four. Over and out."

With the Remington pump and flashlight in hand, I hiked up to the generator. The fuel tank was half-full. I adjusted the choke and yanked the starter cord. It caught on the second pull. With the sound of the motor chugging behind me, I ducked beneath the upper lip of the rockshelter's frowning entrance. The string of caged work lights glowed inside.

It could've been the memory of the whorl of frightened brown bats or Jelly's fear of balls of rattlesnakes or thinking an ancient spirit might be angry because someone rustled his bones, but something was making the hairs on the back of my neck stand up. I shifted the 12 gauge from port arms to against my shoulder so that the tip of the barrel was leading the way.

29

The walk to the fork in the rockshelter seemed to take longer than before. I turned left when I reached it and relied on my flashlight to pick a route over, under, and around the obstacle course of stalagmites and stalactites. Once inside the chamber where the Ancient One had lain, I re-examined the walls, palming the surfaces and poking and prodding the nooks and crannies. I pushed aside large rocks to make sure nothing was under or behind them.

Standing in the middle of the chamber, I held my flashlight straight out and turned around slowly. The lighthouse maneuver revealed no surprises. There were no hidden tunnels or passageways, no evidence left by the person or persons who'd taken the old bones. Nor had any new bones been added. For Stephanie, Tuhudda, and Nagah's sake, I was relieved about that.

I returned to the fork and followed the string of caged works lights into the larger righthand cavern, walking on top of the hard vein of carbonate that ran down the middle. It didn't take long to reach the grids where the two graduate assistants had dug, scraped, and brushed away dirt in search of stone tools under the learned eye of Professor Sizemore. I paused at the square where Stephanie had exhumed the Clovis point and wondered if things would've turned out differently if she'd never discovered it. Would Sizemore still be alive? Harry Silver? Had the fates of the missing trio been determined by the Stone Age weapon as well?

Only the last question still held the possibility of an answer, but I'd have to find the three—dead or alive—to learn it. Signs of digging in the gridded squares became more sporadic the farther I ventured. The team had been conducting random test sampling. A spadeful of cavern floor was unearthed here and a chiseling of rock there. Two squares remained untouched while the third one had trowel marks. The team had been hopscotching their way deeper and deeper into the cavern.

The lights grew dimmer as the distance to the power generator grew greater. I shined my flashlight on the walls to check for openings to other chambers, but the rock faces appeared scoured smooth as if an underground river had once rushed through.

The last bulb in the string of lights was dimmer than the others and flickered weakly. I pointed my flashlight past it. The beam stabbed the darkness to reveal the cavern continued while the gridwork didn't. I remembered Sizemore saying the rockshelter had qualities unlike others, that depth and size were among them.

Before going on, I turned to unhook the protective cage around the flickering light to check if the bulb was loose. As I reached for it, a puff of air ruffled my hair. It came from the dark end of the cavern. I stood stock-still, wondering if I'd imagined it. Seconds passed and then another puff blew. I scooped a handful of dirt from the floor and tossed it up so it would fall in the beam of my flashlight. It billowed rather than rained straight down. I ran my tongue across my lips and tasted grit.

The puffs of air meant there was an opening somewhere. It

could be as small as a hairline fissure or large enough for bats to use as a back door. I resumed walking with the pump shotgun snugged to my shoulder again.

I counted strides as I went. At twenty-two, the ceiling sloped precipitously. At thirty-four, I had to stoop. No glimpse of sky or rays from a winter sun revealed the opening's whereabouts. At forty-one strides, the beam from my flashlight mushroomed as it struck the end of the cavern.

Or was it?

A bite had been taken out of the bottom of the mushroomed beam. I focused the flashlight on the black spot. The mouth of a low tunnel swallowed the light. That I'd nearly missed seeing it explained why the deputies searching the crime scene had never mentioned it. Perhaps they'd never ventured this deep or maybe they'd seen the tunnel but chose not to stick their heads in it. Jelly Welch might not be the only one frightened by stories of rattlesnake balls and vampire bats.

Getting on all fours and holding the flashlight in my teeth, I pushed the shotgun into the tunnel and started crawling. The rotten egg smell of something sulfuric soon filled my nostrils. I held my breath and crawled faster. The tunnel finally opened up. The odor of sulfur dissipated. I stood without bumping my head and swept the flashlight. I was in a chamber much larger than the one where the old bones had lain. There was no crack in the wall or opening in the ceiling to explain where the puffs of air had come from.

Dark vertical smudges like soot on the glass chimney of a kerosene lantern streaked the walls in places. Beneath each streak lay a circle of blackened rocks. Sizemore had pointed at the fire ring near the mouth of the cavern and explained carbon dating, but the purpose of these fires wasn't for heating or cooking or warding off wild animals. They were lit to provide light while painting.

Red and black handprints speckled the walls. The most ancient of self-portraits had been made by placing a palm in a mixture of ground minerals, plants, water, and blood, and then pressing it flat against the rock. A group of stick figures holding spears was drawn in charcoal. They were stalking a four-legged creature with huge, curving tusks. In another drawing, a pair of seated stick figures banged rocks. More animal figures were painted with an ochre pigment. They resembled the pronghorns that lived at the Hart Mountain refuge I patrolled.

The artwork appeared older than any I'd seen throughout Harney County. The drawings and paintings were beautiful in their simplicity and their colors were still sharp. Hidden inside a rock vault deep inside a mountain, they'd never been exposed to the history-erasing forces of sun, wind, and rain.

I turned a hundred-eighty degrees to examine the opposite wall. A large-winged black bird with oversized talons and a curved beak dwarfed everything else. Above it shined a red disk that could only be the sun. As I panned my flashlight, the bulb dimmed. The batteries were growing weak. I kicked myself for not grabbing a spare from the box of flashlights the dig team kept at the rockshelter's entrance.

I smacked the butt to coax more juice out of it. It generated a raspy echo. The sound was strange, but caverns were known for their peculiar acoustics. I smacked the flashlight again and got another raspy echo. The two noises weren't even close in pitch and tone. Curious, I gave a sharp whistle. The gruff echo sounded again, but it didn't bounce off the walls. It rose from the chamber's floor.

I aimed the flashlight down. The beam haloed around a black hole. I walked toward it slowly, carefully. When I was steps away from the edge, I began shuffling my feet as if testing the thickness of ice on a pond. The raspy echo grew louder. I leaned forward and angled the flashlight into the shaft.

A hand reached up and grabbed for the beam. I jumped back.

The rasping grew shrill. I leaned forward and shined the light down once more. The hand shot up again. Rather than trying to snatch my flashlight, it was trying to block the beam from shining in eyes, eyes that had seen nothing but total darkness for days, eyes that instinctively closed as if to keep from staring directly at the sun, eyes beneath the hem of a soft wool cap with alpacas running across the crown and tassels dangling from earflaps.

"Stephanie!" I called, quickly swinging the beam beneath my chin to reveal my face. "It's Nick Drake."

She rasped pitifully, her voice shot from hours on end yelling for help in a shaft in the floor of a cavern so far from the entrance and so deep in the mountain, she would've become nowhere bones if I hadn't discovered the tunnel.

"I'll get you out. Keep your eyes shut while I check your position."

The grad student was huddled in her down parka on a narrow ledge about ten feet below my boots. The walls above her were smooth and nearly vertical. I saw no footholds or handholds. I pointed my flashlight past the edge of the ledge. The beam never found bottom.

I wanted to know how she got there. Had she fallen or was she thrown? Did she grab for the ledge as she dropped or was it divine intervention that landed her on it to prevent her from plunging into oblivion? But Stephanie didn't have strength in her voice to answer any questions and I didn't have time to ask them. Now that she knew rescue was possible, I didn't want her to panic and risk falling off her perch.

"Here's what we're going to do," I said. "I'll pull you out, but I need a rope. I have one in my pickup. I'll get it and be right back. In the meantime, stay calm, keep still."

Stephanie tried to speak, but all that came out were squawks.

"I'll be back. I promise."

"Don't. Leave. Me," she finally croaked.

"I have to get a rope. It's the only way."

"Please! Don't leave."

Her plaintive words haunted me as I crossed the chamber and began crawling back through the tunnel. Once again, the rotten-egg smell filled my nostrils. Sulfur deposits were common in the volcanic areas of southeastern Oregon and there must've been a lot of iron and lead sulfides trapped in the rocks that lined the tunnel. It smelled bad, all right, but not enough to make me puke.

I emerged in the main cavern and broke into a run. As I raced toward daylight, I remembered something other than a mineral that produced a sulfuric odor too. I could see myself sketching it and writing down its taxonomy in my notebook. *Animalia, Chordata, Mammalia, Carnivora, Mephitidae, Mephitis, Mephitis mephitis.*

Striped skunk.

I'd surprised a big male one time. The buck instinctively raised his bushy tail and sprayed me with a mix of sulfur-containing organic chemicals from glands on either side of his anus. I had to soak my jeans in vinegar and tomato juice to get the stink out.

I reached the pickup and radioed Orville. "I found Stephanie. She's in a shaft in the rockshelter."

"Is she alive or deceased?" The young deputy didn't do a very good job masking his excitability this time.

"Alive. Send an ambulance. Alert Pudge too. I'll have her out by the time they get here."

"Ten-four."

"Wait. Find out which bus Jelly is on. Pull it over, pull him off, and bring him in."

"On what grounds?"

"On the grounds he stinks."

I clicked off, grabbed a couple of candy bars from the glovebox and a coil of climbing rope and plastic jug of water from the back. I ran with dread urging me on, dread that having come so close to being saved, Stephanie would lose whatever willpower she had left and make a final, fatal mistake of trying to climb up the steep, slick rock wall. I barely broke stride as I passed through the gapped-tooth entrance, plucked two flash-lights out of the box, and raced to the fork.

Blowing past it, I sped down the righthand cavern, not worrying about stepping on buried ancient artifacts or breaking the strings that outlined the dig team's grids. No one would blame me if I did, least of all Stephanie. I reached the tunnel.

"I'm almost there," I yelled.

I held my breath, dove into the low, narrow passageway, and pulled and kicked my way through as if swimming the length of a pool underwater. Once inside the painted chamber, I sucked in air, turned on both flashlights, and waved them wildly as I approached the edge of the hole.

"Told you I'd be back." I shined both lights into the shaft.

It seemed to take forever, but Stephanie finally raised her hands to block the beams. She clenched her fists and flashed two thumbs up.

"Hang on while I fix the rope."

The cavern was free of stalagmites and stalactites, meaning no water dripped from the ceiling, another reason the cave art was so well-preserved. But a large slab had broken off one wall and it was heavy enough and tall enough to loop my rope around and anchor it. As I tied it off and tested the knot, I thought about options for getting Stephanie out. I quickly rejected lowering the rope, instructing her how to tie a loop around herself, and then pulling her up. I didn't know what kind of shape she was in, how weak she'd become without food or water, or whether her fingers had the strength to tie the knot correctly. That left only one choice.

I shook the rope out and began making small loops in the tail every couple of feet by tying them with figure eight knots. I tied the plastic water jug to one. When I reached the end, I looped the tail twice around my waist and tied it off with a bowline knot. If I fell climbing down, it would arrest my plunge. Or so I hoped. I balanced one shining flashlight on the lip of the shaft and jammed the other into my pocket. Then I pulled in the slack to the rock anchor, turned my back to the hole, leaned back, and stepped off the edge.

The rope twanged as I pressed the soles of my boots against the shaft's wall and rappelled down to the ledge. When I reached it, Stephanie grabbed my legs and sobbed.

The glow from my pocketed flashlight revealed a smudged face and cracked lips. I wished I'd brought a tube of ChapStick like Pax Sizemore always carried, but at least I had the jug of water. I held it to her lips. Stephanie gulped, retched, and gulped some more.

"Out now," she croaked, her strained vocal cords loosening from drinking.

I peeled one of the candy bars. "Hope you like almonds in your chocolate." I held it out. She grabbed my hand and wolfed the bar down. I peeled the second. It disappeared as fast.

"Let's check you first." I took her wrists and gently moved them up and down. I did the same with her ankles. She didn't cry out. "How about your arms and legs? Can you move them without pain?" She raised her arms and bent her knees.

"Any trouble breathing? Do your ribs hurt?"

The alpacas ran as she shook her head. "Don't think so."

How she'd been able to survive a ten-foot drop onto hard rock and not sustain any broken bones was something I didn't want to question too closely while perched on a ledge in a shaft in a chamber deep inside a mountain that had been decorated by ancient people. It was the same as the puffs of air I'd felt that led me to her. Living among *Numu* had taught me many things were better left accepted than doubted.

"Ready? Let's go," I said.

I untied the bowline knot and undid the double-loop around my waist. I retied the rope around hers, but kept two extra arm-lengths of the tail which I used to form two more loops, one around each thigh. The three loops formed a climber's harness joined at the center with a bowline knot at the front. I tested it. The knot held fast.

"I'm going to take your wrists now and raise them over your head." I closed her fingers around a figure eight-knotted loop. "Hold on to this. I'll climb out first. Once I'm up, I'll pull you. All you have to do is stand when I tell you and keep hold of the loop."

She croaked again, but eventually formed words. "I'll fall."

"I won't let you."

"Too heavy."

"I've lifted heavier. Once we start, don't look down. Keep your eyes closed."

I didn't give her anytime to think about it. Keeping the slack piled around her, I began climbing. It was the ropes course in basic training all over again, only this time without a drill instructor calling me a maggot while yelling obscenities.

Once I pulled myself over the lip, I stood and began reeling in the slack. When it was taut, I called down. "Okay, Stephanie. Here we go. Keep hold of the loop. Stand up!"

I pulled hand over hand, knowing it was a rough ride for her. The harness would be pinching her waist and thighs. Her body would bounce and scrape against the shaft's wall. She'd get a few bruises and lose some skin, but she'd be out.

The flashlight propped on the edge of the shaft illuminated the rope. I counted the loops as they crossed the lip. One empty loop, two empty loops, three, and then up came the half-full water jug tied to the fourth. Finally, a loop with fingers clenched around it showed. I stopped pulling and held Stephanie in place while I reset my feet, took a deep gulp of air, and then pushed my arms straight up in a weightlifter's overhead press. Stephanie's elbows cleared the lip, then her head, her shoulders, and then her chest. I lurched backward and sat down on the rock floor. Stephanie popped up, shot forward, and landed in my lap.

"Gotcha!"

30

We sat away from the edge of the vertical shaft. When Stephanie finished emptying the water jug, she said, "Where's Pax?" Her voice was much less croaky now. "Why isn't he here with you?"

I needed her to stay strong to make it the rest of the way through the rockshelter; there would be plenty of time to tell her later. "It's a long story. Let's get you out of here first."

To distract her, I shined the flashlight to illuminate the cave paintings. "Aren't they beautiful?"

Stephanie gasped. "This whole time, I had no idea I was in here!"

"You've been in this chamber before?"

"The day Nagah discovered it. Pax had him working the grids with us after we finished with the old bones. Nagah ran ahead to look for big rocks to move and came back super excited."

"Did everyone crawl through the tunnel?"

She nodded. "Even Jelly, though he freaked out when he was half way through and tried to turn back."

"Bats and rattlesnakes," I said. "Did you see the shaft in the cave floor then?"

The tassels on her cap swung back and forth. "I didn't, but others may have. We only stayed a few minutes. Pax didn't want our breath and flashlights to damage the cave art. We made plans to come back later with proper equipment."

"When was this?"

She cleared her throat a couple of times before answering. "What day is it now?"

I told her. Stephanie inhaled sharply.

That she'd lost track of time was understandable. Stephanie couldn't count the days by making scratches on a wall she couldn't see. She'd been forced to dwell in total silence and absolute darkness while fear and hopelessness competed with thirst and hunger to claim victory over her mind and body.

"Ready to go?"

I helped her up and walked her to the entrance to the stinky tunnel. Then I snaked backward into it, expecting I'd have to grab her wrists and drag her. But Stephanie, showing surprising resilience for someone who'd gone days without food or water, crawled through on her own.

When we reached the main cavern, she took my arm for support and stumbled only a few times. When I could see the glow from the string of caged work lights, I asked her if she wanted a blindfold to protect her eyes.

Stephanie shook her head. "I never want to see darkness again."

We reached the grid where the Clovis point had been discovered. She asked again where Pax was. "What happened? How did I get in the hole?"

"All that matters right now is you stayed alive."

I slowed as we drew close to the rockshelter's entrance and asked again if she wanted a blindfold before we stepped into daylight. "The sun is weak this time of year, but still bright. Corneas can get sunburned."

"No. I need to see it to make sure this isn't another dream."

"It's real this time, but if you want, I can pinch you."

I hesitated before passing through the gapped-tooth entrance to see if a jacked-up four-by with a snowplow blade was parked near the tents. It wasn't.

Stephanie, also looking toward the camp, started to shake. "I feel dizzy, like I have vertigo. I don't know how I got in there."

"What do you remember?"

"Feeling sick."

"In the hole?"

"Before then." And with that, Stephanie sat down on a flat-topped rock where Clovis people once perched and told me about the night of the murder.

A stomachache woke her up. She thought it was something she'd eaten for dinner. It was her night to cook, and, as she readily admitted, she was terrible at it. She burned everything because she'd put a pan on the propane stove to heat and then forget about it while she wrote in her logbook and re-examined the relics they'd unearthed. Stephanie said holding the antiquities was akin to taking a ride in a time machine. She would close her eyes and picture people hunting woolly mammoths, building fires, and cooking meat as babies crawled on animal hides spread atop the rockshelter's floor.

Lying in her tent that night, her stomach started to cramp. Feeling like she was going to be sick, she quickly got out of her sleeping bag, pulled on her alpaca cap and down jacket, and dashed up the main trail to the path that led to the outdoor toilet.

As she sat on the white wooden seat fastened atop the metal bucket, she hoped she hadn't come down with a case of food poisoning. To take her mind off it, she went over the plans she and Sizemore made to return to the painted chamber. Loud noises coming from the direction of the tents broke the night's silence. She thought a bear had come out of hibernation, smelled food, and was rummaging through the main tent looking for something to eat. Stephanie grew frightened the bear would sense her too. As she pulled up her jeans, she heard Pax yelling things like, "Get out of here. Go on. Leave."

As Stephanie rushed back to the main trail, the sound of heavy footsteps nearby made her freeze. The bear was coming, she thought. Then she could hear more footsteps running behind it. Hoping it was Sizemore chasing off the bear and not the other way around, she continued toward the tents. When she reached the main trail, she saw a dark figure looming ahead. Fearing it was a second bear rearing on its hind legs, she shined her flashlight to scare it away. Something flashed and a loud bang rang out. Stephanie felt herself falling and then all went black when her head struck the frozen ground.

"How long do you think you were unconscious?" I said.

"I have no idea. When I came to and couldn't see anything, I thought I was dead, trapped somewhere between life and the afterlife."

I moved so daylight would shine on her. I looked at her closely. Not all the smudges on her hands and face were dirt.

"May I?" I asked, reaching for the zipper of her down parka.

"What are you doing?"

"There's a hole in your jacket right there." I pointed at her side. "You have what looks to be dried blood on your face from touching it with your fingers."

I unzipped the parka. She wore a sweater beneath it. It had a hole in the same place. I pulled up the hem. Underneath was the top to a pair of long underwear. The hole was there too. It was also in the T-shirt beneath it. I finally reached bare skin. Dried blood surrounded a blackened wound in the fleshy part of her side right above the waist. I looked behind and saw a slightly larger wound. The bullet was a through and through.

Stephanie cocked her head. "I must've landed on something sharp."

I pulled down the layers of clothing and rezipped her parka. "Is your blood type AB negative?"

"How did you know?"

"Do you feel any pain now?"

"A little when we were walking, but not as much as before. I thought it was a cramp from food poisoning. It felt better when I kept my hand pressed against my side."

"Did you recognize any voices besides Pax's that night?"

Stephanie looked across to the camp again, taking in the parked vehicles and the sagging tents. The tassels on her alpaca cap swung. "Only his. Is he looking for me too?"

"Do you remember anybody picking you up and carrying you?"

She turned to face me. Her chapped lips trembled. "It wasn't a bear, was it?"

"No. It was someone who came to steal relics."

"And Pax?" Her voice quavered as she said his name.

"I'm sorry. He's dead. He tried to stop the thief. There was a struggle and he was killed."

Stephanie gasped, then moaned. Strained vocal cords couldn't hold back her cries of anguish. "No, no, no!" she wailed. "Oh no. Not Pax. Please, no. Please!"

I took her hand, but didn't say anything. Stephanie's sobs eventually turned into sniffles. I handed her a bandana to dry her tears and blow her nose. She looked at her side again. "I was shot, wasn't I? The flash, the bang, being knocked down. The thief shot me like he shot Pax and then threw me in the hole."

"The thief didn't shoot the professor and he didn't shoot you. Jelly did."

"Jelly?" Shock showed among the smudges.

"He told the sheriff and me he exchanged shots with some-body he assumed was the intruder."

"But I don't own a gun. All I had was a flashlight."

"Fear makes people hear and see things. Jelly was afraid for his life."

"Where's he now?"

"He was shot that night too. He's been in a hospital in Burns."

"Is he going to be okay?" When I nodded, she said, "I suppose I should be mad at him, but, well, it was a mistake, an accident." Her voice trailed off.

"In addition to searching for you, we've also been looking for the Wills. Any idea what happened to them?"

"I wouldn't know. I haven't seen them since they left camp."

Adrenaline surged through me. "When was that?"

"The day we discovered the cave paintings. They left after lunch."

"But their car is still here."

"The battery was dead and wouldn't take a jump. Pax said he'd give them a ride home, but Tuhudda wouldn't hear of it. He said, 'Our own two feet will carry us.'"

I could hear the old man saying it in his slow, deliberate manner. "What made them want to leave, especially after Nagah found the tunnel to the cave paintings?"

Stephanie looked down. "It's supposed to be a secret because it's against anthropology department policy."

"What is?"

She sighed. "Tuhudda asked Pax for the bones. He knew once word got out about the cave paintings, people would flock to the rockshelter. Tuhudda said the Ancient One deserved a blessing and burial in the *Numu* tradition. Pax said yes. Tuhudda also wanted to take the buffalo-bone handle knife, sage sandals, and fire-starter kit. He believed they belonged to his lost grandparents,

Bear and Yellow Moon. Pax told him he'd give them to him after he had a chance to take them back to his lab and study them."

"Did Tuhudda say where he was taking the bones?"

The alpacas moved from side to side. "Pax told him not to tell us, that it would be better if no one knew but *Numu* so they could rest in peace forever. There aren't any laws to protect Indian relics and cultural sites, including burial grounds."

Stephanie's answer still didn't tell me where the old man and his grandson were, but if anyone could walk across Harney County in snow and cold weather, it was Tuhudda and Nagah. They'd be retracing steps their ancestors had taken for thousands of years no matter the season.

We left the rockshelter and returned to the camp. She stiffened when I showed her the spot where her blood was found. "This is where you fell." I pointed to Jelly's tent ten yards away. "And that's where Jelly was shot."

"Where did Pax die?"

"Not here. It was at the base of a postpile that's nearby."

"How was he killed?"

"He chased the thief and caught up to him where he'd parked his pickup. They fought. The thief stabbed him with the Clovis point he'd taken from the main tent."

"The Clovis point I found?" Stephanie started to sag. I caught her.

"Let's get you a chair. I radioed for an ambulance. It should be here soon."

I helped her into the main tent. Stephanie seemed too dazed to notice that everything was turned upside down. I righted a camp chair and got her seated. Then I rummaged through the clutter and found a jerrycan with H2O stenciled on it. I shook it, heard a slosh, and filled a tin cup that had been tossed on the floor.

Stephanie clutched the cup with both hands and sipped tentatively. "I loved Pax," she said softly. "Not in a romantic way, but as a friend, a colleague. He was my teacher, my guide. He showed me there was another world out there from the one I'd grown up in, that I could be anybody I wanted. Pax always treated me with respect and as an intellectual equal."

I righted another chair and sat so I wouldn't be towering over her. She sipped more water and appeared lost in thought. I assumed she was replaying memories of being with him in a lecture hall, around a seminar table, in the field, shoulder to shoulder unearthing a stone tool handcrafted by people who'd walked across continents, over a frozen sea, along the edges of glaciers, and into the unknown, playing their part to build an unimaginable future for members of their species who one day would fly a rocket ship a quarter of a million miles through space and plant a flag with stars and stripes on the dusty, lifeless surface of the moon.

"Stephanie, we owe it to Pax to find his killer and bring him to justice."

She was nodding, but I wasn't sure she was listening, either locked in remembrances or imprisoned by shock.

"Do you understand?" I said. "He must pay for what he's done. Pax wasn't the only person he killed."

"How do you know that?"

"Because the police in Eugene removed the Clovis point from the back of a dead pawnbroker named Harry Silver."

Her body jerked. "My find killed two people?"

"We think the thief was trying to sell it to him and there was a disagreement over the price."

Her hands trembled as she sipped more water.

"I think you know who raided the camp that night. You may not have seen him or heard him speak, but you know who it was.

You know he's violent and what he's capable of doing. Help us find him before he kills again."

Stephanie drained the tin cup. She breathed in deeply through her nose, held it, and then exhaled. Her shoulders straightened. Her chin came up. Even though the sunlight in the tent was diffused from being filtered through the nylon roof and walls, the golden flecks in her brown eyes shone with determination.

"It had to be Flip. He was my boyfriend in high school. I broke up with him years ago, but he's never taken no for an answer. He's made my life a living hell. The only thing that's saved me is paleoanthropology."

"Flip Carson," I said.

She couldn't check her surprise. "You know him?"

"Pax told me about him the first time I was here. Later, a detective in Eugene told me more, including Flip's run-ins with the law and his arrest record."

"He's obsessed with me. He took a job at the university so he could watch me. Flip followed me around. It felt like he was hunting me. In the dorms, outside classrooms, everywhere on campus. When I moved into an apartment, he started parking his truck out front. Sometimes he'd be in it watching. Other times he'd leave it there for days on end. If he ever saw me talking to a male student, he'd scare him off, either right then and there or he'd follow and threaten him. Flip threatened Pax more than once even though there was nothing between us. He can be very intimidating. Scary."

"I met him. It was in the parking lot of a tavern in Springfield."

"It was probably The Lumberjack, his hangout," she said. "What did Flip say to you?"

"That he'll never stop looking for you."

Her body jerked again. "He won't. I should've transferred to another college, moved out of state. I should've gotten as far away from Oregon as I could." Her voice caught. "But I knew it wouldn't help. I'd never be free of him no matter where I went."

"You can be if he's arrested. He'll spend the rest of life in prison."

"No, he won't. He'll escape and come after me. I'll never be free of him. You don't know Flip like I do." Her eyes narrowed. "Do you think he'll come here?"

"He might."

Stephanie bit her bottom lip. It peeled away a piece of chapped skin. "I don't understand. If he came here that night and stole things, why didn't he take me with him? It's what he'd do."

"I think he intended to, but couldn't find you because, well, you were answering the call of nature. Pax heard him and chased him off. When Flip killed him, he didn't come back for you because he'd just committed a murder and needed to get far away from it."

"Then how did I end up in the hole?"

I started to answer, but the sound of tires crunching on gravelly snow and an engine idling filled the tent. "That's probably the ambulance. Wait here while I tell them where we are."

Stephanie didn't question why I told her to stay put, nor did she say anything when I clamped the shotgun to my shoulder and quietly slipped out the tent flap.

31

A red-and-white Chevy Suburban with a silver siren horn mounted between two emergency flashers on the roof idled between my rig and Tuhudda's lidless junker.

I lowered the shotgun and called to the ambulance driver. "Over here."

He was sitting behind the wheel, but didn't acknowledge me. Thinking he must on the radio telling dispatch he'd arrived, I went to escort him to the main tent.

Silver flashed to my right. Something whistled overhead. Steel clanged on steel as a hook attached to the end of a choker cable whipped down, wrapped around the barrel of my shotgun, and yanked it from my grip. Flip Carson jumped from behind Tuhudda's old sedan and bullwhipped the steel cable again. It ensnared my ankles, and before I could draw my sidearm, he jerked the choker and my legs went out from under me.

Carson dove on top of me, stretching a length of cable between his hands. He pinned me by the neck with it and started choking me. I managed to slip my left hand between the garrote and my throat while kicking out of the loop around my ankles. Black spots swirled as I tried to keep him from crushing my windpipe.

"Told you I'd kill you," he growled.

I hammered his side with my right, but Carson didn't even wince. I gave up slugging and patted around for my gun. My fingers curled something curved and hard, but it was the hook attached to the cable's eye, not my revolver's grip. I clenched the shank and swung. Carson roared and arched his back. He straightened his arms and locked his elbows as he tried to drive the cable through my throat and into the ground. I hit him again with the hook's point, this time aiming for his kidneys. I kept swinging it, jamming the point, raking him with it.

Carson howled again and finally rolled off. He jumped up. "I'm gonna set you like a log."

He jerked the cable. I let go of the hook. The sudden release of tension snapped it straight back. It smacked him in the chest and rocked him. By the time he regained his balance, I was on my feet with the .357 in a two-handed grip.

"Drop it," I tried to yell, but coughed the words instead. I was sucking air as deep as I could. Carson dove behind Tuhudda's junker, his reflexes honed by years of dodging chainsawed trees and runaway logs broken loose from winches. I pulled the trigger anyway, hoping the sound of a bullet clanking against a fender would make him stop.

It didn't.

I sprinted to the lidless trunk and leapt onto the boxes, using them as a stairway to reach the rusty sedan's roof and command the high ground. Carson was running toward the tents.

"Give it up!" This time my voice box worked.

Carson didn't pause. I aimed at his calf and fired. The slug went high, but not too high. It caught him in the left hip and spun him around. Somehow he stayed on his feet.

"Drop the choker," I said. "Face down on the ground."

Carson's eyes burned at me. He started swinging the hook back and forth like a hypnotist's pocket watch. "Tell me where my Steffi is."

"Drop it!"

"Tell me where she is and maybe I won't kill you."

The loop in the cable was growing longer as he kept swinging the hook. I didn't want to shoot him again and I sure didn't want to kill him. I was days away from getting married and weeks from having a baby. I didn't want his death walking down the aisle with me or be there every time I rocked my newborn to sleep.

Carson sensed my hesitation. He quickly bullwhipped the choker cable and sent the heavy hook snapping toward my head. I ducked before I could pull the trigger, but an explosion thundered anyway and the smell of gun smoke filled the air.

The big logger crashed backward. He landed sitting up, his plate-sized hands clutching his chest. Stephanie stood with my 12 gauge against her shoulder. She pumped in another shell and stepped toward him.

Carson looked at her in disbelief. Blood streamed between his thick fingers and his cough was filled with phlegm. "Why, Steffi? Why won't you love me back?"

"You don't want love," she said. "You want control."

"But I love you."

"No, you confused it with hate."

Carson tried to speak again, but only air bubbles bright with blood came out. The light faded from his eyes and his head slumped forward, but the big man still didn't topple as he died.

I hopped down from Tuhudda's car and took the shotgun from Stephanie's hands. "It's over."

"It'll never be over."

"He's gone. He can't hurt you anymore."

The alpacas and tassels disagreed. "It's a hurt that lasts a lifetime."

Stephanie walked back to the main tent. I watched her go, but didn't follow; she needed time to heal, not empty words. I went to the ambulance to check on the driver. The window was rolled down. He sat slouched with his head tilted back, but was breathing. What happened was clear. Carson had approached like he had something to tell him and cold-cocked him.

Gravel crunching beneath tires and the thrum of a powerful V8 sounded again. I spun around, leveling the 12 gauge. Pudge Warbler parked his pickup behind the ambulance. As the sheriff strode toward me, he took it all in in a glance, the unconscious driver, me looking the worse for wear, the pump shotgun, and the dead man slumped on the ground. His hand was a blur as he drew his .45.

"Any more of them?" he said, sweeping the camp with his gun.

"Only him. It was Carson all along."

"What the Sam Hill, son?" the old lawman said as he holstered his weapon. "I thought I told you to take it easy down here."

"I fought with him, but I didn't kill him. Stephanie Buhl did, to save my neck."

"You don't say? What about him?" He meant the ambulance driver.

"Some smelling salts will rouse him."

"And where's Miss Buhl now?"

I hooked a thumb at the tent. Pudge hitched his gun belt. "I best go in and have a chat with her. I'll get your version later."

"Go easy," I said. "In addition to what Carson's put her through, she's been in a black hole for days with no food and water and a through and through in her side courtesy of Jelly Welch."

"So, she *is* the one Jelly shot that night. Goes along with what I've been cogitating on ever since I saw that inchworm alongside his thick skull. The only one who could've snuck up on him and put a gun to his head was Jelly himself."

"A home shot," I said. "We had a couple of those in 'Nam, but usually in the foot or hand in exchange for a seat on the next Freedom Bird."

"Only a no-'count coward would do that."

"Or someone desperate to throw off suspicion. Jelly grazing his own head made it awfully convincing."

"You'd think someone going to a fancy school like the University of Oregon would be a little brighter than that. He must have a mighty big incentive to risk his life to cover up what any judge would've ruled as a tragic mistake."

"Was Orville able to track down which bus he's on?"

"He did better than that. He used his calculating machine not only to figure out which bus, but where'd it be at any given time. Worked out when it left Burns, what the speed limit is, and how fast he'd have to drive to intercept it. Said the formula was based on a test question he took to get into college. Orville lit out in that new hands-only rig of his and chased down the Dog before it crossed the county line. Red lighted it and used his loudspeaker to order the bus driver to deliver him Jelly right then and there."

"Orville's quite a lawman."

"You can tell him yourself. He's bringing Jelly here directly."

The sheriff disappeared inside the main tent and I rummaged around the back of the ambulance. I found a bottle marked ammonia carbonate, shook out an ampule, and snapped it beneath the driver's nose. It did the trick.

"What? Who? Where am I?" he mumbled, coming to with a start.

"Among the living. Where's your partner?"

He wiped away the tears caused by the ammonia and blew his nose on his sleeve. "Dispatch said it was a non-emergency transport. I came alone."

"They got it wrong. Are you a medic?"

He nodded and then saw Carson. "I got to tell you, boss, from the look of it, there's nothing I can do for him."

"The patient is in there." I pointed to the main tent. "She has a GSW in the side, but the bullet is out. Make yourself known before you go in. The sheriff is with her and doesn't take kindly to being surprised."

I went to my rig to radio Loq. He didn't pick up. I tried him on another channel. Still no response. For a moment, I wondered if Carson had parked his jacked-up rig down at the postpile again and got the jump on him, but I batted it away. The chance of anyone surprising the Klamath was less than zero. He must've found something worth following.

Carson had to have hidden his pickup somewhere close or Pudge would've seen it when he drove in. I hiked past the parked vehicles. I didn't have to go very far before I spotted a new track. Carson had carved a short route around a pile of boulders. The four-by was behind it. I searched the cab and found a gunnysack shoved under the seat. Inside was the buffalo-bone handle knife, sagebrush sandals, and fire-starter kit. They were more than evidence of a robbery and two murders; they were touchstones to a people's past.

I swung the gunnysack over my shoulder and was hiking back to camp when Orville drove up.

"Good afternoon, Ranger Drake," the young deputy called through the open window of his customized Jeep.

"The tents are straight ahead," I said. "Pudge is waiting for you in the largest one."

Jelly Welch was sitting in the backseat. He sported a shiny new pair of handcuffs.

"Welcome back," I said.

The grad student scowled. "This is false arrest. It's a total putdown."

"The sheriff isn't waiting alone. Guess who's with him?"

"As if I care."

"That's right, you don't care about anybody but yourself. You sure didn't care when you discovered you'd shot Stephanie and carried her up to the rockshelter and dumped her in the shaft inside the painted chamber."

His mouth fell open. Surrounded by the scraggly beard, it reminded me of the angry skunk lifting his tail and aiming his anus.

"I don't know what you're talking about," Jelly sputtered.

"Tell it to the sheriff." I waved Orville on.

When I reached the camp, I put the gunnysack in my rig. Orville had already gotten out of the Jeep and into his customized wheelchair, though with its sporty frame and over-sized rear wheels, it looked more like a dragster. It even sported a gold seven-point deputy's star painted on the back of the seat. He ordered his prisoner to get out.

Jelly refused to budge. I stepped aside, giving him a clear view of Carson. He took one look and slid out as fast as he could. "You got to protect me, Deputy. He's crazy."

"Like a fox," Orville said. "Now, march."

Jelly stumbled toward the main tent and Orville followed, propelling himself over the rough terrain and patchy snow. I gave another look at Carson before joining them inside the tent. The dead man still hadn't toppled.

Pudge was sitting on the camp chair I'd recently vacated. Stephanie was in the other chair while the ambulance driver tended to the wound in her side.

"I got to get you to the hospital," he said. "It doesn't look infected, but I only have this topical antiseptic. A doctor needs to take a look."

Pudge acknowledged Jelly's arrival by saying, "That would be the same Dr. Goldman who bandaged up this numbskull's thick head."

If Jelly had any illusions people were going to go easy on him, they surely disappeared a second later when Stephanie waved off the ambulance driver and said, "I might've been able to forgive you for being scared and shooting me in the dark, but the sheriff told me you threw me in that hole. How could you?"

"I didn't," he said. "I tell you, I didn't."

"Horsepucky!" Pudge said. "I got you dead to rights. No one else knew about the shaft but you, Miss Buhl, and the professor."

"The Indians did," Jelly said quickly. "The kid is the one who found it."

"Funny you didn't mention the Wills had lit out before the shooting started the first time I questioned you. Slipped your mind, did it?"

Jelly raised his handcuffed wrists and meekly touched the side of his head. "I have hearing and memory loss from being shot. Dr. Goldman said so."

"Then I'll speak a little louder, you halfwit. You expect a jury to believe an old man and his grandson discovered you and Miss Buhl unconscious, picked her up, and threw her in a hole?" His short-brim Stetson waggled. "If they were gonna throw anybody away, it'd be trash like you."

"You can't talk to me like that. It's slander."

"It's not if it's the truth." The sheriff paused. "What I want to know is, did you even check to see if Miss Buhl was dead, or did you know she was alive and elected to finish her off?"

Jelly's eyes darted back and forth. "Okay, I shot her, but it was an accident. It was dark and I thought it was a badass looter coming at me. I fired. When I saw it was Stephanie, I panicked. I thought she was dead. I felt bad, real bad. But it was an accident and accidents happen. They do, Sheriff, all the time."

"And no one shot at you first. That was a lie."

"I couldn't wait to see if they would. I had to defend myself, didn't I?"

"Shooting Miss Buhl may've been an accident, but throwing her over your shoulder and hauling her into the cave and dumping her into a hole in the ground?" Pudge shook his head. "That took it from a mistake to attempted murder, open and shut. Why'd you do it?"

Jelly hung his head. "I was afraid I'd be put in prison. Do you know what's in prisons? Rats and cockroaches and real badasses." His belly jiggled when he shuddered.

"Did you shoot yourself before or after you dumped her?"

"After."

"Where's your gun? Drake looked for it. My deputies looked for it. No one's found it."

"I hid it in the crapper so it couldn't be traced."

"That's a five-gallon bucket with a toilet seat back of the tents," I said.

The old lawman squinted at Jelly. "Didn't think anybody would look in there, did you? Well, I got news for you. You put it in, you're gonna fish it out."

Jelly groaned. "That's a putdown. A total putdown."

"Son, I'm only getting started."

Pudge turned to Stephanie. "How you feeling, Miss Buhl? Ready for that ambulance ride now?"

"Not yet. This is the best medicine I could ever get."

"Well, if you're sure. You've been through one helluva lot. I didn't get a chance to say it, but I'm sorry for your loss. I never met the professor personally, but Drake here speaks highly of him."

Stephanie's chapped lips tightened as she fought back tears. A few escaped. "I still can't believe Pax isn't going to sweep aside that tent flap and walk right in here."

"And the man outside, Flip Carson—"

"Don't be sorry for him," she said quickly. "And I'm not sorry I shot him either. Not one bit."

Jelly staggered backward. "You killed him?" She turned her brown eyes on him and let the gold flecks speak for her. "Oh my god!"

"Now, Jelly," Pudge said, "You're in a heap of trouble for what you did to Miss Buhl. But you can make it easier on yourself if you help me make sense of what happened. It could persuade me to put a good word into the judge for you. And, yes, there is gonna be a judge because there is gonna be a trial."

"But what about her?" he whined. "She's admitted to killing someone. You're not going to do anything to her?"

"Maybe give her a medal for saving Drake's life."

"Always the teacher's pet. Okay, okay. If I tell you what you want to know, how do I know you'll keep your promise and make them go easy on me?"

Pudge slapped his chest. "See this badge? I've worn it longer than you've been alive. Do yourself a favor here and don't question my word again. Ever. You hear?"

Jelly flinched. "It wasn't supposed to happen like this. No one was supposed to get hurt. We never planned on that."

"Who's we?"

"Oliver and me."

"That being your advisor, the professor with all those names."

"Cecil Edwards Oliver."

"That's the one. See, you're already being helpful. Keep it up. Now, what were you and Oliver fixing on doing? Pocket an arrowhead when no one was looking and sell it later?"

"That's nothing you can plan for. There's no guarantee of finding anything. Most digs turn up squat. The odds of finding something are a hundred to one at best."

"He's right," Stephanie said.

Pudge said to her, "You mean, you drill more dry holes than gushers in your line of work?"

"I suppose that's one way of putting it."

"Then you certainly hit the jackpot here." The sheriff cocked his Stetson at Jelly. "Son, quit circling the bush and start digging. What were you two after?"

"Money."

"But if you weren't going to pocket relics and sell them later, how were you going to get it?"

"By suing the university. They settle fast to save legal bills and protect their precious reputation."

"I should've guessed." Pudge rubbed his jaw. "You asked me for the name of a lawyer in the hospital. Said you were gonna sue the university for not warning you about Carson having threatened Sizemore before the dig started. Were you and Oliver working with him to salt the mine?"

Jelly hesitated, as if sensing a trap. "I changed my mind. I want to speak to a lawyer before I say another word."

"Why?"

"I don't need to tell you why."

"You think me knowing that you and Oliver were working with Carson makes your trouble worse?"

"I don't have to answer that."

"But you knew about Carson before you got to Catlow Valley. That's a fact."

"No, I didn't," he said quickly.

"Yes, you did," Stephanie said. "Everyone in the department knew about him because I told them. Flip barged into every classroom I was ever in since I enrolled. I warned all the professors and the grad students about him, especially men. I warned Professor Oliver because he was always making passes at me. And I warned you too. It was in Pax's graduate seminar on stone toolmaking by the Fremont culture. Flip was lurking outside the door." She turned to me. "Fremont is younger than Clovis by eight to ten thousand years."

I could all but hear Sizemore say, "Sorry, it's the teacher in me."

"I don't remember that," Jelly said.

"Liar."

"I am not."

Orville Nelson rolled his wheelchair closer. "Sheriff, a word?"

"What is it?"

"I was in such a rush to intercept the bus Mr. Welch was on, I neglected to mention that Detective Skinner sent a fax this morning." He patted his breast pocket. "I believe it could shed some light on this. I could read it out loud if you'd like."

"If it can get us out of here before dark, go right ahead."

The young deputy backed up and pulled out a folded square of shiny papers. He unfolded it. "This is a copy of a bail bond receipt from the Eugene municipal jail. The Muni, I believe they refer to it locally. The receipt is for five hundred dollars for the release of Philip 'Flip' Carson. He had been arrested for being drunk and disorderly and was banging on the front door of a private residence. It was later determined to be the home of Professor Paxton Sizemore."

"Who paid for his bond?"

"The signature on the receipt says Cecil Edwards Oliver."

"Now, isn't that a coincidence." The old lawman didn't try to hide his grin.

"Okay, so Oliver knows him," Jelly said. "It doesn't mean I do."

"Looks like you got two pages there, Orville," Pudge said. "What's the second one say?"

The deputy shuffled the pages not once, but twice. His head bowed as he studied the shiny piece of fax paper. He was either stalling or trying to make sense of it.

"My apologies," he said. "The ink is smeared in places. It is a copy of a report from the telephone company. Detective Skinner had been searching for the location of Carson's hideout in Springfield by tracing a call that had been placed by the bartender at The Lumberjack tavern. The report shows that multiple calls from another number were also placed to the same house. They are circled and he has written next to them Jelly Welch's name."

"That's a lie," Jelly shrieked. "I never called Carson."

"This report says otherwise," Orville said.

"Let me see that."

Orville pulled the pages close to his chest. "I cannot let you. This is official evidence linked to a double homicide."

"He has to prove it or I'm not going to say another word," Jelly cried.

Before Pudge could respond, Orville started reciting numbers. With each digit, Jelly's jaw dropped lower and lower.

"Looks like you're smart enough to recognize your own telephone number, son," Pudge said. "Now, before you waste any more of my time, let me tell you what happened. Oliver and you got to grousing about Sizemore, how he got him fired and was tough on you. You two cooked up a scheme whereby you could get back at him and line your pockets at the same time by pulling some kind of stunt that would make him look bad and give you grounds for a lawsuit against the university."

The old lawman leaned toward Jelly. "To make it all the more convincing, you hired Carson to do the dirty work and dangled the fact that Miss Buhl would be there to get him to agree to go along. He did his part, but everything went to hell in how he went about doing it."

"That's all speculation," Jelly said. "And everything you have is circumstantial evidence. You have no real proof."

"Naw, there's plenty of proof and an eyewitness to boot," Pudge said. "Your buddy Oliver is gonna spill it and say it was all your idea in hopes the Eugene PD will go easy on him."

"You're bluffing. Oliver wouldn't say a word," Jelly said.

"He will when Detective Skinner sits him down in an interrogation room and shows him how thick a copy of the Eugene telephone book is by measuring it against the side of his pointy little head."

Jelly started to swoon. "I don't feel so good. I need to sit down."

"The old bad back acting up on you?" Pudge said.

"It is."

"How do you think it's gonna feel when you're out on the chain gang busting rocks all day long?"

"They don't do that anymore."

"They do where I'm gonna recommend the judge sends you."

"All right, all right. It's like you said. We got the idea after hearing about how Carson accosted Sizemore in his lab one night and threatened him with a stone axe. But we never told him to hurt anyone. Honest." Jelly wouldn't look in Stephanie's direction.

Pudge eased out of his camp chair. He stretched as he stood. "Orville, take Jelly back to Burns, get an official statement from him, and them put him in a cell. Miss Buhl? I suggest you take that ride to the hospital now and let Dr. Goldman have a looksee."

As Orville ordered Jelly out, Pudge said, "Hold up there,

Deputy. Best give me that fax from Detective Skinner for safe-keeping."

Orville hesitated. "Are you sure, Sheriff?"

"I am. Wouldn't want it to fall in the hands of some shady defense lawyer."

The young deputy frowned, but did as ordered, and then used the front of his wheelchair to herd Jelly out of the tent.

Stephanie came up to me. "Thank you for saving my life."

"Likewise," I said. "I wish I could've done more for Pax."

"I'm going to make sure the rockshelter becomes his legacy. Who knows, maybe those paintings in the chamber were made by people older than the Clovis."

"He'd like that."

The old lawman and I watched them load up in the two vehicles. When they were gone, Pudge unfolded the two shiny pieces of fax paper and looked them over. "Well, I'll be a son of a gun."

He handed them to me. The first was a handwritten note. It read, "Orville, my love. Quit working so hard and come home early. Mom made axoa d'Espelette for supper—that's chopped veal stew since you don't speak Basque yet, but that's another special thing I'm going to teach you!" The second page was a big heart with an arrow through it and two sets of initials: O.N. and L.L.

"Lucy Lorriaga," I said. "Looks like she faxed these from the physical rehab place she works at. No wonder why Orville keeps them in a pocket close to his heart."

"That boy is smarter than those calculating machines he's always fooling with, able to pull Jelly's phone number out of his memory bank from when he was researching all these folks the other day and coming up with that bail-bond bluff. Remind me never to play poker with him."

I handed back the faxes. "You better hope the FBI he always dreamt of joining doesn't come steal him away."

Pudge pointed at the hand-drawn heart. "This tells me I won't be the only one who fights to keep Orville right here in Harney County."

32

The sun had risen by the time I got out of the narrow bunk in the lineman's shack. I wasn't one for sleeping past dawn, especially on a work day, but I wasn't about to feel guilty for getting a full eight hours either—especially after spending a couple of nights in the front seat of a freezing pickup and surviving a choker fight with a killer. I scarfed a bowl of steel-cut oatmeal, filled a thermos with cowboy coffee, and hit the road to the Malheur refuge.

I'd driven the two-lane south from No Mountain more times than I could count, but on every trip, I saw something different. It could be as subtle as the sagebrush turning a paler shade of silver or as dramatic as shadows of storm clouds stampeding across the high lonesome. This morning was no different. Snowmelt sparkled as it ran off the shoulders of the blacktop and a murmuration of starlings painted Rorschach inkblots in the sky. Nature was heralding that wintertime was finally drawing to a close.

I turned onto the Central Patrol Road. A hundred-pound bale of hay thumped in the bed as I bounced along. I made a mental note to haul in some gravel to fix the potholes, but then remembered I wouldn't have time. Marriage, a honeymoon, and, quite possibly, a new job in a big city were all in the offing. After the vernal equinox, my life was going to change. How it would, I couldn't tell, but I did know being a husband and father were for starters.

I reached the field where I'd last seen the elk herd. It was empty. The windrows of snow were shrinking in the stubble like bleached bones sinking into a sand dune. Piles of the elk's oval-shaped droppings looked parched. I got out, picked up a pellet, and squeezed. It disintegrated easily. A wide trail of hoof prints led east. The herd had left for its usual foraging grounds near Riverton.

The disappointment stung. Not only had I come to check on their well-being, but to sketch a portrait as a wedding gift for my future father-in-law. My earlier drawings of the elk weren't bad, but I could do better. Sketching a new one from memory or a photograph wouldn't do. I needed to breathe the same air and stand on the same ground as my subjects. It was the only way I could capture their true spirit.

As I was about to get back into my pickup, I spotted the signs of another trail. It was less traveled and the hoofprints that made it were fresh. I powered up the four-by and followed the tracks to a row of cottonwoods that served as a windbreak from one field to the next. The trail went between trees too close together to drive through. I parked, took my sketchpad and pens, and started walking. As I entered the adjoining field, a female elk that was lying on the ground abruptly jumped to her feet.

The bright white patch on her rump and cougar claw mark scars on her hindquarter were unmistakable. It was the pregnant cow, but she had slimmed. Movement next to her explained why. A gangly newborn struggled to stand, finally wobbling on long, stick-like legs. The pair stared at me, but it was as if the cow recognized me too. She didn't bolt. The calf took its cue from its mother, ducked its head beneath her belly, and began to nurse.

I edged around them to get a better perspective and began sketching. Within minutes a bugle blew. The younger of the two bulls smashed through the cottonwoods. Strong and fiercely protective of the cow and calf, he lowered his head and charged down the field.

There was no time to run and hide among the trees. All I could do was stand my ground. At the last second, the bull skidded to a stop, sending old snow pelting against my shins. Twin streams of steam blew from his nostrils as he snorted and pawed the ground. Bulls were notorious for coating themselves in their own urine as perfume to attract mates, but this young male had really outdone himself. He stunk worse than Jelly Welch.

I couldn't blame him for his instinctive behavior, and so I broke off our stare-down and retreated to my pickup. I dragged the haybale out of the bed with a pair of hooks and strongarmed it back to the field. The bull had joined the cow and calf. He watched suspiciously as I dropped the bale and broke it apart with the hooks.

My gift was accepted. As the adults ate and the calf nursed, I began sketching the trio until I was pleased with the portrait. Waiting for the ink to dry, I thought of Pax Sizemore and his life-long dream of finding evidence that humans lived here before the Clovis culture. Maybe he was right and others had made their way to Harney County thousands, even tens of thousands of years before, but no matter how long ago *Homo sapiens* might have arrived, we were newcomers compared to our fellow mammals like the ones in front of me. Elk roots in North America were twenty million years long. Surely, there was a lesson in their ability to adapt and survive for humankind to learn.

With the drawing for Pudge secure in a folder, I bid farewell to the elk family. I got back on the Central Patrol Road and continued my rounds, checking the fields for wildlife and poachers, inspecting the irrigation channels that ran alongside them to make sure they hadn't become blocked with old tumbleweeds.

I paused to watch a flock of blue-winged teal settle down on a pond after flying all night. They, like the majority of birds, migrated in the dark because the skies were less turbulent and the air temperature cooler. Night flying also made it easier to avoid predators, hawks and humans alike. Plants were announcing the coming of spring too. As I circled the fields, I could see the green shoots of new life poking among the old grasses of last year and buds swelling on bushes and trees recently freed from Jack Frost's grip.

I took my time so I could soak in the quiet beauty of the wildlife sanctuary that had proved to be my own refuge from the trauma that followed me home from Vietnam. It was doing the same again by providing solace and understanding after being exposed to Grazier and Flip Carson's mad and cruel interpretations of love.

Eventually, I wound up on a seldom-used track that led back to Malheur Lake, the heart and soul of the refuge. The twin ruts led me up and down a chain of low black-capped buttes. As I crested one, I could see across to the top of the next. Sunlight glinted off the chrome bumper of a pickup. I grabbed my binoculars and zeroed in on it. The vehicle matched my own. Loq had finally surfaced, and he wasn't alone. A bright yellow, late model Ford Bronco was parked alongside.

It took several minutes of jarring and bouncing and shifting into compound low to reach them. I left my pickup next to the rigs and walked toward the edge of the butte. Loq was seated cross-legged on a striped Pendleton blanket beside a circle of porous red rocks. I recognized them as vesicular basalt, a type of lava whose pores were created by gas bubbles and the brick-like color by trapped iron. I also recognized the four people seated around the circle with him.

"Hello, my old friends," I said.

Tuhudda Will gave his customary greeting without getting up from the blanket he shared with his grandson.

November tsked at me. "I told you I would get here on my own."

"I never doubted you would," I said.

"Actually, I gave Girl Born in Snow a ride in my brand-new yellow sleigh," Wyanet Lulu said with a sly grin from the colorful blanket they shared.

The two women had grown up together, and for years, along with Tuhudda's late wife, had traveled throughout *Numu* lands performing ceremonial dances at sacred gatherings. In contrast to November's traditional appearance, Wyanet Lulu had a beauty-shop hairdo and wore bold prints and lots of jewelry. Her carefully tended look befitted her name, which translated to Beautiful Rabbit.

"We have been giving the Ancient One a blessing," Nagah said. "We have also been giving a blessing for Professor Sizemore." The teenager's head dipped. "Mr. Loq told us what happened."

"Now they are traveling the spirit world together," Tuhudda said. "This is so."

"I'm sure Pax appreciates that, for they have much to talk about," I said.

The three tribal elders nodded. All had lost spouses and took comfort in believing they would be reunited in the spirit world along with their friends and ancestors.

Loq motioned to me. "I circled the postpile after you left and found tracks leading north. I followed them on foot before switching to my pickup. I stopped on the high grounds and swept with my binos. I finally caught up to them."

"We were following the river home," Nagah said. He meant the Donner und Blitzen, which arose as a stream on the flank of Steens Mountain and ran through the refuge before emptying into Malheur Lake. The Will family's camp was on the north shore. "Mr. Loq offered us a ride and Grandfather asked him to call the Warbler ranch on his radio so he could speak to Girl Born in Snow."

"I told her where the blessing would take place," Tuhudda said.

"And the Ancient One?" I said. "Have you already buried his bones the traditional way?"

The old man's red bandana headband bobbed up and down. "He is nowhere bones no more forever."

The perch on the edge of the butte provided a sweeping view of the shimmering lake beyond and the river valley below where herds of pronghorn, deer, and elk roamed and birds passed overhead as they had for millions of years. The sun shone on the special place as it traveled from east to west in a continuum as old as time.

"This has a good view of eternity," I said. "It's a good place to rest."

"A very good place," Tuhudda said.

"I have something for you." I opened the gunnysack and handed the old man the buffalo-bone handle knife, sage sandals, and fire-starter kit.

Tears welled in his eyes and coursed down the crags in his face as he clutched the relics. "These belonged to my grandparents. I felt their spirit in them the first time I touched them. I feel it now."

"*Padooa* and *Ohalune* are with us again," November said solemnly. She raised her hands to the sky and looked up. "Those who were lost are now found."

Though I'd never met them, I pictured Bear and Yellow Moon, first as children, then as husband and wife, then father and mother, then grandfather and grandmother, now two souls forever bound by their love for each other. What caused their disappearance and how they died didn't matter. What did is that their family and friends had never forgotten them nor ever would.

"You've done a good thing bringing these here, brother," Loq said. "Does this mean you finally caught up to who stole them?"

"I did, after I found Stephanie alive in a shaft in the rockshelter. Jelly had shot her by mistake and then panicked thinking he killed her and dumped her there. He's in jail."

"The thief had to be the choker setter, Flip Carson. What happened to him?"

"He's somewhere bones now."

Loq looked down his high cheekbones. "That's also a very good thing."

November stood. "Let us give blessings to the Ancient One and *Padooa* and *Ohalune* and all who have come before us and all who will come after. As are the sun and moon and stars above and the rocks below, we are all part of a circle that has no beginning or end."

We joined hands around the ring of red basalt that was spewed from a volcano when mammoths and mastodons lived in the valley below. As the Paiutes sang to their ancestors in *Numu*, and Loq to his in *Maklak*, I sang to mine in English. If I'd known the words, I would've sung in Old Norse and Old English too, for those were the tongues of my ancestors. Like the Clovis people, they'd been hunters and gatherers living in rockshelters along the fjords in Scandinavia before traveling in narrow wooden boats across the North Sea to a new homeland in the British Isles and eventually on to North America. In all their wanderings, over all these centuries, they'd carried their traditions and beliefs with them, including the family name, *Draki* in Old Norse and then *Draca* in Old English, a word rooted in Latin via the Greek meaning "dragon."

As our blessings rose to the heavens, my thoughts turned from the past to the future, to Gemma and our child still to be born, and I prayed it'd be a very long time before anyone had to gather on the top of a butte in the high lonesome and hold a Cry Ceremony for us.

33

THE TRAVOIS

F at drips into the plane's spinner dome from the duck cooking on a spit straddling the fire inside the wickiup. It's dark outside, but the embers cast my wife and daughter in radiance. Gemma is sitting up on the pine-bough bed cradling the baby. Both grow stronger with each passing day.

"You're becoming quite the hunter," Gemma says. "That duck makes three in a row."

"If the word spreads in the bird world, I'll get divebombed next time I step foot onto a refuge." I give her a grin, but Gemma doesn't return it. "There will be a next time. We will get back."

"I know. It's that I'm still not sure where it is we'll be going back to."

"Let's not worry about that now, okay? We have our work cut out for us to be ready to leave in the morning."

I dip the end of a cluster of pine needles into the bubbling juices and brush the duck with it. The skin is browning nicely with the basting. For the past three days, I've returned to the same pond where I shot the snow goose. A blind made of branches set close to the pond gives me an edge when waterfowl discover the open water. The meat is keeping us alive for now, but we also need grains and vegetables. I've tried foraging, but the snow is still too thick and the temperature too cold for plants to bloom in the mountains.

While mother and child appear to have come through the birth without complication, they still need to be examined by a doctor. And then there's Gemma's broken ankle. I splinted it the best I could under her direction, but the fracture surely requires surgery.

Gemma moves the infant to her shoulder and gently pats her back to elicit a burp. "November appeared in my dreams again last night," she says.

"Was it the same dream as before or different this time?"

"Mostly the same. I could see her surrounded by smoke and hear her chanting as she hovered over me while I gave birth, but this time she spoke."

"What did she say?"

"The plane went down for a reason. That our time here is also for a reason and we need to learn from it."

"A crash is a harsh teacher. We could've been killed."

"But we weren't."

"What is it we're supposed to get out of all of this?"

Gemma kisses the top of the baby's head. "Don't you know?"

I turn the duck on the spit. "I didn't need to go down in an airplane to appreciate what we've got and fight like hell to keep it."

"November said something else last night. What she calls the baby."

"Not Hattie after your mother like we decided?"

"Her *Numu* name. Girl Fell from Sky."

"Figures."

"We can give her a nickname, if you'd like."

"She already has one. Hattie is short for Henrietta."

"I mean for her *Numu* name."

"Henrietta, Hattie, Girl Fell from Sky, or just Sky, we'll call her whatever suits her as she grows up because we're going to be there with her every step of the way. But tomorrow she needs to be Girl Rides a Travois."

Gemma laughs. "I won't tell Wovoka and Sarah you pulled us if you won't. They'd be jealous."

"What I wouldn't give for those two horses and a double buggy with sleigh runners right now."

As I finish cooking the duck, I go over tomorrow. We'll get up before first light. I'll load sweaters and coats we use as blankets on the silver space blanket I've already fastened to the two poles of the travois. The lightweight but strong material will serve as the platform for Gemma and Hattie to ride on. It's not a rope net like the Paiute braided out of rolled sagebrush bark for their sleds, but it'll do the trick. I'll wrap the duck in a folded square of the space blanket along with leftovers from the other birds to preserve the meat from spoiling so we'll have food for the journey. I don't know how long it'll take to reach the shiny object I saw from the pond. Binoculars might've told me what it is, but all I have to go on is it must be man-made.

"We could wait a while longer to see if another search plane flies overhead and spots us," Gemma says. "They haven't given up looking for us."

"I know they haven't, but it's been too long now since the only one flew by. We must've been blown off course farther than even Orville can calculate."

"It's that I feel so helpless not being able to walk out on my own. You know I don't like asking someone to do something I wouldn't do myself."

"You sound like your father, but you're doing the most important thing there is." I stroke Hattie's head.

"I can't wait to introduce her to Pudge," Gemma says.

"Grandpa. That's a title he'll wear as proudly as Sheriff. And November? I'm sure she'll have a strong opinion on what she wants Girl Fell from Sky to call her." I bank the embers, but leave the duck on the spit to slow-cook through the night. "Let's get some sleep. Dawn will be here before we know it."

We rearrange the pine boughs and Gemma tucks Hattie under her sheepskin coat and I lie down beside them.

"Who needs a fancy hotel?" the horse doctor says, touching the side of my face. "A fireplace, a comfy bed, even room service. This is the best honeymoon a girl could hope for."

Dawn comes fast and I don't stoke the fire. I go about the business of packing up as quickly as I can. While I'm working, Gemma hobbles out of the wickiup using a crutch made from a stripped pine branch. The cradleboard is strapped to her back. Hattie's coos and gurgles come from it. They sound like laughter.

"I want to walk with her on my back for a little way before we get on the travois."

"Did November tell you in your dream to start teaching her *Numu* traditions already?"

Gemma nods. "She'll ride looking behind us to see where we came from so she'll always know which path to take going forward."

I buckle myself into the makeshift harness made from the wrecked plane's seatbelts and start pulling as Gemma limps beside me. The two poles of the travois leave wakes of snow as they drag.

I glance back at the wickiup. Outside of the old lineman's shack, it's the best home I've ever known. "Thank you for your gift," I whisper.

We stop when we reach the wrecked plane. It saved us too by not breaking apart in the sky despite being struck by lightning and battered by the violent storm, and then providing us with materials for cooking, chopping wood, and making the travois. "Thank you for your gift," I whisper again.

Gemma eases the cradleboard off her back and settles onto the space blanket with Hattie on her lap. I arrange clothes around them to keep them warm and cushion the bumps.

"Are you sure about this?" Gemma says.

"As sure as I am about us."

"Then I only have one thing to say."

"What's that?"

She makes a kissing noise and mimics snapping reins. "Trot on!"

We pass the pond and the going is smooth, the snow forgiving. I know it won't always be so easy, but neither is life. There are always bumps, always hills, always cliffs, always crashes lurking around each bend. The trick is not to give up, to keep moving forward.

I fall into a rhythm as I let the natural fall line of the mountain slope guide me while sticking to the course I've plotted with the aid of my compass. Sometimes Gemma sings to Hattie, and her songs give me bursts of strength.

Other times I pull in silence, lost in my own thoughts, running back through the chapters of my life. Growing up on military bases. The occasional visits from my soldier father when he came home from some mission he never would speak about. My mother's quiet and steady faith. Grade school. High school where I ran track. Enlisting in the Army. Basic training. Landing in Vietnam. My first firefight. My first promotion. Leading a squad of men into the jungle. The first man I lost. The ambush where I lost all my men. The first taste and false courage of heroin. The Freedom Bird home. The padded cell at Walter Reed. Moving to No Mountain. Meeting Pudge and Gemma.

As daylight fades, we stop to make camp. I tip the travois on its side to create a lean-to. We eat last night's duck; it's still warm from its cocoon in the space-blanket wrapper. I don't sleep as I tend a campfire and listen to the soft breathing of mother and child as tree branches whisper and the moon glides in and out of clouds.

In the morning it's another meal of duck, though cold this time. I buckle back into the harness as Gemma and Hattie retake their seats. I know the ride for them is uncomfortable as I slog through the snow, the bounces jarring, the slip-sliding down the mountainside frightening, but Gemma never cries out, never complains. One hour becomes two and then three and then more. The day passes. I know we're making progress, but it's impossible to tell how many miles we've covered.

We spend the second night of the journey under the makeshift shelter again, huddling together for warmth as I keep watch over the campfire. I focus on the flames and whenever despair starts to creep into my thoughts, I throw them in the fire like lies. In the morning we eat the last of the cold duck and suck the marrow from the bones. I haven't seen any game on our trek. The going will get tougher on an empty stomach.

Late in the afternoon on the third day, we climb out of a steep, icy gully. I have to rest at the top to catch my breath and slow my heart rate. My head hangs as sweat drips from my brow and the salt stings my eyes.

"Look!" Gemma cries.

"At what?" I say, not bothering to raise my head.

"I'll show you."

I'm moving too slowly to unbuckle the harness to aid her. She scrambles off the travois on her own, clutches Hattie to her breast, and hops one-legged toward me.

"There!" she says.

I follow her pointing finger across the snowy forest that slopes downhill. The shiny object I saw at the pond now looms large. A transmission tower rises a mile away, the first in a chain that runs down a river gorge, carrying thick power cables. The tower stands next to a hydroelectric dam. Smoke curls from the chimney of a shingled cottage next to the dam.

Gemma and I are struck dumb by the sight, rendered immobile as the weight of having survived the crash, bearing a baby in the wilderness, and being lost now collides with imminent salvation. Our eyes meet.

"I could fire off a few rounds to get the dam keeper's attention," I finally say, not making a move to reach for my pistol. "He must have a snowcat and can give us a ride the rest of the way."

She hesitates. "Is that what you want?"

"No, we've come this far."

Gemma holds Hattie up so she faces forward. "That's where we're going," she turns her around, "and that's where you were born. It isn't nowhere, it's somewhere, because we were there together."

"You two ready?" I say.

"For anything," Gemma says.

"That makes three of us. Let's go home."

AFTERWORD

In 1976, two hundred years after the signing of the US Declaration of Independence with its immortal clause stating all men are created equal, Iowa enacted the first law in the nation to protect Native American graves and provide for repatriation of human remains. It came into being thanks to one woman and her five-year-long fight for justice. Maria Darlene Pearson (her Yankton Sioux tribal name, *Hai-Mecha Eunka*, translated to "Running Moccasins") had learned that, during a highway construction project, the remains of twenty-six white settlers were dug up and promptly reburied in a nearby cemetery while the bones of a Native American woman and her baby were sent to the state archaeologist's office instead.

Determined to end discrimination and disregard of Native American spiritual beliefs, she tried to meet with the Iowa governor, but was ignored. Undeterred, she sat outside his office dressed in the traditional attire of her people and vowed to wait, no matter how long it took. The governor finally relented and asked what she wanted. "You can give me back my people's bones and you can quit digging them up," she declared.

Her victory in Iowa set a national precedent. Fourteen years later, the US Congress enacted the 1990 Native American Graves Protection and Repatriation Act (NAGPRA). At the time of its passage, hundreds of thousands of Native American human remains and an untold number of sacred objects and relics were held by museums, universities, and private collectors around the world. The Smithsonian Institution alone possessed some fifteen thousand dead Native Americans and tens of thousands of cultural artifacts.

NAGPRA provided legal teeth in the form of civil and criminal penalties for knowingly selling or purchasing sacred objects stolen from graves, or trafficking in Native American human remains, but the law only applied to federal lands. It was also very slow to become adopted and enforced. Twenty years after its passage, key federal agencies such as the Bureau of Indian Affairs, Bureau of Land Management, and Army Corps of Engineers had not fully complied. As of this writing, outcomes of NAGPRA repatriation efforts remain sluggish and the law cumbersome, forcing many tribes to spend considerable time and money documenting their requests.

Compliance with the act can be complicated and controversial. An example is the fate of Kennewick Man, a nine-thousand-year-old skeleton found in 1996 near Kennewick, Washington. The Umatilla, Colville, Yakama, and Nez Perce tribes had each claimed Kennewick Man as their ancestor, and sought permission to rebury him, but some scientists wanted to keep him for study, claiming that because of his great age, there was insufficient evidence to connect him to modern tribes.

The dispute continued for nearly twenty years, but, finally, in 2015, a DNA test was performed. It concluded that Kennewick Man was more closely related to modern Native Americans than to any other living population. The following year, Congress passed legislation to return the bones to a coalition of Columbia Plateau tribes for reburial according to their traditions, and on February 18, 2017, members of five Native American tribes gathered at a secret location and returned the Ancient One to the earth.

GET A FREE BOOK

Dwight Holing's genre-spanning work includes novels, short fiction, and nonfiction. His mystery and suspense thriller series include The Nick Drake Novels and The Jack McCoul Capers. The stories in his collections of literary short fiction have won awards, including the Arts & Letters Prize for Fiction. He has written and edited numerous nonfiction books on nature travel and conservation. He is married to a kick-ass environmental advocate; they have a daughter and son, and two dogs who'd rather swim than walk.

Sign up for his newsletter to get a free book and be the first to learn about the next Nick Drake Novel as well as receive news about crime fiction and special deals.

Visit dwightholing.com/free-book. You can unsubscribe at any time.

ACKNOWLEDGMENTS

I'm indebted to many people who helped in the creation of *The Nowhere Bones*. As always, my family provided support throughout the writing process.

Thank you to the University of Oregon, my alma mater, for opening doors and minds. A shout out to Kenneth Mitchell for alerting me to Paisley Caves that spurred an exploration of the many prehistoric wonders of south-central Oregon.

I'm especially grateful to my reader team who read early drafts and gave me very helpful feedback. Thank you, one and all, including George Becker, Terrill Carpenter, Ron Fox, Jeffrey Miller, Kenneth Mitchell, Annie Notthoff, John Onoda, and Haris Orkin.

Thank you Karl Yambert for proofreading and copyediting. Kudos to Bun Lee for your spectacular photograph taken in Harney County, and to designer-extraordinaire Rob Williams for creating the stunning cover.

Additional thanks go to the Harney County Library's Claire McGill Luce Western History Room and Archivist Karen Nitz.

I humbly offer my respect to the Burns Paiute Tribe of the Burns Paiute Indian Colony of Oregon for your inspiration and to the Klamath Tribes, whose mission is to protect, preserve and enhance the spiritual, cultural and physical values and resources of the Klamath, Modoc and Yahooskin Peoples by maintaining the customs and heritage of their ancestors.

Any errors, regrettably, are my own.

ALSO BY DWIGHT HOLING

The Nick Drake Novels

The Sorrow Hand (Book 1)

The Pity Heart (Book 2)

The Shaming Eyes (Book 3)

The Whisper Soul (Book 4)

The Nowhere Bones (Book 5)

The Forever Feet (Book 6)

The Jack McCoul Capers

A Boatload (Book 1)

Bad Karma (Book 2)

Baby Blue (Book 3)

Shake City (Book 4)

Short Story Collections

California Works

Over Our Heads Under Our Feet

Made in the USA
Coppell, TX
27 April 2022